THE CHALET SCHOOL AND BARBARA

Also in Armada

Chalet School Fête
Mary-Lou at the Chalet School
Jo of the Chalet School
Shocks for the Chalet School
Eustacia Goes to the Chalet School
New Mistress at the Chalet School
The Chalet School and Jo
The Chalet School and the Island
Peggy of the Chalet School
The Chalet Girls in Camp
The School at the Chalet
The Chalet School in Exile
Three Go to the Chalet School
A Rebel at the Chalet School
A Problem for the Chalet School
The Coming of Age of the Chalet School

First published in the U.K. in 1954 by
W. & R. Chambers, London and Edinburgh.
This edition was first published in 1967 by
Fontana Paperbacks,
14 St. James's Place, London SW1A 1PS.

This impression 1982.

Printed in Great Britain by
Love & Malcomson Ltd.,
Brighton Road, Redhill, Surrey.

THE CHALET SCHOOL AND BARBARA

ELINOR M. BRENT-DYER

CONTENTS

CHAPTER ONE

Beth and Barbara

BETH CHESTER laid the book she had been reading on her knee and looked across with an amused smile at her younger sister. Ever since they had left the dining-waggon after breakfast, Barbara had spent her time gazing out of the window. As Beth reflected, at fourteen, she was behaving as if she were seven.

"Still, there's a good deal of excuse for her, poor babe," the elder sister thought. "She's been so shut away until just lately that it's little wonder that she goggles at everything like a kid at a Sunday school treat!"

She turned her wrist to look at her watch and the window-gazer caught the movement and turned her head to ask, "How much longer before we reach Basle now?"

"I'm not too sure," Beth replied. "I've never been this way before, any more than you have, so I can't say."

"But you *have* been in Switzerland before. You came three summers ago with Daisy Venables and Gwensi Howell."

"Yes; but that was Geneva and Lucerne. All this is quite new to me. Judging by the time, I should say we ought to be there in another half-hour or so. Are you tired?"

Barbara's flaxen curls bobbed wildly as she shook her head.

"Not likely! I'm a lot too thrilled for that!" She squirmed round in her seat to face her sister. "Oh, Beth! You don't *know* how much I've longed to travel and now it's come at last!"

Beth's lovely face broke into a smile of sympathy. "I mayn't know, but I can jolly well guess. You wait till the school begins to run expeditions! You'll see something of the country that way before the term is many weeks old or I don't know my Chalet School!"

Barbara bounced excitedly up and down in her seat. "Do you really think so? How marvellous if you're right!"

Beth laughed. "Babs! Do behave like a civilized being! Of course I'm right. You ask Aunt Jo when we see her if you don't believe me. I've always heard that in the old Tirol days they did quite a lot of expeditions every term. And naturally they'll run them early on, this term. I don't suppose it'll be easy to get about once the snow comes. When it snows in these parts it *snows*."

Barbara, who had spent a good part of her life in Guernsey where snow is by way of being a rarity, chuckled "And that'll be another thrill! Oh, I *have* been so looking forward to school *at last*! You simply can't think!"

Beth regarded her young sister thoughtfully. "I wonder how you'll really like it? You've never been away from Mummy in your life before."

"But that's just it! Don't you *see*, Beth? I've never been anywhere in my life away from her since I could remember. All the rest of you went off to boarding-school quite early——"

"Not me," Beth interrupted her decisively. "It didn't happen for me until I was thirteen."

"Still, even that is a whole year younger than I am now," the younger girl argued. "And Nancy and Janice and the boys went when they were seven."

Beth gave it up. "Well, you'll be able to see how you like it very soon now. I expect you'll love it, once you've settled down. Only, Babs, it *will* be different from home and I'm not sure how you'll like it just at first. Do remember that it takes time to get accustomed to anything new. You stick it out, and you'll soon be enjoying yourself. And, of course, I'll always be there in the background if you want me."

Barbara's rejoinder was unexpected. "I know that. But I'm not going to come running to you every time something happens that I don't quite like. That *would* be like a baby! How much longer do you think the journey will be?"

"I told you I couldn't say exactly. Half an hour or so, I imagine. We're due in at Basle at noon. It's just on half past eleven now."

Barbara nodded. "Thanks a lot." She turned back to her window and Beth was left to pick up her book again and smile to herself behind it. All the same, there were times when she wondered to herself just how Barbara would get on at school after being such a complete home-bird for the first fourteen years of her life.

Barbara had been born at a bad time in the family's history and had proved such a frail baby, that her father had baptized her almost on the spot. All through her early childhood she had been the cause of alarms.

As the centre of attention in her family, with all the others taught to give up to her in every way, she had had every excuse for being selfish and self-centred. As Beth reflected now, it was little short of a miracle that she had grown up as sweet of nature as she was.

"It's about the only time I've ever known measles to be a blessing in disguise," the elder sister mused. "If it hadn't been for that when she was ten, she might still be lounging about at home, the pet of everyone and getting more and more egotistical every day."

She went on remembering those early years. Barbara had been protected from all infection so thoroughly, that she had had none of the usual childish illnesses until, at ten, she had come down with measles to everyone's consternation. It had been a sharp attack and for two or three days, they had been very anxious. Then she had turned the corner, and after that she had gone ahead by leaps and bounds. By the time measles was a thing of the past, she was a different girl. By the time her twelfth birthday came, she was considered fit enough to go to a small private school near at home. For the past year she had been begging to be allowed to join her second and fourth sisters at the Chalet School, which had then been on an island off the South Wales coast.

To that, however, Mrs. Chester would not consent. Then the news came that the school originally begun in the Austrian Tirol, was to move out to the Oberland as a prelude to returning to the land of its birth. Dr. Chester had leapt at it.

Anne Chester was the more ready to agree because an

old friend, Joey Maynard, once Joey Bettany and sister of Lady Russell who had started the school in the days when she was still Madge Bettany, had gone out to make her home on the Görnetz Platz where the school was to open. Dr. Maynard, her husband, had been appointed head of the new Sanatorium to be opened up there, so Joey and her long family of eight would be close at hand and would be able to watch over the once delicate Barbara. As a final inducement, Beth, the eldest of the Chester family, was to join the Maynards as nursery governess and mother's help to Joey.

Beth surveyed her third sister meditatively.

"What a change!" she thought. "She's always been such a little misery, but now she doesn't look particularly delicate at all. I wonder how she really will get on? I know she thinks it's going to be all jam; and it won't be, of course. No school ever is. I'm jolly glad on the whole that we're to live with Aunt Jo and let her go for the day. It won't be so awfully different from going to Miss le Marchant's. And thank goodness I won't have all the responsibility!"

She looked at her watch again. Then she shut up her book, leaned forward and touched her absorbed sister's arm. "Babs! We must be nearly there and you look positively *wild*! Here's your comb and a face-cloth and towel. For goodness' sake scoot along to the toilet and make yourself fit to be seen. If whoever meets us sees you looking like that, they'll think they're importing the original Wild Girl of the Woods!"

Barbara giggled. "What a shock for them! Any soap? You do get filthy on continental trains!"

"It's the soft coal they use, I suppose," Beth replied as she rummaged in her case. "Here you are! Scram! I don't suppose you have any too much time."

Barbara scuttled away and Beth, after a quick glance at herself in the mirror of her compact, powdered her pretty nose, pulled on her hat at the latest angle and then began to lift down the suitcases from the rack.

Barbara came back presently, looking decidedly better.

Her sister had all the cases piled up at her feet and the books and magazines packed safely away. She looked up at the younger girl as she appeared in the corridor and nodded. "That's a lot better! You look like a Christian now. Pull on your beret—here it is. We should be in Basle in a few minutes more. Let me look at you? Yes; you'll do. You're clean and tidy, at any rate."

Barbara grinned at her. "O.K., Grannie! I say, Beth," she added more seriously as she tugged on her gloves, "I hope you don't propose to try and run round after me all the time, do you? Because I warn you I've had all I want of that sort of thing for the rest of my life."

Beth stared at her speechlessly for a moment. Then she burst out laughing. "Well! You cheeky brat! There's gratitude for you! Oh no, my child. *I* shan't run round after you once we're at the Görnetz Platz. That will be Aunt Joey's job. And if that's the way you're going to take it, I don't envy her, either. Hello! This must be Basle—the outskirts, anyhow. I don't know how long the train waits, so we'd better make for the door."

Barbara subsided and her Declaration of Independence was left unfinished for the moment. She picked up a case and her raincoat while Beth saw to the rest of their possessions, and once she had Barbara and their hand-luggage safely out of the train and on the platform, she looked round anxiously, searching for their escort. The school proper would not come till the following day, but Mrs. Chester had been anxious to have Barbara settled safely at Freudesheim, the Maynards' house, before term began so they had been sent off a day sooner.

No one who looked like an escort seemed to be there. Beth began to tell Barbara to stay where she was by the cases while she herself went off to the van to claim their trunks, when she felt a gentle touch on her arm and swung round to find herself facing a very fair, slight person, pretty as a picture, with her shady black hat framing an apple-blossom face.

For a moment Beth wondered who it could possibly be. Then she remembered. "Frieda!" she exclaimed. Then, reddening, "I beg your pardon—I meant Mrs. von Ahlen.

I didn't recognize you just at first," she added apologetically. "It's so many years since I last saw you."

"But I recognized you," Frieda von Ahlen smiled. "You haven't changed, Beth, except to grow up."

Beth laughed. "You'd expect that. I've been grown-up for ages. Have you come to meet us? How lovely! Barbara, this is Mrs. von Ahlen, Aunt Joey's chum. Are you staying with Aunt Joey?" She turned back to Frieda.

That lady shook her head. "But no! Most certainly not! My husband works in a bank here and our home is here, too. But, Beth, where are your trunks? Surely you have more baggage than this?"

"Yes—two trunks in the van. I was just going to see about them when you spoke to me," Beth replied.

"Then come with me and we will have them taken to the car," Frieda said. "Barbara, you will stay here with the cases, will you not, *mein liebling*?"

Barbara nodded shyly, so the two grown-ups went off and presently came back, followed by a porter who brought the trunks. They picked up the cases, and then led by Frieda they left the station and were quickly tucked into the little car waiting outside.

"How tall you are, Beth," Frieda said, with a glance at the beautiful girl beside her as she started the car. "But I remember both your parents were tall."

Beth laughed. "At one time I was the despair of the family, I grew so fast. But I'm no taller than Aunt Jo," she added as they swung into the traffic stream.

"No," Frieda agreed. "Jo always was the giantess of our quartette."

Beth looked at Barbara who was gazing round excitedly. "Babs, Mrs. von Ahlen is one of Aunt Jo's greatest pals. I've heard her talk about you," she added to Frieda. "You stayed with her in England during the war and didn't you have two little boys while you were there?"

Frieda von Ahlen laughed. "Louis and Gerard. And since then I have had Gretchen and, just this year, Joey's god-daughter, Carlotta Josephine. The boys are at school at this hour, but you will see Gretchen and Carlotta when we reach home. You come with me for *Mittagessen*, Beth.

Then I will take you and Barbara to the Centralbahnhof again and see you on to the train for Interlaken. Besides," she added, "I have a message for you from Jo."

"That sounds lovely," Beth began, but Frieda stopped her.

"We will not talk now if you do not mind. The traffic is very busy today and I must keep my mind on my driving."

Beth fell silent and the remainder of the journey was taken without much more talk than an occasional word from Frieda, calling their attention to something of interest. At last they turned into a quieter side street and then to others until they were running down a broad road with big blocks of flats either side. Before one of these, the car stopped and Frieda jumped out.

"Here we are! No; leave your cases. Jakob will see to the car and you will be here so short a time, that it is not worth while carrying them up to the flat. Come Barbara."

Barbara tumbled out into the sunny roadway and stood gazing round her. A short, sturdy man in uniform came up and Frieda spoke to him in rapid German which neither of the Chesters could follow, though Beth caught a word here and there and wished that she had not so completely dropped her German when she left school. Then they were led into the block of flats, deposited in the very latest thing in lifts and whisked up to the fifth floor, where the two English girls found themselves entering an airy flat that seemed full of sunlight.

"This is our home for the present," Frieda said as she ushered them into a big room with wide windows. "We are looking for a little house with a garden, outside the city; but we have this for a year."

A little girl came shyly up to them from one of the windows, and Frieda slipped an arm round her. "That is right, *Blümchen*," she said, smiling. "Beth, this is our elder girl, Gretchen, born after we settled down in Innsbruck. Greet Beth and Barbara, *Liebling*," she added to shy Gretchen, who curtsied with a little smile.

Beth bent to kiss her. "How like you she is, Frieda," she began. Then she stopped again flushing to the roots of her hair. "Oh, I'm so sorry! But Aunt Jo never calls you anything else."

"It is all right," Frieda said quickly. "Do call me 'Frieda', Beth. I know Jo means that you shall drop the 'Aunt' now. After all, we are not so very much older than you. Yes; Gretchen is very like me. But wait till you see our baby!"

Barbara, who had been silent from shyness, was moved to curiosity by this and involuntarily demanded, "Why?"

Frieda laughed. "You will see in a moment. Gretchen, run and ask Marie if *Mittagessen* is ready for us. Come and see my baby, Barbara, until the bell rings."

She gave her small daughter a gentle push and then, slipping an arm through Barbara's, took them along a shadowy passage into a bedroom where a big, beautifully carved cradle stood near the bed. Frieda beckoned them over to it and then stood back, her eyes on their faces.

They knelt down on either side. As they looked in at its small occupant, Beth gave an exclamation of amazement and Barbara, after one look, sat back on her heels and exclaimed. "But she isn't like you or Gretchen *at all*!"

"Not in the least," Frieda said placidly. "Gretchen and the boys are like me—fair. Carlotta is the image of her papa who is very dark."

The baby rolled over and opened big dark eyes. She looked up at the strange faces and then gave a chuckle.

"Oh, what a *darling*!" Barbara cried. "Oh, *may* I hold her?"

"Wait until she has had her dinner," her mother said. She glanced at the cuckoo clock on the wall. "Yes; there is just time. Gretchen shall show you the bathroom and you can freshen yourselves. Then, after *Mittagessen*, while we drink our coffee, you shall nurse her, Barbara." She raised her voice in a call and Gretchen came running.

At her mother's bidding, she led the visitors off to the bathroom and when they had washed and generally tidied themselves, she took them back to the big *Saal*. Beth tried to talk to her, but Gretchen was very shy and very little was to be got from her. Barbara was shy herself and remained dumb, too, so, as Beth thought despairingly to herself, there was little to be done about it. Luckily, Frieda came in a few minutes later, carrying Carlotta in her Moses ark and then the bell rang and they all went into the room next door which Frieda called the *Speisesaal*.

Looking round it in the intervals of devouring cold chicken salad, ripe peaches and cream and sponge-cake, all washed down with a delicious fruit drink, Barbara decided that it was one of the prettiest rooms she had ever seen. Stands of flowering plants had been set between the windows and through the open windows with their screens of wire netting was to be seen a blue sky across which great white galleons of clouds drifted lazily. The table was covered with a blue and white checked cloth and the glasses were of all colours—yellow, ruby and sapphire blue.

When they had finished their meal, they went back to the *Saal* and Barbara was thrilled to have the baby taken from her ark and laid in her arms.

Gretchen came and stood beside her, gently stroking the baby's black curls.

"She is pretty?" she said very shyly.

"She's lovely!" Barbara replied quickly. "How lucky you are to have a baby sister! I was only four when Janice was born and Mummy wouldn't let me hold her ever."

"Jolly good reason," Beth said, overhearing this. "You were a tiny thing yourself and Janice was a good hefty baby. You'd have dropped her if you'd held her at that age. No; no more coffee, thank you. But it's the most delicious I've ever tasted," she added.

Frieda smiled. "I am glad you enjoyed it. But now, I'm afraid we must go or you will miss your train."

Beth was remembering something. "Frieda, what was the message Aunt Joey gave you for me?"

Frieda looked conscience stricken. "Yes; I know, Beth. Indeed, I have not forgotten. But it is—well, not very nice."

Beth sat up and Barbara pricked up her ears. Frieda took the baby from her and tucked the small sleepy thing into her Moses ark. When she had done everything, she said slowly: "It is this, Beth. Barbara cannot go to Freudesheim."

"Not go to Freudesheim?"

"Then where *am* I to go?"

The two exclamations came together. Frieda gave Beth a worried look. "The fact of the matter is that this morning Con and Len woke up with rashes and Jo says that Charles is not very well."

"What is she afraid of—measles?" Beth demanded.

"Not that; no. But what you call German measles. There have been one or two cases at one of the hotels and Jo's family were playing with the children. Jo says she is almost certain that it is German measles, but Jack had not come home from San when she rang up——"

At which point, the telephone bell trilled suddenly. The mistress of the flat jumped up and went to take the call. She called Beth in a moment, and that young lady hurried out of the room and took the receiver held out mutely.

"Is that you, Aunt Joey?" she asked. "This is Beth."

"Well, I'm glad you've got so far," Jo's voice came back to her. "The thing is that though *you* may come all right—I remember you had it at school when they had that epidemic—Barbara most certainly may *not*!"

"But what is it?" Beth demanded anxiously.

With the intonation of a tragedienne, Jo replied, "German measles!"

CHAPTER TWO

"Barbara must be a Boarder"

BETH'S FIRST REACTION was to giggle madly. Jo heard her and demanded with great indignation what there was to *laugh* at?

"It's not funny!" she said. "You probably don't realize it, but we must have had the infection for at least a fortnight and Stephen went off to his prep school last Wednesday, probably full of it. That's a nice beginning, isn't it?"

"Oh, *no*!" Beth cried. "How simply awful!"

"*You* are telling me! And quite apart from that, I've seven of them here, including two babies who have their hands full already with cutting double teeth. Margot seems all right so far, but she's practically sure to come down with it. So is Mike. I'm hoping for the best where Felix and Felicity are concerned. They're not a great deal with the others, so they *may* have escaped. But we can't be sure of that for another fourteen days. In the meantime, Barbara doesn't come into this hotbed of germs. She'll have to go straight to school and begin as a boarder after all."

Beth pulled herself together. "Well, it might be a lot worse. She's been dying to *be* a boarder and it was only Mummy's insistence that made Dad agree to your suggestion that she should have this term as a daygirl. And as for your family, once I've handed Babs over you'll have *me*. I'm safe enough so far as German measles is concerned. The entire Fifth had it when I was a Fifth Former."

"I *thought* I was right about you. I'll be thankful to get you! No one is ever really ill with it, but you've got to see that they keep out of draughts and so on and with a lively set like mine, it's none too easy."

"So I should imagine. Well, don't worry. We're just off to the station with Frieda. I'll hand Babs over to whoever comes to meet us and come straight on to you. By the way, if Margot and Mike are going to have it, I do hope they don't linger too long over it. It *would* be maddening if they hung on till the very last day of quarantine and then started!"

"Don't mention it!" Jo cried. "If *that* happened, I should go crackers! Well, I mustn't make you lose your train so I'll ring off. See you presently."

She hung up and Beth returned to the *Saal* whither Frieda had preceded her. "Come along, Babs," she said. "Can't miss our train. Frieda, it's been lovely to see you. You'll forgive us if we fly now, won't you?"

Frieda nodded. "Come and get ready. We shall be in good time, so you have no need to feel flurried." She glanced at Gretchen. "Will you come with us, *Blümchen*?"

Gretchen was slightly less shy of Barbara by this time and she nodded. "Yes, *Mütterchen*."

As they prepared themselves and Frieda settled Gretchen's shady hat, she said in an aside to Beth: "I shall not see you for some weeks now. But I hope you will come to visit us as soon as you can. Give my love to Jo and say that I trust all will go well with her little hospital."

Beth nodded. "Of course. And luckily everyone is on the phone, so we can ring up,"

She meant to delay telling Barbara the latest arrangements until they were in the train and well on their way. Barbara was anxious to know what had been happening, but she was still shy enough to say nothing. They went down in the lift, packed into the car which Jakob had brought round to the great doors again and set out for the Centralbahnhof. They arrived in plenty of time and Frieda saw them comfortably settled in corner seats before she and Gretchen bade them good-bye.

"I want you to see my boys," she said, laughing, to Beth. "When you knew them, Beth, they were very little fellows; but now they are big. Both my boys are like my own father in that." Suddenly she laughed. "Jo used to call *der Vater* '*Onkel Riese*'. That means, 'Uncle Giant', Barbara. He is a very big man indeed, and Louis and Gerard are going to be just like him there."

"That was like Aunt Joey," Beth laughed. "Oh, we're off! Good-bye, Frieda! Thanks more than I can say for meeting us. I'll give Aunt Joey your messages."

She had to shout the last few words for the train was moving swiftly. Frieda waved her hand to show that she understood. Then the station was left behind and Beth and Barbara were alone.

It really *was* alone. The train was barely half-full and they had their seats to themselves. Once they were well away, Beth stopped gazing out of the window and turned to look at her young sister. Barbara got in first.

"Now tell me exactly what has happened?" she pleaded.

"It's not so much what *has* happened as what's *going* to happen," Beth told her. "You're getting your wish, and even Mummy can't say anything against it."

Barbara's eyes became saucers. "What *do* you mean?"

"Just that you'll have to start straight in as a boarder."

"*What?* Beth Chester? Do you really mean that?"

"Barbara Emily Chester, I do—most definitely. Aunt Joey's kids have started German measles so you certainly can't go there. You couldn't possibly go to an hotel by yourself and anyway, I don't see the Head or any of the rest of the school authorities agreeing to that. So it's school for you, my lamb, from the word 'go'! How about it?"

Barbara clasped her hands excitedly. Her eyes shone and her usually rather pale cheeks became vividly pink. "*Oh!* I'm so thrilled, I—I can't think of anything to say! Is it really true? Oh, how simply marvellous!" Suddenly she leaned forward. "Beth, when the kids are all right again, I won't have to come and live at Freudesheim and *stop* being a boarder, shall I? That would be just *too* awful!"

Beth looked at her curiously. "I can't say one way or the other. The Abbess and Aunt Joey will fix all that up." She thought a moment. Then she added, "Look here; if I were you, I'd write to Auntie J. and get her to talk to Mummy. All her girls have been boarders at the school and so have Vanna and Nella Ozanne. You get the aunts on your side. I don't say they'll be able to shift Mummy if she wants you to be a daygirl when it's possible; but if they know how badly you want it, I'm sure they'll do their best. And I'll dig in, too."

"Oh, I will!" Barbara spoke with deep fervour. "Oh, Beth! This really is my heart's desire coming true!"

"If you want it all that much, I hope you get it." Beth looked uneasy, however. She added, "Only, don't imagine it's going to be all jam, for nothing ever is. You'll come up against things you won't like. Everyone does. But if you've anything in you, you'll dig your toes in and stand up to it."

"How do you mean?" Barbara demanded. "It's what I want—more than anything else in the world. And I know it won't all be lovely. I've heard you and Nancy talk—and the cousins, too."

"Well," Beth said doubtfully, "as long as you feel that, I should think it'll be all right. Anyhow, if things get too bad, you'll have me and I'll help you as far as in me lies. And there's always Auntie Jo."

Barbara nodded, but her sensitive lips folded together in an unusually determined way.

Nothing more was said on the sub'ect. Barbara turned again to her window and was soon absorbed in watching the landscape. Once they were among the mountains, she forgot that she was fourteen and bounced up and down on her seat with excitement.

"Oh, isn't it *wizard*?" she cried delightedly. "Oh, look, Beth! What a lovely, sunny lake!"

It was Lake Thun along the north shore of which the line runs to Interlaken. Barbara was so delighted that she actually fell silent and sat quietly, gazing out at the still lucent waters in which they could see the mountains mirrored so clearly. Half-way along, she turned to her sister.

"Beth, do you think the school will ever bring us down here?"

"I expect so," Beth said calmly. "Daisy Venables used to talk of the fun they had on the Tiernsee when the school was there. I should imagine you'll come down quite often in the summer, at any rate. It won't be much fun in the winter."

"Won't it freeze over then? Perhaps they'll teach us to skate."

"Perhaps they will. Now you stop flattening your nose against the window like that and help me with the cases. Do you want these mags or shall we leave them?"

Barbara turned round from the window and gave her attention to the question. When the train finally rolled into the Hauptbahnhof, they were ready. Beth hung out of the window, her eyes roving round for their escort.

"I'm here," said a gentle voice almost immediately below her; and she looked down on Miss Dene, secretary to the Head and an old friend of her own schooldays.

"Miss Dene! How wizard to see you again after all this time!" she exclaimed. "We'll be out in a sec!" She turned round to Barbara who was bobbing about. "Oh, for goodness' sake stop behaving like an inebriated grasshopper! Pick up that case and your mac and follow me."

Barbara did as she was told with a chuckle and the pair left the coach and joined the people thronging the platform.

Miss Dene had hurried along to the door, and she relieved Beth of one of the cases she was carrying and then demanded to be told where their trunks were.

Beth pointed to the van and the secretary spoke a few words in rapid German to the porter standing near and he went off to secure the trunks. Then she turned to the two girls standing beside her.

"Nice to see you again, Beth," she said. "And this is Barbara? Splendid! Beth, I suppose you know what's happened at Freudesheim?"

"Do I not!" Beth broke into a peal of laughter. "Poor Aunt Joey! I told her I'd see Barbara safely into your hands, Miss Dene—by you, meaning the school—and then hurry on to her."

"Well, you can't desert us yet. We go up together. Then I'll run you along in the car. Joey's place is next door to the school, you know. I propose to take you there first and decant you and your luggage. Then I'll go off with Barbara and after that, my dear, you'll be in quarantine till those youngsters are over their German measles—or so far as we are concerned, anyhow. No one is bringing an epidemic into the school at the beginning of term if *we* can help it!"

"I couldn't agree more!" Beth looked at Miss Dene. "It isn't what Mummy meant when she gave way about Babs coming to school, but Babs is all for it."

Miss Dene laughed. "That's good hearing! I hope you'll be as happy with us as all your sisters have been, Barbara. And I hope," she added with a wicked twinkle, "that you won't let us in for quite as many alarms and excursions as Beth and Nancy have both done."

To Barbara's undisguised delight, Beth went scarlet. "Oh, Miss Dene! That's *not* fair!" she cried. "There were a good many worse girls than we were!"

Rosalie Dene pealed with laughter. "Who's denying it? But you must admit that you and Daisy and Gwensi contrived to give us one or two bad moments amongst you. Well, we'd better go and seek our taxi. Come along! I don't want to miss the next train and I'm sure you'll be glad to reach the end of such a long journey and settle down for a few months." She led the way to the entrance "I'm sorry no one could get down to Basle to meet you, but we decided that Frieda von Ahlen could very well do it for us. You contacted her, didn't you?"

"Oh, rather!" Beth said. "She took us to her flat and gave us a simply luscious meal and we saw her little girls."

"And what did you think of Carlotta?" Miss Dene asked with dancing eyes.

"Simply lovely! But talk of a hop-out-o'-kin! I suppose Louis and Gerard are still as fair as ever?"

Miss Dene nodded. "Brown of face, but fair as they can be, otherwise. Carlotta is the picture of her father—the only one, so far. Here's our taxi. Hop in!"

They clambered in while Miss Dene finished with her porter before she joined them. Then the doors were slammed and they creaked off. The taxi swung out of the Bahnhof Platz into the Hoheweg and trundled along to a point where the taxi drew up for them to see the Kursaal with its famous floral clock.

"Oh, how lovely!" Barbara exclaimed. "Can you really tell the time by it, Miss Dene?"

Rosalie laughed. "Why, of course you can. One day we'll bring you people down to explore and then you'll hear all about it." She told the driver to go on and then continued, "We're going to the Bahnhof-Ost, but if we weren't, we could go on to a place called Bonigen which is where the Aare has been made into a kind of canal leading from Lake Brienz. That's another place we hope to visit before the winter makes expeditions too tiresome."

Barbara chuckled. "I think school sounds gorgeous. When do we do lessons?"

"Oh, you needn't be afraid that those are missed out," Miss Dene told her. "Expeditions are only for Saturdays. You'll have plenty of lessons in between."

They had reached the station by this time and the man was busy with a porter who was talking excitedly to him. Miss Dene leaned forward with a quick question in German. The answer made her give an exclamation. Then she embarked on a long speech in such fluent German that the two Chesters stared at her. When it was over, she turned back to them.

"We have just missed the train for which I was heading and there isn't another for forty minutes. I'm leaving the luggage here and our driver will take us to the Jungfraublick. There's plenty of time for you to see that *and* have a drink and some cakes at one of the *pâtisseries*."

The trunks and cases were unloaded and borne off by the porter. The taxi turned and they ran back down the Hoheweg which still looked very gay, with its trees turning golden and red with autumn tints, the big flowerbeds, still full of flowers, and the crowds thronging the pavements. At one point, they stopped and the girls got out. Miss Dene turned them and bade them look. They did as they were told. There before them, austere, remote, beautiful was the Jungfrau herself, her veil of glacier glittering in the late afternoon sunshine.

Rosalie Dene watched their faces for a minute or two, triumph in her eyes. Then she touched Beth's arm. "I wanted to show you this, but you can see it every clear day from Freudesheim. One of the drawing-room windows looks directly towards the Jungfrau. But if we're to have coffee and cakes, we must go on. Come along, both of you."

She took one of Barbara's hands and slipped an arm through Beth's and pulled them back to the taxi or they might have stayed there another hour, just gazing. But she was not anxious to miss yet another train and she had decided that the two needed something by this time. They left their taxi beside a *pâtisserie* not far from the station and she paid the man off, explaining to the Chesters that it was barely ten minutes' walk away. Then she escorted them into the coffee room where, for the first time in Barbara's life, she had the joy of being given a plate and a cake-fork and going to the counter where trayfuls of luscious cakes were set out, and choosing for herself before she sat down at the little table with a big cup of coffee, topped with a blanket of whipped cream before her.

"This is a luxury and extravagance," Miss Dene said, touching her own cup. "Don't go in for cups of coffee, Beth. It'll cost you the equivalent of a shilling every time."

"Not really?" Beth looked up dismayed. "I was just thinking what a treat I should have any time I came down from the Platz. Do you really mean that, Miss Dene?" Then, as Rosalie nodded: "How awful! And what a disappointment!"

"With all this cream on, it's bound to cost the earth," Barbara pointed out.

"Yes; I suppose so. But I *am* disappointed. Oh, well, I must make it a real treat to come only when I'm in funds."

"That's what we all have to do," Miss Dene said philosophically. "We enjoy it all the more, I suppose. Now I don't want to hurry you, but time doesn't stand still."

They made haste over the little meal and then, having paid their score, Rosalie marched them off to the station for the mountain train. Their porter had the luggage loaded in and they had tickets which the secretary had had the foresight to buy when she came down earlier. All they had to do was to find their seats in the glassed-in car of the rack-and-pinion railway and two minutes later they were off, gliding first across the narrow plain, then beginning to ascend the mountain with incredible smoothness.

Barbara had her face glued to the window. Her eyes were with excitement and her cheeks pink. Beth was gazing, too, but whatever she felt, she controlled herself. Rosalie Dene watched them, making mental notes.

"What a lovely creature Beth Chester has grown into—really, something quite choice! I'm amazed that she isn't married yet; or engaged, anyhow. What *can* the men be thinking of?" She turned her eyes to Barbara. "She's a pretty little thing. Poor little soul! I do hope she'll make a go of her school-life after all these years!"

Meanwhile, after the first delight, Beth herself was taking notes. She was moved to wonder if the others had changed as little as Miss Dene.

"We all liked her," the girl thought. "She's just as jolly as she always was. Nancy did say that the rest were just the same, but I wonder. She's not much more than a kid for all her eighteen years—and not a very observant one at that!"

"Görnetz Platz!" Rosalie Dene exclaimed at that moment. "Come along! The train doesn't stop for more than a minute or two and we have the boxes to get out."

She hustled them out on to the tiny platform, spoke to

the man who was at the luggage-van and then hurried her charges out of the station to where a car was standing.

"In you get! I'll have to swing her, I expect. She's been standing here since I left her at thirteen o'clock, so she'll be stone-cold and she doesn't always react to the self-starter on such occasions."

Under the spell of her energy, the girls piled their cases on the back seat, leaving room for Beth, and Barbara scrambled into the front one. The man, the train having gone on, strapped the trunks on to the luggage grid, and Miss Dene, having succeeded in starting the engine, climbed into the driver's seat, slamming the door behind her and they were off on the last lap of their journey.

"Only three miles to go now," Rosalie Dene said as she guided the car along the track. "That big building over there is our new Sanatorium, Barbara. The school is right away at the other end of the Platz. That opening down there is the one and only motor-road down, but the gradient is awful and I don't like it. There *is* another motor-road—the one the ambulances take, but it's fearfully roundabout and adds over twenty miles to the trip. It comes up by way of the other alps."

"I wondered how you got all the school furniture and so on up here if the gradient was so awful," Beth said. "Oh, what a view! Look, Babs!"

Barbara looked out at the view of peaks rising over peaks, and gave a cry of rapture. "Oh, isn't it marvellous! Oh, I'm so glad I've come! This will be school with bells on!"

Rosalie Dene chuckled. "It isn't term-time yet, but I'd better warn you that slang is *not* permitted. So if you've picked up a slang vocabulary at home, I advise you to forget it as quickly as you can. However, with four days a week of nothing but French and German, I fancy that won't be too difficult. Here we are! Beth, that building among the firs is the school. And this is Freudesheim. Jump out and take your case. I'll see that your trunk comes over presently. Say good-bye, Barbara. You won't be seeing Beth—or only at a distance, anyhow—for the next three or four weeks, thanks to German measles."

Beth lifted her case from the top of the pile and set it on the ground. Then she came to the window where Barbara was looking out, a troubled expression on her face.

"Good-bye, Babs. It won't be for long and I expect we'll be able to grin at each other, even if we can't come within speaking distance. And look here, Babs! After the others have come, you hunt out young Vi and ask her to introduce you to Mary-Lou Trelawney. She's a nice kid, if all Vi says is true. And Vi herself will give you a hand. I'm afraid Betsy and the Ozanne twins will be rather grand young women in school. But you'll have Vi and plenty of the others before the end of the week, I imagine. Now kiss me and let me go. Miss Dene wants to get back."

For a moment, Barbara felt panic-stricken. Then she pulled herself together. Her arms went round her sister's neck in a violent hug as she said quickly, "It's all right. Don't you worry about me. Vi's a dear and a cousin's *almost* like a sister anyhow—a cousin like Vi, I mean. I'm looking forward to it all *awfully* and I know I'm going to have a gorgeous time!"

Beth kissed her and then stood aside, Miss Dene turned the car—not without difficulty, for the road was none too good as yet, though there were plans afoot to improve it as soon as possible. Barbara waved pluckily and saw her sister open the gate before she picked up her case and went into the garden. Then they had rounded the curve and she could see no more. She choked down the sob that came into her throat, made a supreme effort and said to Miss Dene, "And now it's my turn and I'm—I'm excited!"

CHAPTER THREE

The School Arrives

"WELL, WE'VE talked about almost everything except our new uniforms. What do you all think of them?"

The eight Senior Middles in the compartment sat up when Mary-Lou Trelawney flung this bombshell among them as the train that was bearing them to Interlaken thundered along on the shores of Lake Thun. What *did* they think of the new uniforms? Most of them had grumbled furiously when the letter came from the school, informing their mothers that the old brown and flame was to be left behind for the use of the English branch and they would make their début in Switzerland in something as different as it could be. They looked self-consciously at each other and then Hilary Bennett spoke.

"I'm bound to say I simply raged when I first heard. Well, I expect I wasn't the only one!" She looked accusingly round at her friends and they all nodded, Mary-Lou with a deep chuckle. Hilary continued. "We've *always* worn brown and flame. People know us by that. All the same, I do see the point of changing now. And you know, looking at you all, I must say I rather like it on the whole. It's such a gorgeous deep, vivid blue."

"It's gentian blue," Mary-Lou told her with an air. "Auntie Jo told me that. I like it myself. I loved the brown, of course, but there's more—more *colour* to this. And the ties and badges and hat-bands are marvellous!"

"Oh, they're marvellous all right," Carol Younger said, "and it suits most of you. But what about me? I haven't any colour to speak of at the best of times and this shade of blue makes me look even worse than usual."

As Carol was inclined to sallowness and had mousey-brown hair and grey-green eyes, there was a good deal of truth in her words.

"I expect living in Switzerland will give you a complexion," Vi Lucy said soothingly. "They say the air's marvellous. And if you come to that, Carol, neither did the brown suit you. I rather love this myself." And she looked down complacently at her well-cut tunic in the glorious blue, with its flared skirt and the matching blazer, with the school badge embroidered on the breast-pocket in silver and crimson.

Carol heaved a deep sigh. "Oh, well, let's hope you're right and Switzerland gives me a colour. Really, the only thing that would do me would be a dark crimson."

"And what about the people with red hair?" Mary-Lou

demanded. She suddenly giggled. "I think I hear Clem, for instance, pronouncing on a crimson uniform with *her* hair!"

The rest joined whole-heartedly in her giggles. Clem was Clem Barrass, a very important person, since she was a prefect this year. She had dark red hair and was debarred from ever wearing reds or pinks as a result. Clem in crimson would have been a shock!

Miss o'Ryan, one of the escort mistresses, came along to warn them that they would arrive at Interlaken in less than ten minutes.

Mary-Lou, pluming herself on the fact that she had not touched her strapped case since they had changed at Basle, glanced at the less provident others who were scrambling with magazines, books, sweets and cases and then tackled the mistress on the subject of the new uniform in the usual calm way which caused so many people to exclaim, "Isn't Mary-Lou the absolute *edge*!"

"Miss o'Ryan, what do *you* think about our new uniform? Do you like it?"

Miss o'Ryan, an Old Girl of the school, surveyed her interrogator with dancing eyes. "Oh, I like it very much indeed. I think it was so wise for us to start in a new place with new colours. 'Tis a glorious blue it is and we chose cream for your blouses as we thought white would make too startling a contrast. But there isn't time to talk about a trifle like that just now. You get everything together and be ready to fly as soon as we leave the train. I'll discuss the matter with you when we've been here a few days—say Saturday week. Hurry now, girls, and don't be keeping us waiting." She nodded at them and passed on to the next compartment, leaving them to tell Mary-Lou what they thought of her coolness.

"Really, Mary-Lou, you are the outside of enough for cheek!" Lesley Malcolm said as she pulled her straps tight.

"How you get away with all you do I just don't know," Vi added as she tried to squeeze a book, a magazine and a box of sweets into a case already full to bursting.

"You'll bust your locks if you try to shut that," Mary-Lou remarked, ignoring all recriminations with the insouciance that was peculiarly hers. "Here; let me! You'll never do it with such a mess!" By the time she had finished, Vi was able to lock it.

"You're a wizard packer; I will say that for you," her friend observed as she put the keys in her purse and then began to fold her raincoat. "Where's my beastly brolley? Oh, here it is. Shove it on top and help me pull the straps tight, will you? Thanks a lot! *That's* all done! Got your own brolley?"

Mary-Lou nodded. "Gran says if I lose it I can just buy another myself—and I'd have to, you know. They make such a fuss about brolleys at school. I'm sticking to this like glue, I can tell you. It would be a ghastly waste of pocket-money to have to buy another and they prob'ly cost the earth here, anyhow."

Everyone agreed with this dictum. They had little use for umbrellas and as for Mary-Lou, she had lost every one she possessed until her grandmother had put a stop to it by issuing this latest ukase. Since then, Mary-Lou had contrived to keep the hated thing safe for the last two terms.

The cases were finished and they sat back, waiting excitedly for the moment when they would leave the train. Vi voiced all their feelings when she said suddenly, "Oh, I'm thrilled to the limit! This really *is* something!"

"I've only one thing against it," Lesley said thoughtfully. "It means that we're a much smaller school and I don't like that. Last year we had over three hundred with the Juniors. Here, we've only about a hundred."

"We've no Juniors at all, of course," Mary-Lou said when they stood in their ranks on the platform, cases in hand, and all ready to march off as soon as the word was given. "That makes a big difference. There were over seventy of them, weren't there? And then quite a lot of our own crowd are staying on at the English branch. Yes; I don't like that part of it awfully much. Doris isn't here, f'rinstance, and we're going to miss her a lot. She's always been one of our crowd."

Hilary went off at a tangent. "I wonder if we'll still be in the same forms as we were last term? That kid, Len Maynard, was Upper IVB—remember?"

"That was only because we were so full up anyhow,"

observed Vi. "Len kept her end up all right, but I know she had to slog for it. I should think that now we've got so much smaller she'll be put down. Where did she come in the end-of-term lists?"

"Ninth," someone replied.

"Well, there you are, then. They'll probably keep her there with this term's new lot."

There was no more time for gossip, for the last girl had left the train with her case and taken her place in the long lines on the platform and Miss Derwent, head of the escort staff, came round to the front and called for silence.

"Straighten your lines, girls," she said. "Now! Buses are waiting to take us up to the Platz. There are too many of us for the mountain railway. Prefects, will you lead out? You will find the buses waiting outside in the Bahnhof Strasse. Four prefects to each bus, please, and leave a front seat for the mistresses. Miss o'Ryan and Miss Armitage, will you go first and begin seeing them in. Have you all got *everything*? Miss Burnett, just take a run through the carriages, please, and make sure."

Miss Burnett, the Physical Training mistress and an Old Girl of the school like Biddy o'Ryan, the history mistress, skipped agilely up the steps into the nearest coach while the girls, headed by the prefects, followed the latter and Miss Armitage, the science mistress, out of the station into the Bahnhof Strasse where the great blue school buses were waiting for them, and began to clamber in.

"How do we go?" Vi Lucy asked of Ruth Wilson, one of the prefects in their bus.

"On wheels!" Ruth responded promptly.

"I didn't mean that. I meant which route do we follow?" Vi returned with dignity, ignoring a piece of primitive humour which she would have snubbed severely if it had come from any of her compeers.

Madge Herbert, another prefect, cast a glance at Ruth, reminding her that such witticisms should be beneath the dignity of a prefect and said in her pleasant voice, "I was asking Miss Derwent about that in the train and she says that we have a long run. The only direct motor-road to the Görnetz Platz is terribly steep, so we go through the mountains by one they built a few years ago for heavy traffic."

"Thank you, Madge," Vi said, still with a touch of reserve in her voice. "That sounds wizard."

Madge smiled at her and went to sit at the back of the bus with Ruth and the other two prefects, Nora Penley and Dorothy Watson, while what was known as "The Gang" in the school settled themselves comfortably.

"What a goop Ruth Wilson is!" Hilary remarked in an under-tone. "Did she think she was being *funny*, by any chance?"

"Probably," Lesley Malcolm returned. "I wonder how old she thinks we are?"

"Oh, well, she's the only one, and she's new to the job," Mary-Lou said tolerantly. "Isn't it weird to know beforehand just who the Head Girl and the Prees are? Generally, we have to wait till after Prayers."

"They'd have to fix all that up beforehand," Hilary said. "The prees will have to hoe in at once. I wonder what sort of a Head Girl Julie will make, Vi?"

"As good as anyone, I should think," returned Vi who held the proud position of younger sister to the new Head Girl. "By the way, we know who the prees are all right, but we don't know who has which job."

"We shall know after Prayers tonight," said a small, silvery voice which had hitherto been silent. Its owner was a tiny, angelically lovely person of fourteen who claimed the distinction of being Mary-Lou's "sister-by-marriage", since the latter's mother had married her father that summer. They had always been great friends, beginning their Chalet School days together.

In her way, Verity-Anne was as great an original as Mary-Lou herself. She was very quiet and retiring, where Mary-Lou, without any idea of being bumptious, forged her way to the front. But once Verity-Anne had made up her mind about anything, it would take, as Lesley Malcolm had graphically phrased it, a herd of wild bulls to make her change. Where Mary-Lou thought and acted like lightning, Verity-Anne was slow and inclined to moon. But she had her own ideas and was quite ready to voice them when asked.

Mary-Lou, tall, sturdy and very grown-up in many ways, protected her "sister" when it was needful and saved her from many a scolding; but there was no doubt to those old enough to realize it that Verity-Anne acted as a brake on Mary-Lou's wilder notions.

The whole Gang decided, in the main, most out-of-school affairs affecting the rest of their crowd, and Mary-Lou and Vi led the Gang by the nose.

On this occasion, they had all contrived to crowd into the same bus, the authorities being too much occupied with other matters to pursue their usual policy and separate them. They had secured seats together and, though Miss Burnett cast a quick glance at them when she entered the bus immediately after Verity-Anne's speech, she decided to let them alone.

"After all, they're all Senior Middles this term," she said in an aside to Miss o'Ryan as she sat down beside her. "They ought to have a little sense by this time."

Mary-Lou had seen the look—very little ever escaped her—and she decided to be very crushing if anyone tried to play the fool. Then they set off and the bus was rolling down the Hoheweg before turning off to the south to run through rising country which became higher and higher until they were passing between great cliffs which awed the girls into a near-silence. They had never seen anything like this before. They went on mounting and soon the busy little towns and villages were left behind and there was no sign of human habitation for some distance except very occasionally a chalet on a little shelf.

"I shouldn't like to live in one of those," Mary-Lou said with a slight shudder as they passed one of these lonely places. "I should think it must be deadly, even in the summer. As for winter, I don't know how they can stand it!" She raised her voice. "The Görnetz Platz isn't like that, is it, Miss Burnett?"

Miss Burnett turned round to smile. "Oh dear, no! It's quite a place. Besides ourselves and the new Sanatorium, there are at least thirty or forty chalets dotted about the

Platz, including a couple of shops, one of which is the post office. The Platz used to be a climbing centre, but there are other places which are better for that sort of thing, so visitors began to leave it. That is how we were able to get the two big hotels for the San and the School. Mrs. Maynard has what used to be a guest-house and there's another, not far from the San, which Dr. and Mrs. Peters share with Dr. and Mrs. Graves. You all remember, Miss Burn, don't you?"

Big Carola Johnston, seated near the back with her chum, Jean Ackroyd, chimed in. "Of course we do! Do you mean that she and Dr. Graves are here? How super!"

"Yes; I thought you'd like that," Miss Burnett agreed "I've heard all about your adventure in the lily pools at Bosham, Carola."

Whereat, Carola went red and said no more. Miss Burnett continued her account placidly. "There is a biggish kind of hall nearby which we can use for concerts and plays and so on; and there are two churches—a Protestant one and a Catholic chapel which is served from an Augustinian convent a few miles away. Plenty of company, you see. And with more than a hundred of our noble selves, you won't lack for any amount of people, Mary-Lou."

"It all sounds simply thrilling," Vi remarked.

Miss Burnett and Miss o'Ryan looked at each other and laughed. "Sure 'tis thrilling for us it is," the latter said. "All those years away and now back in the Alps again at last! Not that they're our own original Alps," she added. "Still, 'tis the Alps, and that's a great thing."

"But Switzerland is lots nearer Tirol than England," Mary-Lou said. "You'll be able to go and see it at half-terms, won't you?"

"Quite right; we will," Miss Burnett agreed. "In fact, I don't mind telling you I've an invitation for this half-term to visit Innsbruck and if I go, I shall certainly make a trip to Tiernsee. Now look out, all of you! This is one of the little villages on the way. It's within walking distance and the villagers do the most lovely wood-carving and the women make lace. I expect we shall have an expedition here one Saturday and let you explore."

A chorus of delight rose from the girls as they gazed out at the village with its chalets with their steeply-pitched roofs, weighted with rocks and tied with ropes, beautifully carved balconies, window-frames and door-posts, and the tiny hayfields now bare and brown, since the hay had been cut and carried three weeks before.

"Isn't it pretty!" Lesley said. "But what have they done with the hay? I don't see any ricks anywhere."

"All under cover in the sheds," Miss o'Ryan informed her. "Sure, you don't leave hay out in the open in a land where the snow is several feet thick in winter. If you did, your poor beasts would often be going hungry."

They passed the village and swung round a hair-pin bend and once more they were rolling along between grim rock walls, broken here and there by shelves. Everywhere they saw clusters of black-trunked pines and firs.

"What lots of firs they have, hereabouts!" Christine remarked.

Miss Burnett heard and turned round again to give more information. "Yes; and they are so important that if anyone cuts one down without permission from the forestry office—if that's what they call it; I don't really know—he is liable to imprisonment or a heavy fine. So never try your hand at felling as a joke!"

Her remark had roused their curiosity. Luckily, Mary-Lou never suffered from shyness and she asked what they were all dying to know.

"What a weird idea! Why are they as important as all that?"

"The forests act as avalanche-breaks," the mistress explained. "You all know what an avalanche is, don't you? Well, trees in bulk break up an avalanche and disperse the worst of it, so long as they are healthy and thickly enough planted. I'm not certain, but I *think* the Government have a department whose job is solely to look after the pines and firs and see that the woods round the villages are kept in proper condition. We have pines and firs all along the back of the Görnetz Platz, though as the mountains round about there are not giants and so lose their snow in summer, there isn't anything like the danger that there is among the Grisons and about the really high peaks. All the same, if we have an unseasonably warm spring, we can have avalanches on a minor scale. So we have the trees as a precaution."

One or two of the girls looked positively scared as Miss o'Ryan noted, so she changed the subject. "Here's another village—Laustadt, by name. 'Tis only five miles we have to go now. We'll be seeing the Maynards' house, Freudesheim, in a few minutes. Oh, and while I think of it, none of you are to go anywhere near it. They've started with German measles and the whole family is in quarantine at present. Len and Con are down, and so is Charles. 'Tis the likeliest thing in the world that the rest will follow—though we're hoping Felix and Felicity will escape."

This caused a sensation. Mary-Lou turned to Vi, exclaiming, "But isn't that cousin of yours, Barbara Chester, to live with them and come daily for this term? That's what you told us in the train, anyhow. Whatever will she do?"

"That's all right," Miss Burnett said cheerfully. "It happened before Barbara arrived and she came straight to school. No one wants her to begin her school career with German measles, so she'll be a boarder at once instead of waiting a term."

Before anyone could say anything else, Miss o'Ryan exclaimed, "Here we are! This is the beginning of the Görnetz Platz and there's the new Chalet School over there, amongst those pines."

She pointed, and everyone promptly crowded to the window on the right to get the first glimpse of their new school and in the excitement, even Vi forgot her grievances. They saw a high fence with a ring of firs and birches inside. Above these rose the peak of a high roof with squat chimneys nestling down to it. They rounded the curve and passed through the wide-open gates and up a short drive. There, their bus drew up. They had arrived at last!

CHAPTER FOUR

Barbara's First Day

BARBARA HAD AWAKENED that morning with a feeling that something unexpected had happened. What it was she was unable to think for the first moment or two. Then she rolled over in her little bed and surveyed the prospect.

She was in a cubicle in what was known as "Leafy" It was walled in by curtains of fresh cretonne whose cream ground had a pattern of leafy sprays running all over it. The rug by her bed and the cushion in the wicker-chair repeated the design and so did the *couvre-pied* on the bed and the counterpane which she had removed and folded the night before under Matron's instructions. There was also a table which had two little drawers and two long ones. One end of it was a locker affair. The top lifted back and showed a mirror with a place for toilet articles, all except one's sponge-bag. For that, there was a hook attached to one of the standards that supported the curtain-rods round the cubicle. A second standard had a hook for your dressing-gown and there was a big closet at one end of the room which had two pegs for her frocks and two for her coats.

When she got as far as this, Barbara sat up in bed and hugged herself with glee. This really *was* school, just as she had always dreamed of it. It was really true. She was at the Chalet School and not just as a daily pupil but as a full-blown boarder.

She looked at the curtains cutting her off from cubicles on either side. When tomorrow came, she would have her own cousin, Vi Lucy, on one side, and the unknown Mary-Lou Beth had talked of on the other. Barbara had heard of Mary-Lou from the other girls in the family and she liked all she had heard. Beth seemed to think well of her, since she had told Babs to ask Vi to introduce them.

"But there won't be any need of that," Barbara thought.

"If we're next door to each other, we're *bound* to talk!"

She twisted round to look out of her half of the window which was divided between her cubicle and Vi's. You couldn't see much that way and it was a glorious September day with the sun shining brightly. Barbara threw back the bedclothes and scrambled out of bed to see out properly. Everything was hung with dew which glittered in the sunlight.

"Oh, it's all simply gorgeous!" she said aloud. "This is a lovely place! I just know I'm going to love being here!"

"Well, that's good hearing, anyway," said a voice behind her; and Barbara turned round, startled, to face a tall lady with a pleasant, clear-cut face. Her wavy dark hair shone with hard brushing and her blue eyes were smiling. "Yes; this is a beautiful place. I'm glad you feel it. And now to introduce myself. I'm Miss Annersley, your Head Mistress. I'm sorry I couldn't see you last night, but I was busy till after ten o'clock. I peeped in when I came up to bed, but you were asleep then. I hope you slept all right?"

A sudden smile curved Barbara's lips. "I don't even remember getting into bed," she said solemnly. "I slept like a log all night and I've just wakened up, really."

"That's good! I shall hope to hear on the last day of term that it's been the same thing every night," the Head said with a clear, ringing laugh. "Well, I expect you've had all the sleep you want for the present, so what about coming out with me for a stroll beforehand? You know which your bathroom is, don't you? Then hurry up and bath and dress and get into your uniform"—Barbara wondered how in the world Miss Annersley could know that she was simply dying to wear it?—"and come down to my study. Don't forget to strip your bed, will you? And lift the mattress into a hump in the middle so that the air can pass under it. But I expect Matron told you all that sort of thing last night."

Barbara nodded mutely.

"I thought so. Put on your walking-shoes and your blazer. The sun is shining, but there's a nip in mountain air as early as this in September. I'll have a glass of milk waiting for you and then we'll take a short walk." Miss

Annersley nodded and vanished through the curtains once more and Barbara hurried to pull on her bedroom slippers and dressing-gown, seize her sponge-bag and towels and then make tracks for the bathroom.

Matron had explained to her that she might have a bath every morning so long as it was either a lukewarm or a cold one. She would very much rather have chosen the former, but she had heard her sisters on the subject of "Sissies" who funked their cold plunge so, repressing a shudder, she turned on the cold tap and ran the bath. Then she tossed off her shoes, drew a deep breath and plunged in, ducking down in a squatting position which sent a lovely tide of water slopping over the edge.

Oh, how cold it was! A gasp broke from her, but by the time she was dry and in her pyjamas again, she was glowing and fresh from the icy sting.

When she was ready, Barbara raced off to the dormitory to scramble into her clothes and give her fair curls a few perfunctory taps with a brush. Then began the delight of putting on the uniform. Of the fact that she had committed all sorts of sins in leaving the bathroom in the state she had done, she was cheerfully unaware. At home, someone had always tidied up after her. She tied her shoe-laces and then stood up, ready for the supreme moment.

It is doubtful if any uniform was ever put on with more reverence. First the blouse with its smart little collar and tie. And, incidentally, that tie gave her any amount of trouble, but it was done at last. Then she drew the well-cut, flared tunic over her head and settled it with fingers which had inherited her mother's gift of putting on her clothes daintily. There was only the blazer left. She slipped her arms into it and then surveyed herself once more. She considered her head and shoulders which were all she could see in the locker mirror, and decided that all was well there. Then she stood on tiptoe to see as much as she could of the rest of her person and was on the verge of climbing on to her bedroom chair to see the rest when the curtains were flung open again and Matron stood before her.

"Good morning, Barbara," she said.

"Good morning, Matron," Barbara replied very properly.

She stood in deep awe of the trim little lady who was no taller than herself and who looked so very smart and trig in her stiffly starched blue linen dress with its big white apron and the "angels' wings" cap.

Matron looked her up and down. "Yes; well, your hair won't do like that," she said briskly. "Have you brushed it *at all* this morning?"

"Oh, yes, Matron," Barbara assured her.

"Not very well, I'm afraid. Here, slip on your dressing-gown, sit down at the mirror and give it a good hard brushing. A curly crop like yours needs that twice a day if you're to escape tangles and pullings. I'll strip your bed for you and show you how you are to do it for the future."

Barbara did as she was told; but after watching her attempts for about half a minute, Matron took the brush from her. "My dear girl! Has no one ever shown you how to brush your hair properly. What were Nancy and Beth thinking about?"

"Mummy always did it for me," her victim explained humbly.

"I see. But here, you must do it for yourself, you know. Start at the crown of your head and draw the bristles down with a firm, steady stroke. Go all round your head and if you do it rightly, your scalp should be tingling by the time you've finished." She watched Barbara essaying a stroke or two and nodded. "That's the way. Now never let me see you *patting* your head again. Turn round and watch me strip your bed. No; don't stop brushing. You can do two things like that at once."

Barbara turned round to face the bed and Matron proceeded to show her the one only way of stripping a bed that she approved.

Matron then examined the fair curls which were beginning to shine, said that would do for now and ordered her victim to look round and make sure everything was tidy before she left the cubicle. When it was all done, the little abode passed Matron's keen scrutiny and she nodded.

"Yes; that will do very nicely. Now remember; this has to be done every morning. And every other day, you must turn the mattress so that it wears evenly. Do you understand?"

"Yes, Matron; I think so." But Barbara was thinking rather dismally that she would have little time for dressing if this had to be seen to before she went downstairs in the morning. She was yet to find that practice helps you to be quick; and also that there was generally someone in the dormitory who would give you a hand—strictly against rules, of course!—if you really couldn't manage.

At present, Matron merely said, "Excellent! Well, now come with me."

Wondering what was to happen *now*, Barbara meekly followed the school tyrant, who was also one of the most beloved persons there, to the bathroom. That lady flung the door open wide and revealed it exactly as it had been left. Barbara eyed the mess and shook in her shoes. She could guess what was coming.

"This sort of thing won't *do*!" Matron told her firmly. "After you've had a bath, you must leave the bathroom as tidy as you leave your cubicle. And how on earth did you manage to make such a swim on the floor? You mustn't do that." She went to a cupboard and produced a mop, a bucket and two cloths. "Mop up that flood and squeeze the mop into the bucket. Then take *this* cloth and rub the floor over. Wipe out the bath with this other one and *never* leave a bath unwiped after you've used it."

Barbara went at the unaccustomed task feeling that she had certainly blotted her copybook forever, so far as Matron was concerned. She was slow and awkward, for, apart from the fact that she had never done such a thing before, she was hampered by the need for keeping her new tunic unsplashed. Matron took pity on her and squeezed the mop and cloths herself, before returning everything to its proper place. Then she nodded and said, "Yes; that's more like it! Now remember what I say, for I haven't time to keep running after you all to see that you leave places tidy. And talking of running, *you'd* better run now. Down those stairs, turn to the right and go along the passage and you'll come out at the back of the entrance hall. Go right across to the front-door and the study is the door nearest to that. Oh, and while I think of it, this is the staircase you girls will use—never the front stairs. Now off you go!"

She gave Barbara a friendly clap on the back as she spoke and then hurried off to some other duty, leaving that young woman to find her own way to the study. It was easy enough, and Miss Annersley was waiting for her with a glass of rich, creamy milk and a slice of delicious, holey French bread, simply smothered in butter.

"Come along, dear," the Head said briskly. "Dispose of that and then we'll go for our stroll. Have you put on your stout shoes? The dews are very heavy at this time of year. And *have* you left your cubicle in order?"

"Yes, thank you. Matron came to show me," Barbara said soberly, not seeing the laughter in the Head's eyes as she put the question.

"Then it will certainly be all right! Eat your bread-and-butter, dear. You'll be very hungry before we come in if you don't."

Barbara obeyed and found that what with her long sleep and the cold tub, she had the kind of appetite she had never known till then. The Head waited till she had finished and then marched her out into the morning sunshine. The air was crisp with a sharp tang to it and the dew was so heavy that it looked like hoar frost. Miss Annersley kept to the path and told Barbara to do the same.

"I won't show you our grounds now," she said, laughing. "You must wait for the others to come. Now shall we go along the road a little way? Suppose we walk round to Freudesheim? We might catch a glimpse of Beth. You can't go near her, of course, but we're fairly isolated here, so if you like to call a few remarks to her, I don't mind."

Barbara's cheeks went pink and her eyes shone. How did Miss Annersley know that Beth was the one person she wanted to see just then? "I'd love that!" she said fervently.

"Then come along." She opened the big gate as she spoke and they went out and into the road.

Miss Annersley led the way, talking gaily as they went. But instead of rounding the curve behind which Freudesheim lay, she kept on and presently drew Barbara to the edge of the shelf and bade her look over. Barbara came close and stared down. To her amazement, she was looking down into a sea of white mists that looked almost solid. Across the valley, it lapped up the mountain slopes, making the peaks on the other side look as if they were washed by a real sea so that the summits almost seemed to float.

"Oh!" Barbara gasped.

The Head laughed. "I thought you'd be surprised. At this time of year you get very heavy mists in the early morning. Presently, as the sun grows stronger, they will draw off; but early in the morning, the valley is always full of them. Well, having shown you that, I propose that we turn back and go to Freudesheim and see if we can pick up any news of the invalids. Turn down here, dear. There's Freudesheim, just in front of you."

Barbara scanned the tall house with its heavily carved balconies and steeply-pitched roof with eager eyes. Someone was on the lower balcony, hanging pillows over the rail. The next moment they were seen and a long arm waved to them. The Head waved back and the next moment the figure had disappeared. Two minutes later, Beth and Mrs. Maynard appeared at the top of the steps that led to the door.

"We aren't coming nearer," Joey Maynard called in her golden voice. "We're as infectious as we can be and I know all too well what would happen to me if we handed on German measles to the school at the beginning of term!"

"That sounds suspicious," Miss Annersley replied. "Who's the latest victim?"

"Mike—started this morning, for he was all right at bedtime last night. But he woke up thoroughly whingey and whiney and when I examined him, his chest was covered with rash and so was his back. Margot still seems all right and so are the twins, for which may Heaven be praised! They're both cutting back teeth and we had a night of it with Felix, poor little man! Hello, Babs! I expect you'd like a word with Beth. Go on round the fence at that side and stop at the corner and you can yell to each other there. *We* shan't hear you. I've too much to say to Miss Annersley." She turned to Beth who had been waving excitedly to her sister. "Off you go! But keep well away from the fence." She turned to the Head. "She hasn't been near the family so far, so she is free from infection at the moment. But we'll be safe rather than sorry, I think."

Miss Annersley laughed. "I certainly agree with that! Run along, Barbara, and keep as far from the fence as Beth does. I'm trusting you, Beth," she added.

Beth nodded. "We'll be very careful. Come on, Babs!"

They ran along the fence and once they had reached the corner, Beth stopped a good three feet away from it and began to ask questions at express speed. "How did you get on last night? Did you sleep all right?"

"Yes; like a top. But oh, Beth, I did such an *awful* thing this morning!"

"What was that?" Beth asked quickly.

"I left a most *awful* mess in the bathroom!" Barbara could hardly have sounded more horror-stricken if she had accidentally murdered someone and been caught trying to dispose of the body.

Beth's eyes danced. "And I suppose Matey got hold of you and told you *all* about it for the good of your soul? Don't I know it!"

"I'm awfully sorry, but I honestly didn't know we were supposed to clear up," Barbara said defensively.

"Keep cool, my child; keep cool! Of course you didn't. And Matey's had to deal with that sort of thing times out number. The thing for you to remember is that you haven't anyone to run round after you now and try to keep from making messes. If you do, clear them up at once; that's all. Which dormy are you in?"

"Leafy. It's awfully pretty, Beth! And I've got a lovely view from my window. Matron came in this morning to show me how to strip my bed. Oh, and she says I don't brush my hair properly. She asked what you and Nancy had been doing not to show me."

Beth groaned loudly. "She would! She'll jump on me with both feet and all her weight the first chance she has! Nancy, too, when she comes up from Welsen."

"I don't think she will. I explained to her that Mummy had always done it for me."

"Oh well, let's hope she passes that." Beth paused a

moment, frowning slightly. Then she looked up. "Look here, Babs, when you get into difficulties, you get hold of young Vi and ask her to help you out. I suppose you don't even know if Vi's in the same dormy or near at hand or shoved right away at the other end of the place?"

"But I do," Barbara said triumphantly. "She has the cubicle next to mine and Mary-Lou Trelawney is on the other side. Matron told me last night."

Beth's face cleared. "That'll be all right then. You tell those two that I said they were to give you a hand for the first week or two until you can feel your feet."

"Do you think they'll like that?" Barbara asked.

"What on earth does it matter whether they do or not? You're quite new—newer than most to it all—and it's the only decent thing for them to do. After all, Vi *is* your cousin! Tell her what I say and when she gives you any tips, you take them in. You'll soon know all about it and then you needn't hang on to either her or Mary-Lou."

"Very well," Barbara said submissively. "But I do mean to stand on my own feet as much as I can."

"Good for you! It won't last long—needing to be told, I mean."

Barbara tilted her chin. "I'll see that it doesn't. How do you like it here, Beth?"

Beth laughed. "It's going to be fun. Well, you'd expect that with Aunt Jo at the head of things. Listen! There's the Head calling you! Scram!" She blew a kiss across the fence and Barbara went off to join Miss Annersley and walk back to school for breakfast which, she found, was what was meant by *"Frühstück"*, feeling much happier.

Once the meal was over, she found that the Head had spoken the truth when she said that they would all be very busy. Matron came with her to show her the one way of bedmaking which she approved. When that was done, she marched the new girl off to one of the trunk-rooms where her trunk was unpacked and she had to put away her clothes neatly and properly. Each drawer had its own correct belongings and Barbara was warned that when dormitory inspections were made if hers were untidy, she would be called from whatever she was doing to set them to rights.

When it was all done, she was borne off to the staff-room for milk and biscuits and then Miss Dene demanded assistance in the stock-room and they were hard at it until a gong sounded as a warning that *Mittagessen* was due. Miss Dene sent her to wash her hands and tidy her hair which was wild by that time and she found that in future she must use her form cloakroom—called "the Splashery"—and keep a comb and towel there.

"But you can go upstairs today," Miss Dene said. "No one will know form places until tomorrow after Prayers. Hop along! "

Barbara was very quiet during the meal, only speaking when spoken to. She felt shy among so many grown-ups, so she held her tongue and used her eyes and ears and found to her amazement that mistresses off duty were exactly like Beth and *her* chums.

The meal came to an end and she was sent out into the garden to amuse herself while the staff retired to the Head's sitting-room for half an hour with coffee and chatter.

"I wonder how that child will get on?" Matron mused.

"Who—Barbara? Quite well, I expect," Rosalie Dene said. "She's sister to Beth and Nancy, and they got on perfectly well."

"I think you can hardly judge Barbara by them," the Head said, stirring her coffee thoughtfully. "They have had the usual life of schoolgirls; but Barbara has been so delicate that she has never been away from her mother before. That was why it was first arranged that she should live with Jo and be a daygirl with the triplets."

"Unfortunately, Len and Con have put a stop to that." Miss Denny said. "What's been wrong with the child, Hilda?"

"General delicacy, I gather, with a tendency to bronchitis, Matey."

"Ah! " said Matron. "So that accounts for her! "

"In what way?" two or three voices promptly demanded.

Matron obliged with an account of the bathroom and the Head nodded. "That's exactly what I meant. I don't suppose Barbara realized that she must clear up her own mess. Ride her gently, Matey. It's a big change for her."

"So long as I know! I thought it was just schoolgirl carelessness. As for the bronchitis, I'll keep an eye on her when the cold weather starts."

Then they had to break up and go back to work which continued until the gong sounded for *Kaffee und Kuchen* which turned out to be cups of milky coffee and twists of delicious fancy bread. After that, everyone drew breath for a little until Miss Denny, sitting in the entrance hall with the rest, exclaimed, "I can hear the buses!"

Everyone jumped up and they all surged out to the drive, Barbara going with Miss Dene who slipped a hand through her arm and told her to come along and see the fun. The big buses rolled through the gate and came up the short drive, one at a time, to unload its burden of girls, cases and mistresses. When the last had gone and the girls were standing in long files, the Head spoke.

"Welcome to our Chalet School in Switzerland, all of you! Come along in and take possession of your new school."

The files marched forward, four abreast and filled the entrance hall. Barbara, standing shyly to one side, suddenly felt a hand on her arm and looked up to see her cousin Vi Lucy who, having made up her mind to help her out, was going to do the thing in style.

"Here you are!" she said. "Come along and join our crowd. The Head will have a few words to say and then we'll find out where our dormies are and school can begin properly. Here's my chum, Mary-Lou Trelawney—Oh, and her sister-by-marriage, Verity-Anne Carey. I'll tell you about the rest later. We'll all help you through for the first week or so. Come and hear what the Head's got to say."

Mary-Lou gave her a grin and formed up on her other side and the three wriggled through the crowd to join a cluster of girls, all their own age. So it was that, guarded on one side by Vi and on the other by Mary-Lou, Barbara made her first real acquaintance with the Chalet School.

CHAPTER FIVE

Settling In

THE HEAD did not keep the girls long on this occasion. She gave them her usual friendly welcome back to school and then told them that in Hall they would find a plan of the buildings which would help them to find their way about. Dormitory lists were pinned below and, last of all, the list of dormitory prefects. Then she dismissed them with a gentle reminder that though this was the first night of term and rules were more or less in abeyance until the next morning, talking on stairs and in the corridors should be limited and subdued in tone; and they must, of course, not use the front stairs at all.

"That last remark does not mean the prefects," she added, flashing a smile at a group of very grown-up young ladies. "To use the front stairs is a prefect's privilege."

She and the staff withdrew after that, leaving the girls to see to themselves, and a crowd at once surged into Hall which was a big place, running from back to front of the building.

"*We* needn't bother with plans or lists," Vi said with an air to her clan. "We've got Babs here to tell us. You came yesterday, Babs, so you ought to know all about it. Which dormies are we in? That's the first thing to see to."

"You and Mary-Lou are in Leafy," Barbara said, having studied her own dormitory list thoroughly that afternoon. "So is Verity-Anne and someone called Catriona Watson. And there are two more girls called Emerence Hope and Janet Forster and the prefect is Katharine Gordon."

"Might be worse," Mary-Lou observed. "I like Katt Gordon and Jan Forster is quite a decent kid. Catriona is one of us. I suppose you don't possibly know where the rest of our gang are? Oh, well, that's enough to be going on with. You others will just have to go and see for yourselves.

I hope Matey hasn't shoved you miles away from us."

"So do I! But you bet she has," grumbled a girl with wavy brown hair. "I think she might have put Catriona and me together and left young Emerence out of it."

"If you ask me," Mary-Lou said with her most grown-up air, "she's shoved Emerence in with us because she thinks that we can suppress her if necessary."

"And *that* wouldn't surprise me," Vi put in, drowning Christine Vincent's remark, "Whose trumpeter's dead now?" and giving a chuckle. "You know what Emerence is like! It's hard luck on you and Catriona, Chris; but then it's just as hard luck on us and Lesley. Go and find out where you all are, anyhow, and let us know later. Come on, you others—oh, we'd better get hold of Emerence and Jan, I suppose."

"They've gone into Hall," said Verity-Anne in her composed little voice.

"Oh, bother them! Well, I suppose they'll find the way sooner or later. Lead on, Babs!"

Barbara turned and led the way from the entrance hall, down a long passage, round a corner and so to a flight of uncarpeted stairs. "Up here," she said.

"O.K.! Come on, folks!" And Vi set off up the stairs, two at a time, secure in the knowledge that no one would call her to order for that tonight. The others raced up after her and once they were at the top, she delegated the leadership to her cousin with a grin and the remark, "Seems rum for *us* to have to get *you* to show us the way, seeing we've been at the school for years and you've just come! But that's your luck!"

Barbara laughed self-consciously and led the way. "This is Leafy Dormitory," she said shyly as she opened the door. "That cubicle there is yours, Vi. I come next and then Mary-Lou and Verity-Anne on the other side. Catriona, your cubicle is opposite Vi's and the other two are next and Katharine Gordon has the one opposite Verity-Anne's."

The four strode into the room and stood looking round critically. Finally, Mary-Lou spoke. "New curtains and everything! I rather like the new pattern on the cretonnes, don't you? I suppose the old ones have been left for the English branch."

"Rather nifty!" Vi agreed. "Barbara, you and I share a window. And Mary-Lou and Verity-Anne have another. What about Katharine? The prefect *always* has a window cubey."

"Yes; she has one, too," Barbara said. She was still standing by the door while the other four strolled round the room examining everything and commenting freely.

A sudden clatter of feet down the corridor recalled them and Barbara had just time to move to one side when two more girls came bursting in. One was a small, slim person, possessed of a fair, sharp prettiness. The other was a tomboyish creature with brown hair cropped close, a cheeky nose and a mouth that always seemed on the verge of breaking into a smile.

"Which are our cubeys?" demanded Janet Forster.

"Over on that side," Vi pointed. "You're next to the door and Emerence is between you and Chris."

Emerence's face fell. "Do you mean we haven't window cubeys? How foul!"

There was a moment's silence and Emerence suddenly turned red—for no reason that Barbara could see. She was speedily enlightened. Mary-Lou straightened up.

"Look here, Emerence," she said. "You'd better look out for your language if you don't want to be minus pocket-money for most of the term. You know we aren't allowed to use 'foul'. It's a horrid word, anyway!"

Emerence looked sulky. "Oh, tosh!" she said rudely. "Anyhow, there aren't any rules going yet, so you just shut your trap and mind your own business, Mary-Lou!"

The others said nothing—and said it very pointedly. Then Janet turned to Barbara who was still standing silent and asked, "You're a new girl, aren't you? But," with a puzzled look, "I seem to know you somehow. Your face rings a bell."

It was Barbara's turn to look puzzled. She had never met that particular phrase before. Vi, however, understood. She gave Barbara a look and then explained. "It's my cousin, Barbara Chester. She's an awful lot like Nancy—

you remember her last term. I expect that's what makes you think you know her, Jan."

Janet nodded. "That's it! But you're lots older than young Janice. How is it you haven't come to school before?"

Barbara was dumb from shyness, so Vi stepped once more into the breach. "She's always been ill up to date. But she's all right now, so she's joined us."

"And that's enough about that," Mary-Lou remarked. "The bell for *Abendessen* will be ringing and we shan't be ready. Pull your curtains and get cracking. Barbara, you know which is our bather. Will you show me?"

Barbara guessed that Mary-Lou was asking the way to the bathroom, so she nodded and turned to lead the way. Mary-Lou followed, and when she returned she sent off Verity-Anne.

Emerence, who was nearly as quick as Mary-Lou, emerged from her cubicle, ready to go as soon as Verity-Anne came back. She looked at Barbara. "Who's dormy prefect?" she demanded.

"Katharine Gordon," Barbara said briefly. She did *not* like Emerence so far.

Emerence made a face. "Oh, cripes! We'll have to mind our P's and Q's, then! " She looked round in a dissatisfied way. "And where's Margot Maynard? Oh, but you wouldn't know, being new and all."

"But I do know," Barbara said quickly. "They've got German measles at Auntie Jo's, so Margot and Len and Con won't be coming to school for a few weeks. Margot hasn't got it, but she may start at any time, so we aren't to go near their house."

Emerence's face lengthened. "How ghastly! I've heaps to tell Margot."

"Well, you'll have to sit on it—or write to her," Vi observed, coming out of her cubicle. "Burney told us in the bus coming here that we weren't to go near Freudesheim for the present. Are you next for the bather, Emerence? Then bags me after you! "

Emerence said no more though she looked very glum. She and Margot Maynard were great friends though there was a good three years between them.

Verity-Anne arrived back from the bathroom just then, still drying her hands, and Emerence darted off. The rest followed rapidly in turn. Meanwhile, Barbara, who had gone to her cubicle, was considerably startled when the curtain between it and Mary-Lou's was pulled aside and that young lady appeared with a request that the new girl would plait her hair for her.

"I *can* do it myself, of course," she explained, "but if I try to do it at the back I practically always get it squint; and if I Kenwigs it, it gets into everything. There's such lots of it, you see."

Barbara, looking at the masses of fair hair streaming to her waist, saw the point. "I'll do my best," she said. "But—what did you mean by 'Kenwigsing' it?"

Mary-Lou giggled infectiously as she turned her back to have her hair done. "I forgot how mad it would sound! You've read *Nicholas Nickleby*, haven't you?"

"Bits of it," Barbara said.

"Well, do you remember the Kenwigses in it—Morleena and the rest? Nicholas goes as tutor to them."

"Ye-es; I think so. But why?"

"Well, the one we have in the school library has a gorgeous picture of them, all with a pigtail hanging down each side of their faces. *Now* do you see?"

Barbara saw and giggled in her turn. "How funny!—Oh, sorry! I didn't mean to pull!"

"O.K.," Mary-Lou said serenely. "You didn't hurt much. Ready for a ribbon?" She waved a broad band of gentian blue ribbon over her shoulder. "Don't plait it right to the end—only about two-thirds of the way down. And for goodness' sake tie it tightly. I don't want to have to pay fines to Lost Property for bows."

Barbara tied the ribbon in a smart bow, plaited the other pigtail and then Mary-Lou coolly lifted the lid of the bureau-dressing-table and examined the effect. "You don't mind, do you? Yes; that's awfully nice. And what swish bows! Mine always look as if they'd been well-chewed! Vi!" She raised her voice.

"Hello!" Vi responded.

"Your cousin's going to be an acquisition in one way. She can tie bows!"

"So can most folks," Vi returned, suddenly appearing from the other side. "But I know what you mean. Did you do those, Babs? Mary-Lou's right. They're nifty."

Barbara blushed at this stately praise. She had been afraid that Vi might resent having to look after her, but it was plain that Vi did nothing of the sort. It was at that moment that the elder girl—Barbara was a few months the older—put forth a tiny rootlet in the Chalet School.

"Well, are we all ready?" demanded Mary-Lou, who seemed to have constituted herself sub-prefect of the dormitory. "Then we'd better go downstairs. D'you know where the Senior Middle common-room is, Barbara?"

Barbara nodded. "Just under this."

"O.K.; then let's get cracking. Line up at the door, folks."

They lined up and, led by Barbara who was hastily shoved into position by Vi, marched along the corridor and began to descend the stairs. Half-way down, they were met by a big girl whose brown locks were worn in a clubbed plait on her neck.

"Good!" she said as she saw them. "Thank Heaven some of you Middles seem to realize that even though rules don't begin till tomorrow, you can't go haring about all over the stairs and passages, making a bedlam of the place! Do you know where your common-room is?" Mary-Lou said, "Yes, thank you," with a wide beam. "Go there until you hear the gong for *Abendessen*. Then you can march to the *Speisesaal*, which is just opposite."

"What did you say?" Mary-Lou gasped.

"The *Speisesaal*. It's German for 'dining-room'. Naturally, we shall use the proper terms here."

"Oh, I see," Mary-Lou murmured. "Thanks for telling us, Valerie."

"I'll tell you something else. Miss Dene says that table-lists are on the notice-board in each common room. Have a look at yours and see where you're sitting. Then you can take your places without a fuss. You might pass that on to the rest of your lot." She smiled at them and hurried on up the stairs. When she had gone, they pursued their way and finally reached the common-room where fifteen other girls of their own age or a little older were standing about.

"Mary-Lou! Thank goodness!" exclaimed a jolly-looking girl of fifteen. "Come and give us all the gen. You're safe to have found out a lot by this time!"

Mary-Lou chuckled. "I've had as much time as the rest of you," she reminded them sweetly. "All the same, our crowd's in luck. We've got Barbara Chester here—Nancy's sister, you know—and she came yesterday, so she knows quite a bit. First of all, though, have you all looked at the table-lists and found out where you're sitting?"

"Table-lists? But, *ma chère*, where, then, are they?" demanded a girl whose general appearance stamped her as French, quite as much as her accent.

"On the notice-board, of course! Mean to say you didn't think of that? Where *is* the board?"

She looked round the big, pleasant room and then shot off to the farther wall. "Here we are! Now stand back and don't crowd, and I'll tell you exactly where you all are."

They did as she told them and she stood before the board and scanned it closely.

"Top table for staff as usual. Then there are three lines running down the room and a long table across the bottom. Now, where are *we*? Oh, good! All our crowd—and that includes you, Barbara—and Ghislaine Thomé, Mollie Woods and Clare Kennedy are at the middle one nearest the windows. Clem Barrass takes it, so that's all right! Maeve, you and Betty and Heather and Emerence and a pack of Junior Middles are at the next. The rest of the Junior Middles seem to be at the bottom one that goes across. Janet, Yvonne, Nancy Wadham, Connie Winter, Dorothy Ruthven, Barbara Kitson, Peggy Harper, Francie Wilford *and* Nesta Williams, you're in the middle row top table nearest the staff. And you have the Head Girl *and* Nora Penley to take you. Matey's evidently running no risks," she added, obscurely so far as Barbara was concerned, though the rest broke into delighted laughter.

Peggy Harper—Barbara had heard someone use her

name—made a face at her. "And what's wrong with our crowd, may I ask?"

A chorus promptly told her. "Worst lot in the school!" Hilary Bennett said.

"You—and Barbara Kitson—*and* Connie Winter!" exclaimed someone else. "*Some*one's made a bad mistake."

Vi asked gently, "Are they sitting together, Mary-Lou?"

"No; it isn't as bad a mistake as that," Mary-Lou replied. "Peggy's next door to Julie and Connie is on the other side. Barbara is right down at the far end next to Nora. The rest seem to be well and truly mixed up with Fifth Formers."

"The remainder of our crowd are at the next table, with Valerie in charge. Oh, well, at least we can sit as we like for *Kaffee und Kuchen*," Mary-Lou wound up.

After that they lost interest in the notice-board and strayed over to the windows to look out. The dusk was rapidly closing in now and there was very little to be seen. Clare Kennedy, an Irish girl with a Madonna-like face which could be very deceptive, ran across the room and switched on the lights and they came over to the big centre table which was strewn with papers and magazines.

"My only aunt!" Lesley Malcolm exclaimed as she picked one up. "Only three of these seem to be English! The rest are French and German! Do you mean to tell me that we've got to read French and German for *fun*! How utterly ghastly!"

Catriona Watson eyed the collection gloomily. "Evidently everyone's out to make sure that we learn languages whether we like them or not." She picked up a Swiss magazine and began to turn the pages. Her face suddenly brightened. "Oh, but I say, I rather like this one!"

"Let me see!" Vi craned over her shoulder. "What gorgeous pictures! I wonder if they're all like that?" She reached over and picked up another. "I say, you know, I don't think they're too bad. Anyhow," she added, "you bet we'll have to talk foreign languages all the time here, so I quite expect we'll be able to read decently before long. This looks rather fun." And she began to translate a story, haltingly, it is true, but making enough sense of it to rouse the interest of the others.

"P'raps it won't be too bad," Hilary said cautiously. "Oh, hello, you folk! What ages you've been coming down. I say, we're taking French and German mags."

"How simply awful!" wailed a fat podge of a girl. "Aren't we to have *any* English ones, then?"

"Yes—three," said Mary-Lou, who had picked up a French paper and was giggling over a comic strip. "Don't yawp like that, Ursula! By the end of this term you'll be reading them as easily as anything."

"Never!" said Ursula. "It just isn't in me."

"You will!" Vi spoke with certainty. "And some of them have gorgeous pictures and that'll be a help."

A bespectacled young person turned from the notice-board which she had been studying to remark, "When I read a magazine, it's for the stories and articles. I'm not frightfully interested in illustrations."

"Well, the language isn't going to worry *you*," Catriona told her. "You're a wizard at languages, Zena, and well you know it! But it's jolly hard lines on the rest of us."

Zena smirked. "I *like* languages. I like *all* lessons if you come to that—except maths," she added.

"Yes; that's something else we've got to find out," Mary-Lou put in. "Anyone know who's taking Miss Slater's place?"

Vi swung round on her cousin who was keeping close to her. "Do *you* know, Barbara?"

Everyone looked at her with interest. Barbara went scarlet and faltered, "I—I don't really know. But Miss Annersley did say something yesterday about her not being able to come till Saturday."

"When did she say that?" Zena demanded, eyeing her with amazement.

Vi answered for her. "Oh, everyone! This is my cousin, Barbara Chester—Nancy's sister, you know. She came yesterday so she knows a bit here and there."

Before anyone could comment on the statement, the booming of a gong filled the building and at once the girls hurried to the door to form into lines with due care for the table-lists. Vi pulled Barbara along with her and shoved her in front of her, hissing, "Stand there. You're on my left hand at table. We always line up in proper order so's there's no scrimmage in the dining-room. Now don't forget."

The gong sounded again and at once they marched out, headed by Christine Vincent, with Zena at the end of the line. At the door of the *Speisesaal*, they had to halt, for a long line of elder girls was already filing in. When those important persons had finally entered the room, Christine followed on and led the way to one of the tables by the windows where a big, red-haired girl was already standing at the head. She greeted them with a pleasant smile which they all returned. Later, Barbara was to learn that Clem Barrass was a great favourite with everyone.

Another thing that Barbara noticed was that though they had all talked hard enough in the common-room, as soon as the second gong sounded, everyone was silent and, even when they had taken their places at table, no one spoke. At the table at the top the Head was standing by the centre seat with most of the staff on either hand.

When the last girl, an impish-looking twelve-year-old, had taken her place at the bottom table, the Head touched a bell standing beside her place and everyone bowed her head while the beautiful voice, which was the first thing the new girl had noticed about Miss Annersley, spoke a brief Latin Grace. Then chairs were pulled out and everyone sat down to their first really Swiss meal.

They began with a creamy onion soup which was followed by slices of cold stuffed veal with a salad of lettuce sprinkled with grated cheese. The sweet consisted of thin leaves of delicious pastry, served with a jam sauce.

"How simply luscious!" Mary-Lou sighed as she finished hers. She sipped at the creamy milk in her glass and looked round the table. "Isn't it different with these checked cloths? And I do like the glasses! The different colours make it all so gay."

She clearly had plenty more to say, but she got no further for at that moment, the bell sounded again and the hum of chatter and laughter round the table ceased at once.

Miss Annersley had risen and was looking smilingly round the room. "I have very little to say to you now," she began. "You will hear more after Prayers. But I have to warn you all that the servant question is as difficult here as it is in England and we shall still expect the help from you that you gave us there. When *Abendessen* is over, you are to take your plates and so on and put them on those trolleys standing by the wall. Glasses on the lower shelves, please. Your table napkins will go into the drawers as usual and the prefect in charge of each table must see that the cloth is swept and folded and put with the napkins from her own table. When that is done, you may all go to your common-room until the Prayer-bell rings. Protestants go for Prayers to Hall and Catholics come back here. After Prayers, all Junior Middles will go straight up to bed. The rest may return to their common-rooms until their own bedtime. That is all. Stand!"

Every girl stood. Then they once more folded their hands and bent their heads for Grace, after which, the staff left the room and the girls, table by table, marched over to the trolleys, each carrying her glass, plate and cutlery and with her napkin in her blazer pocket. Prefects stood to see that everything went into its right place and when that was done, two girls from each table swept up the crumbs and folded the cloth which was put in its own drawer. Then they were free to march to their common-rooms and amuse themselves until the Prayer-bell rang.

It was all done quickly and quietly and with the minimum of fuss and Barbara was surprised to see how quickly the *Speisesaal* was cleared and emptied.

In the common-room, she asked Vi, "Are there lots of Catholics here that they have a different room for Prayers?"

"A good many," Vi replied. "Anyhow, you wouldn't expect them to have Prayers with us, you know."

"What about unpacking?" Christine Vincent asked. "When do we do that?"

"Tomorrow, I expect," Mary-Lou said. "I wonder how Matey will manage about it? I mean, there's such crowds of us and we all came at the same time, of course. No one's going to love us very much if she keeps on hoicking us out of lessons for unpacking."

"I know about that," Barbara said shyly. "Matron told me that some of the mistresses and all the prefects will help and everyone will unpack at once."

They were all agog at this. "Not really?" Hilary Bennett exclaimed. "I *say*! That really is something quite new! What piles of differences there are!"

"Rather fun, though," observed Beth Lane, a quiet-looking girl of the same age as the Gang. "Do you know what we are to do after that?" She spoke to Barbara.

"Matron didn't say," Barbara replied in her soft, half-scared voice which was only just audible, for this was a real ordeal for her. "Miss Annersley did say that we were to get in all the walks and expeditions we could while the weather was good, because when the winter came there would be days and even weeks when we couldn't cross the doors."

Mary-Lou nodded. "I can quite believe that! Didn't Burnie say in the bus that the snow was *feet* thick in winter? I can imagine that when it gets really going we shan't be able to show our noses out of doors. Well, let's hope they'll remember that and give us plenty of chances while the weather remains decent! Though, of course," she added, "when the snow comes we'll be having winter sports, won't we? I'm dying to ski and skate!"

"There's the bell for Prayers," Verity-Anne said suddenly. "The Abbess will tell us all about it after that. She said she would."

"Yes; get into your lines and buck up about it!" Mary-Lou said, taking the leadership as usual. "Catholics, this side; the rest that. Everyone in her place? Oh! What about hymn-books? We haven't got them."

"I expect they'll be given out in Hall," Hilary said, taking her rosary out of her pocket. "Weren't they all taken in last term? Well, then! Shall we go first, Mary-Lou? We've only to cross the corridor."

"Yes; that would be best," Mary-Lou agreed.

The Catholic girls vanished and then the rest, led by Vi, marched along to Hall and Barbara found herself sitting between her cousin and a total stranger in Hall, with rows of other girls in front and behind. A carved lectern stood in the centre of the dais at the top of the room and a semicircle of chairs was behind it. At one side was a grand piano with three rows of seats filled with girls of all ages at its side. At the other were three rows of chairs where the grandees of the school were already sitting. Barbara saw red-haired Clem among them. Julie Lucy was seated on the one chair that stood a little apart from the rest and there was rather more colour in her face than usual.

Vi saw it, too, and giggled wickedly. "Julie's feeling her position keenly," she murmured.

Hymn-books were passed along the benches. Then a second bell rang and the staff came in and took their seats on the dais. Barbara noticed that some were missing and guessed that they were with the Catholic girls. The Head entered, very dignified in her gown and M.A. hood, and took her place before the Lectern. The girls had all risen as she entered. Now Julie stepped forward and, in a voice that shook a little with nervousness, announced the hymn. The head of the music, sitting at the piano, struck a chord and the young voices took it up and the singing of the beginning-of-term hymn filled the Hall. When it ended and the girls were seated again, Julie stood up and read the Parable of the Talents, this time in a clear, steady voice. They all knelt and said "Our Father" together. The Head read the "Lighten our darkness" and two other collects. Then she called for the school's own prayer and they said it together.

"Oh, God, our Father, we come to Thee at the end of the day to ask Thee to forgive us all our wrongdoings, and to guard us with Thy Fatherly love through the night. Bid our guardian angels watch over us, and grant us sweet sleep and a joyous awakening, ready for the tasks of the new day. For the sake of Thy Son, our Elder Brother, Jesus Christ. Amen."

"I *like* it," Barbara thought. "It's a lovely prayer and it does make God and Jesus seem so real."

When the blessing was spoken, the girls rose from their knees and sat down. Three minutes later, the door opened and the Catholics came in quietly and took their seats while the Catholic mistresses, headed by Mlle de Lachennais, appeared through the top door. When everyone was seated, the Head came forward again and leaned on her desk.

"There is a great deal to tell you," she began. I want you to know that all unpacking will be done tomorrow morning after Prayers in your cubicles. Everyone will unpack at the same time. You will be divided into groups and a mistress or a prefect will be in charge of each group. When you have finished, you will have your elevenses and then you will go for a good walk. Lessons begin in the afternoon at fourteen-fifteen, and finish at sixteen-fifteen. *Kaffee und Kuchen* will be ready at once and you will have another walk." She stopped, for a gasp had come from the whole school at the mention of the hours. She gave them a laughing look and added, "My dear girls! You know that we are in Central Europe and naturally we must use Central Europe times. Don't worry! You'll soon grow accustomed to it.

"One other thing I must say now. Until Monday, you may use any language you like. On Monday, we go back to our old way. That day and Thursdays will be French days. Tuesdays and Fridays we speak German. English on Wednesdays and Saturdays. Sunday, you do as you choose. But please remember that no excuses will be taken if you speak the wrong language on any day. New girls, we are rather more lenient with you, and for the first three weeks you will be excused for forgetfulness. After that, the rule applies to you.

"Juniors, when I dismiss you, you go to bed at once. Middles have an extra half-hour and Seniors an hour. The prefects need not go up before half-past twenty-one." Once more she stopped and this time she broke into a peal of laughter at the startled faces below her. The staff joined in and the girls followed suit, not quite knowing why. At last she held up her hand for silence and got it.

"My dears, I'm so sorry!" she exclaimed. "But really, your faces! However, as I said before, you'll soon be used to it. Now that is all. Stand!"

Everyone stood and she smiled at them. "Good night, girls!"

Like one girl, the school responded, "Good night!"

She nodded to Miss Lawrence who was sitting at the piano again and struck up a lively quickstep. The girls swung round and, bench by bench, marched out. The Head waited until the last girl—Julie Lucy—had gone. Then she turned to her staff with dancing eyes.

"Well, so ends our first evening! They'll have plenty to discuss and the prefects will certainly keep them in order, being mainly very new brooms. It's time we had a break ourselves. Coffee will be served in my sitting-room in ten minutes' time. Need I say more?"

With one voice, the staff cried: "No!"

CHAPTER SIX

Prefects in Council

JULIE LUCY sat on the edge of the table in the prefects' room, swinging her crossed feet and gazing resignedly out of the window. They had spent the first morning as the Head had suggested, in unpacking followed by a walk about the Platz when they had enjoyed themselves, exploring everywhere. But the day had begun grey, with the clouds well down over the valley and it remained a grey day. Just before they got back to school for *Mittagessen*, the rain had begun to fall and by the time the meal was ended, it was coming down with a grim determination that showed that it meant to keep on for the rest of the day.

After the usual half-hour's rest, most of the school had gone to the form-rooms to settle in as soon as might be. The sole exceptions were the new girls and the prefects. The new girls had been shepherded off to a vacant room where they were set down to test papers so that they might be placed. The prefects had been told to finish off their room and then hold a prefects' meeting so that they might know what their especial posts were.

They had all worked hard at the room and, as Clem Barrass had said after an hour's toil, it only needed some flowers and it would be itself. Flowers must wait for the moment. No one was going to let them go out gathering flowers in rain like that.

That chore finished, they had departed to wash their hands and tidy their hair. Julie, the fortunate owner of a crop of short black curls, was speedily ready. All the rest had to undo pigtails, brush them out and replait their locks, so she had come along to wait for them.

Julie was a slender, handsome creature, so dark that she looked more Latin than English. She was much the cleverest of the family and her great ambition was to follow her father's footsteps and become a barrister. With that end in view, she had steadily worked towards three years at Oxford reading Law.

Normally, she would have left at the end of the previous term and gone to the finishing branch at Welsen with her cousin and great friend, Nancy Chester. During the Easter term, however, she had had a severe attack of peritonitis, involving a dangerous emergency operation; and though she had been allowed to return to school after Easter, it had been with a good many reservations. As a result, what should have been her last year had, to quote herself, been regularly messed up and it had been decided that she should have one more year at the main school to make up what she had lost. She and Nancy had been chums all their lives and though she was friendly enough with everyone else, she was a reserved young person and had no other special friends. This year, therefore, as she meditated mournfully, looked like being on the lonesome side for her.

She did not get very far in her reflections, for she had just got to this point when the door opened and Madge Herbert, another of the prefects, came in.

"Hello!" she said. "Are we the first?"

Julie roused herself from her melancholy thoughts. "We are! The rest will be along presently, though. Then we can get down to business. I say, Madge, what do you think of it all? Think it'll be as jolly as it's always been?"

Madge stared at her. "Why, yes; of course! What's wrong with you?"

Before Julie could answer, the door opened again and

admitted tall Clem of the ruddy locks, very spick and span, with her hair clubbed as usual and her red-brown eyes dancing as she closed the door behind her and came to drop down on the broad window-seat.

"What's the joke?" Madge demanded.

"It's just it seems so funny. I was strolling along when I ran into Emerence and Peggy Harper. Goodness knows what they were doing up here at this time of day. But you should have seen their faces when I appeared! Peggy said, 'It's all right, Clem, Miss Armitage sent us.' And then they scuttled off at the rate of no man's business!"

The other two joined in her peal of laughter.

"The fruits of being a prefect!" Julie said. "Thank goodness it's always meant something in this school!"

Clem nodded and turned to look out of the window. "What weather! If this is glorious Switzerland, we might as well have stayed where we were."

"We couldn't have done that, anyway," Julie reminded her. "The Christys wanted the Big House again and we'd have been somewhere else, whatever happened. Anyhow, I don't suppose we'll get a lot of rain like this yet—though Auntie Jo says that in November we can expect any amount of rain and mist if it's anything like Tirol."

"What a cheerful prospect! Oh, well, we must just make the best of it and hope for better things later on," Madge said philosophically. "Anyhow, we'll probably be up to the eyes, rehearsing the Christmas play by that time. Here come the others, judging by the row. Unless the Head's turned a herd of cows loose!" she added, laughing.

It proved to be only the rest of the prefects who had come in a body. Julie sat down in the chair at the head.

"Come on, folks!" she invited. "*Squattez-vous!* Valerie and Annis, you sit on either side of me. Sort yourselves, the rest of you."

The others settled themselves as they chose and then all sat looking at Julie, who rose to her feet and said, "Well! Here we all are. There are no minutes to read as we're starting a new minute-book with the new school. The old one has gone on with the English branch, so we'd better get down to business at once. You all know that Valerie is

Second prefect and Annis is Games. We've got to settle the other jobs. I'll read them out and then we'll vote for them. Here you are: Library—Magazine—Music—Art—Hobbies—Staff—Stationery. Those are the main things. But the Head asked me to tell you that she thinks we had better have a second Games prefect to help Annis out. Have you all got paper and pencils? Then I propose that we begin at once and vote for Library prefect. Write the name of the person you think most suitable on a slip, fold it over and pass it along to Valerie."

She then sat down to attend to the matter on her own account and there was silence for a minute or two as the girls considered before writing down their choice. When they had done and all the little slips had been dropped by Valerie into one of the compartments of a shoe-box she had fitted up for the occasion, Julie called for the choice for Magazine prefect, explaining that they would go through the list before counting votes.

"What happens if the same girl is chosen for two or three jobs?" Madge asked.

"We'll have to vote on them again, of course," Valerie said. "That's so, isn't it, Julie?"

The Head Girl nodded. "I don't suppose it'll happen, though," she added. "You'll naturally choose the most appropriate person for each job. No use picking Ruth, for instance, for Music, since she doesn't learn."

"And for pity's sake don't anyone try to vote me into Art!" implored Rosalie Way, a very pretty girl whose ideas on art had so infuriated the art master, Herr Laubach, that her lessons had been stopped the previous term.

The prefects laughed at the idea and settled down to tackle Magazine prefect. Julie kept them at it without a pause, for there was not much time left and at last Valerie had collected two remaining slips and dropped them into their compartment.

"We've got them all now, Julie," she said.

"Then you and—let's see—Edris, *you*—can act as scrutineers and go through them," Julie said promptly. "Get down to it and let's know how we stand."

Edris moved from her seat near the foot of the table and

she and Valerie took the box to the window-seat. The rest sat silent, waiting for the results. Finally, Valerie stood up and brought a handful of slips to the table.

"Here you are, Julie. I think we've got them all now." She handed the slips to Julie who scanned them rapidly. Then she looked up with such a deep sigh that Annis protested.

"Hi! Don't sigh like that! You'll blow us all out of the room!"

Julie laughed. "Sorry! But I *am* relieved that no one's thought fit to let us in for any wild experiments!"

A chorus of protests rose at this statement. "What on earth put such a mad idea into your head?" Clem demanded. "We've enough on our plates without doing that!"

"I couldn't agree more!" Pat Collins cried. "Stop nattering and tell us the worst, for goodness' sake!"

Julie laughed. "O.K. Here goes!" And she read out: "Library—Madge Herbert; Magazine—Edris Young; Music—Rosalind Wynyard; Art—Dorothy Watson; Hobbies—Ruth Wilson; Staff—Rosalie Way; Stationery—Zoe Wylie."

"I'd like to say," Valerie put in, "that Clem Barrass was runner-up for no fewer than three jobs—Library, Magazine and Hobbies."

"Well, thank goodness she didn't get one of them!" Julie said fervently.

They all stared at her in amazement. "*Well!*" gasped Madge. "What's the why of that?"

Julie looked round on them with a pitying smile. "Don't you see, you—you goops? The Abbess demands that we shall have a second Games prefect. Well, you tell me who's better fitted for the job than Clem? I believe it was a toss-up between Annis and Clem which got the job of Games pree, anyhow. She's the only one of us who can touch Annis when it comes to Games."

"When it comes to cricket," Annis put in generously, "she can beat me hands down."

"Ye-es," Clem agreed with this. "But when it's a case of tennis, you're the best by a long chalk."

"Well, yes; I think I am," Annis said consideringly. "But

you know, Clem, it's mainly because your service is so chancy. On your day, you're untakeable, but——"

"I know," Clem interrupted with a grin. "It so often doesn't come off. Anyhow, we shan't have to worry about either cricket *or* tennis this term. Julie," she turned to the Head Girl, "what games *are* we to play during the winter?"

"Search me!" The prim and proper damsels who had begun the meeting were rapidly becoming a thing of the past. "I haven't the foggiest. Who are we to play, for instance?"

"There's our own crowd at Welsen," Rosalie said.

"That's only one lot—two matches, at best, unless they can provide two teams. And which will it be—hockey or lacrosse?"

"Netball, perhaps," Madge suggested. "And we can always have our inter-house matches."

"Yes; but what's the betting that that's what it will chiefly mean this year?" Clem demanded. "Tennis, we shall probably be able to manage easily enough. We may even get a few cricket matches. Winter games are going to be rather a wash-out, though, unless some genius can produce an idea or two."

"Well, I'm no genius, but I think I can produce *one*," Julie said.

"Produce it then, and don't sit there looking like a cat that's stolen the cream!" Valerie told her promptly.

"I doubt very much if we can do anything about our usual games. But isn't there such a thing as ice hockey?"

They were silent. Then Rosalie said timidly, "I know there is; but haven't you to be awfully good on skates for that? I mean—which of us can skate?"

"I've skated—a little," Madge said at last. "I've got my balance, anyway."

"Well, that's something. Anyone else do anything?" Julie demanded. "I've never done anything at it myself, so I'll have to begin at the beginning."

"I can skate," Clem said. "Tony and I both learnt the winter we were in Norway with Dad and Mother. I don't say I could play any games, though, or do anything but skitter about the ice a bit."

Julie was doodling on her paper. Now she looked up. "You know, I rather think that, apart from what we can arrange between ourselves, we'll have to give matches a miss this season. But we needn't mind too much."

"How's that?" Annis demanded. "I must say I think it'll be very flat if we can't manage a *few* fixtures this season. What do you propose instead, may I ask?"

"We'll have snow, won't we—*and* ice? Sure to be any amount of both. Most of us will have to learn to skate and that'll be fun all right. And then, what about ski-ing? I know we're to have that. Don't you think if we've got two more or less new things like that to tackle we'll have as much on our plates as we can manage?"

"I'd forgotten about that," Annis said. "It sounds good, doesn't it? Clem, when you were in Norway, did you do any ski-ing as well as skating?"

Clem nodded. "Trust us! Tony and I were into everything! It's frightful fun. And isn't it fun to watch beginners!" she added with a giggle.

"Why?" Rosalind asked suspiciously.

"Well, for one thing, when you begin your skis seem to have a fatal attraction for each other. No matter how hard you try, nothing seems to keep them from simply *rushing* at each other. And then over you go!" She chuckled again.

Julie dropped her pencil, swept her papers into a heap and rapped on the table. "Order, please! We still haven't decided about Clem—or we haven't voted on it, anyway. And let me remind you that we've got duties—prep and supervision and so on—to settle and time's simply *hurtling* past! I don't think we need bother with paper and pencils for that. A show of hands will do. All who think that Clem is the one for Second Games prefect, hands up! Those who don't? No one! Clem, you're elected unanimously. So *that's* settled! Now let's get on with the rest." She fished in her case and produced a time-table sheet. "This is for prep duty. The Head says there won't be much of that at present as the three lowest forms all have prep in the afternoons this term and next and the staff will see to most of that. But there is an hour and a half in the evenings. That's in Hall and it includes the forms below Upper IVB. The rest work in their own form-rooms with the form prefect in charge. There are five evenings in the week and the first half of Saturday morning. I vote that we each take one evening a fortnight—or one Saturday morning, of course. Do you all agree?"

They did. It was the easiest way. Besides, as Madge pointed out, if you knew that you had to take prep on Wednesday, you could see to it that you got the worst of your own work done at another time. They all knew that the prefect on duty had little chance of doing steady work herself.

"Right!" Julie said. "Then, as Monday is generally the worst night, I propose to take one myself and hand the other over to Valerie. Friday is about next worst, so will you and Clem take Fridays, Annis?"

They were quite agreeable and the rest of the preparation periods were easily fixed.

"In Hall, you say?" Pat Collins asked. "How do we manage, then?"

"Each girl brings her folding desk in as soon as she's changed for the evening. The prefect on duty sees that the benches are moved to the back of the hall and that they set their desks well apart. It means about fifty of them, I think."

"Quite enough, too," Valerie said crisply.

"Especially with characters like Emerence Hope and Enid Roberts to liven things up," Nora Penley interjected. "What about the Maynards when they get over their German measles? Len and Con are fairly all right; but young Margot can be a demon when she chooses. Do they stay for prep or not?"

"They stay. They're all in one of the Lower IV forms and they finish at half-past six—I mean half-past eighteen," she put in hurriedly. "Isn't this time business hair-raising? I suppose we'll get used to it presently, but it's the outside of enough just now. About prep. Whoever's on duty must see to it that Margot and Emerence are at opposite ends of the room. But that isn't going to worry us for the next three or four weeks."

"Thank Heaven for that!" Nora said devoutly. "And we shove Peggy Harper into the middle, I suppose?"

"Yes—if you want a moderate amount of peace! And don't forget that Connie Winter's another imp who'll bear watching. I should put her to one side of the middle and Peggy at the other."

"You can add Norah Fitzgerald to that lot," Rosalind Wynyard chimed in.

"I'd forgotten Norah. Oh, well, it's only what you can expect of Lower Middles," Julie said resignedly.

Clem looked up. "Isn't our one and only Emerence fourteen now? Then she'll be a Senior Middle. It's time she tried to reform a little."

"Well, at least we may be thankful we aren't landed with the Dawbarns and all that crew," Pat observed. "*Five* demons are more than enough. If we'd had those two added, my hair would be white at the end of term!"

"We don't know what the new girls may be like, either," Ruth put in. "Your young cousin, Julie, which is she—imp or angel?"

"I couldn't say. Don't forget that she's always been more or less of an invalid until the last year or two. A good deal depends on who she chums up with."

"Better keep an eye on her pals, then," Ruth advised. "Having got better and coming to school may go to her head at first."

Julie shot a quick glance at her. Ruth Wilson was quite a pleasant girl on the whole, but she was apt to be domineering and if she disliked anyone, she tended to ride her hard. The Head Girl hoped that she was not going to take a dislike to Barbara.

"I doubt if Barbara is likely to chum up with anyone like Emerence or Peggy," she said carefully. "So far as I've been able to judge, Vi's seeing to her and that means that Mary-Lou and the rest of the Gang are on the job. *They'll* attend to her manners and morals all right. In any case, *we* can hardly interfere."

"Oh, she'll be all right if that crowd have taken her up," Madge said. "I know they can be the limit when they like, but it's rather what you'd call—*nice* naughtiness. They do have a limit and they stick to it. Besides, last term I really thought they showed signs of beginning to grow up and develop some sense of responsibility. And, of course, Barbara may be in Upper IV, in which case she won't come to general prep. She's about the same age as Vi, isn't she, Julie?"

"Two or three months older," Julie said. "But I doubt if she manages A. What you folk don't seem to realize is that for the first years of her life Babs was so frail that there was simply no question of lessons for her and then only baby ones for ages."

"Poor little soul!" Madge said compassionately. "What a lot of fun she must have missed! She's all right now, though, isn't she, Julie?"

"Must be, or my aunt would never have agreed to her coming to school. I rather expect you'll find that she's so thrilled to be at boarding-school at last, she'll keep rules scrupulously. It won't go to her head in the way you think, Ruth. Babs isn't the adventurous kind."

Ruth subsided and the Head Girl turned to the question of supervision and dormitory work, with the remark that time was flying and they'd have to stop nattering if they wanted to finish before *Kaffee und Kuchen*.

"And I don't mind telling you I've no wish to come back for more meeting," she continued. "I've to interview the Abbess at six—I mean eighteen!—about my work this year and I'll have to change first."

Most of the others were in the same boat, so they turned to the rest of the duties and arranged them without much argument.

CHAPTER SEVEN

Plans for Saturday

"THE SUN'S shining again!" Mary-Lou announced.

Barbara, who had wakened ten minutes before to find the sun pouring into her cubicle through her half-window, decided that she had been patient quite long enough and sat up. At the same time, there came two thuds from what were known as "the wall cubeys", telling any whom it might concern that two people had left their beds with a view to looking out of the windows. They received an immediate check, however. Katharine Gordon in the prefect's cubicle had been awake and reading for the last twenty minutes or so and her voice came from behind the curtains.

"Emerence and Janet, go back to bed till the bell rings!" she said. "It's not twenty to seven yet."

A full year at the Chalet School had taught Emerence that when a prefect—dormitory or otherwise—gave an order like that, it was as well to obey it. She uttered a loud groan, but she got back into bed.

"It's rotten luck having a cubey with no window," she grumbled. "Why should *we* have to take the wall ones?"

"Because you might do such mad things," Vi Lucy told her sweetly.

Emerence uttered a squawk of indignation, but Katharine's influence restrained her from making a dive for Vi's cubicle and punishing her as she deserved for such a remark.

From Mary-Lou's domain came a speculation as to whether they would have an expedition or not, seeing that the day was so fine.

"I'd love to visit that lake we came past on Thursday," Vi said. "I thought it looked simply wizard. Do you think perhaps they'd let us go rowing there?"

"Certainly not!" came from Katharine, who had shut up her book. "I know it's a fine day, but rowing on a lake can be a tricky job and a sticky job if you don't know the place thoroughly."

"Why ever?" half a dozen voices demanded.

"Because of the mountains. Sometimes the wind rushes madly down them and then a storm blows up before you know where you are. When we know what to look for, I expect we'll have rowing all right; but it won't be *this* term!"

"I'd like to go and see Unterseen," Mary-Lou decided. "It used to be a village outside of Interlaken, but Mother got a book about Switzerland and it said that Unterseen is a suburb of Interlaken now."

"Why do you want to see it?" Barbara asked, her curiosity getting the better of her shyness.

Mary-Lou explained. "Well, you see, we have a picture of it in the drawing-room at home. Gran did it when she was a girl at school. It's a pencil sketch and it looks simply sma—I mean wizard. I'd love to see how much it's altered"

"Was your gran in Interlaken when she was a kid, then?" Vi demanded incredulously.

"Of course not, ninny! I asked her about that and she said that in her day when they had art they used to be given pictures to copy and that was one of them."

"What's it like?" Vi was not noticeably crushed by her chum's diatribe, being, in fact, quite accustomed to that sort of thing.

Mary-Lou considered. "It's a kind of farmyard with horses drinking at a trough and some women watching them. The farm-house is behind and it's got a tremendous roof, same as the houses have here. There's a church behind the house—at least, you can see the steeple—and mountains behind that. It's not a bad sort of picture," Mary-Lou wound up with much condescension.

"I've seen it before," Katharine told her. "I doubt if

you'll find your farm-house now, but I expect the church is still there."

"Well, anyway, that's where *I'd* like to go."

"*I'd* like to visit that place where they have all the ski-ing," came from Christine in the corner. "What's it called—Candy—something, or something like that."

"I think perhaps it's Kanderstegg," Barbara offered shyly. "I know a friend of Mummy's was there two summers ago. She said it was marvellous."

"That's it!" Christine agreed. "I wonder if it's near enough for us to go? D'you know, Barbara?"

But beyond the name, Barbara was more or less ignorant, so they had to let it go. In any case, the rising-bell clanged out at that moment and they were out of bed at the first sound, for a wonder.

"You and I are first for bathers, Chris!" Mary-Lou cried. "Come on!"

She was at the door by this time, her sponge-bag swinging from her wrist and her towel slung round her neck. Christine followed a minute later and Katharine called to the next two to be ready as soon as they came back.

"That's you and Jan, Babs," Vi said from the bath-list which she had flown to study. "Emerence, you and I are after Babs and Chris. Strip your bed while you wait, Babs. Goodness knows there isn't time even to breathe in the mornings!"

Mary-Lou came hurtling back and dived between her curtains, intent on dressing and finishing cubicle duties in short order so that she might be able to help Verity-Anne. That young lady had been born slow and not even her years at the school had been able to do much for her in that line. Luckily for her, all concerned were understanding and though it was more or less a rule that girls must manage for themselves, they turned a blind eye to Mary-Lou's activities where she was concerned. As Matron truly said, if they insisted that she must manage for herself, she would only be late every morning and it was no use trying to hurry her as she got flustered and was worse than ever.

"Scoot, Babs! You're next after Mary-Lou!" Vi ordered, her quick ears catching a suspicious sound. She opened her curtains. "Hi, Emerence! You come back! It isn't your turn yet. I *told* you you went with me. I'm after Barbara and you go after Chris. So it's not even your bather."

Emerence, who had been about to take advantage of the new girl's ignorance, came back from the door reluctantly and Barbara scuttled off. Warned by what had happened on her first morning, she was careful to take her bath with as little splashing as possible. The sting of the icy water was no encouragement to loitering and she was little longer than Mary-Lou. Vi was at the door waiting, and as she shot out, commented on her cousin's face, which was glowing.

"I wish Auntie could see you now! You've got cheeks like beetroots!" Then she vanished, joining the long procession of hurrying girls on the corridor and Barbara made for her cubicle where she scrambled into her clothes.

She had reached the stage of hair-brushing when Vi came tearing back to pause before she went through her curtains and hiss to the rest, "Expedition! Matey's door was open when I went past and I heard her say something about it to Miss Dene. Get cracking, all of you and let's get downstairs and find out what's happening!"

After that, Leafy dormitory simply tore through their duties. It is to be feared that hair-brushing was reduced to the minimum and most folk simply gabbled their prayers. Even Katharine who was too dignified to show her excitement as plainly as her Juniors was ready sooner than usual this morning. As for Verity-Anne, she was in such a state of thrills that if it had not been for Mary-Lou she would have gone down half-dressed.

Once in their own room, and free from the supervision of even Katharine, they let themselves go with vim.

"I wonder where we're going?" This was Mary-Lou. "Oh, I *hope* it's Interlaken! They've a marvellous floral clock as well as Unterseen, and Auntie Jo told Mother in one of her letters that the shops are marvellous and you get a marvellous view of the Jungfrau at one point."

There was no one about to point out to her that there are more adjectives than one, so she got away with her perpetual use of "marvellous".

"What are you talking about?" Lesley Malcolm demanded. She slept in Violet at the other end of the building and had just arrived in time to hear Mary-Lou's remarks.

"Expedition! We're to have one today! Vi heard Matey and Miss Dene talking about it! "

"Not really? I say, how simply wizard! I hope they'll take us down to the lakes. I'm dying to see them properly."

By this time, the rest of the Senior Middles were coming in and as they entered the room the folk from Leafy spread the glad news. As a result, when the gong sounded for *Frühstück*, it took all of a minute to hush the babel of chatter. Mary-Lou finally dealt with it. Jumping on to a chair, she clapped her hands vigorously and when the noise had died down remarked scathingly: "About time, too! D'you *want* us all to be stopped going? Line up and for pity's sake try to remember that we're *Senior* Middles this term! Emerence! Stop shoving! You can get into line quite well without behaving like a battering-ram gone mad! "

Her hint sobered them all and it was a very prim and proper line of Senior Middles that finally marched off to the *Speisesaal* and stood quietly behind their chairs until Grace had been said. All the same, once they were seated and busy with milky coffee, rolls and butter and black cherry jam, it was impossible to hide their excitement. By this time, too, the news had spread to the others and the Head, after she had sipped her coffee, set her cup down and turned to Matron with a twinkle.

"Look at those girls! They've got wind of our plans; that's evident. Oh, don't ask me how! They have a grapevine of their own! I believe they absorb news from the air! I'd better make the announcement at once or they won't be able to eat any breakfast and that won't do at all! "

Mlle laughed. "But, Hilda, *chérie*, will it not be well to teach them to use a little self-control?" she asked with a wicked look at the Head.

"Cruelty to dumb animals! " Miss Derwent put in. "How can you, Mlle?"

"Nothing much *dumb* about them! " Matron said crisply. "This noise must be heard out on the road! "

"Yes; I must put a stop to *that*," Miss Annersley agreed, stretching out her hand for her bell. "There are limits to all things."

She pressed it sharply and at the "Pr-r-ring!" the noise died down and the girls turned from their rolls and coffee to look at the staff-table. The Head had risen and was regarding them with mock sternness.

"Less noise, please," she said. "If this goes on, we shall have to set you all down to writing out King Lear's words about Cordelia!" She stopped there for a moment, enjoying the expressions which varied from extreme horror to sheepishness. Then she went on: "By the way, I may as well tell you that as today has turned out so fine, and none of you *can* have any mending to do yet, we are taking you on an all-day expedition."

She had to pause there, for Mary-Lou—it *would* be Mary-Lou, as Clem said later to the rest of the grandees of the school!—began to clap and the others joined in vigorously. She gave them their heads for a minute. Then she held up her hand as a signal that that was enough and they quieted down at once to hear what more she had to say.

"Sixth Forms—Miss Wilson has sent you a hearty invitation to spend the day at Welsen and meet our branch there. Mlle is going with you and you may walk down. Upper Fifth, Miss Derwent is taking you up Lake Brienz in the ferry. Lower Fifth go in the opposite direction, also by ferry, with Miss Armitage. You go to Thun at the head of the lake and then walk back to Interlaken by degrees. Miss Dene and I are taking both the Upper Fourths to explore Interlaken and then go on to visit Unterseen, a charming suburb just outside. Lower IVA are to visit Lauterbrunnen and the two great waterfalls—the Staubbach and the Trummelbach. Lower IVB, you are coming to Interlaken, too, but once we are there, you go off with Matron, Miss Burnett and Miss Moore who will take you to Harder where there is a wonderful park full of wild animals. I have only one more thing to say. We are the foreigners here. The school is a new venture in these parts. On your behaviour depends the sort of reputation we are given. If I have any complaints about *bad* behaviour, that ends any more expeditions for the culprits for the rest of the term. I hope that is clearly understood. You are to obey orders instantly and without argument and you are not to make yourselves conspicuous by yelling or rushing madly about. We want you to enjoy yourselves, but remember there are limits. Now go on with your meal, please. We want to start off by the ten o'clock train. Lower IVA, you will go by bus and it will be waiting at the gates by the time you are ready. Thank you! " And she sat down to go on with her own meal.

It was an effort for the girls not to lose their heads with all this excitement, but they remembered her first words and contrived to rein themselves in, though it was clear enough to everyone that a good many people were bursting to let themselves go. No one wanted to be left behind, however, and the prefects were on the look-out. So though there was plenty of talk it was slightly subdued. The only persons who were at all doubtful, were the ten new girls who still did not know where they had been placed and so had no idea which expedition would be theirs.

Miss Denny, placidly munching her roll, remembered this and suddenly lifted up her voice. "What about the new girls? Do they know where they've been placed yet?"

"No; I meant to ask Rosalie to put up the lists after *Frühstück,*" the Head said. "Rosalie, run and bring them, dear. I may as well tell them and put them out of their agony at once."

Miss Dene left the room to return in a moment or two with a couple of lists which she handed to the Head. "We hadn't quite decided on Barbara Chester," she murmured.

"Oh, I think we'll put her into Upper IVB," Miss Annersley said. "Most of her work reaches their standard and she can have coaching for the odd subjects."

"Then that will make thirty-one for us."

The Head touched her bell as she rose again and read out the lists telling the new girls to which forms they would belong. Barbara was thrilled to hear that she was to be in Upper IV. It is true that it was B division, but if she worked hard—and she meant to do that—she might manage to get herself promoted to A by the end of term. Beth had taught her for the last eighteen months and had seen to it that she was well-drilled in the kind of work the school asked for and she had plenty of brains.

"And, anyway," she thought to herself, "I'm with Vi and the rest for today. I'm thankful for that. I'd have hated being with total strangers and the Maynards won't be back at school for ages yet, Beth said."

There was one new girl for Lower V and two for Lower IVA. The rest were all in Lower IVB the bottom form of all here. Two of them were at the school for sad reasons, for they had mothers in the big San at the other end of the platz, though neither had any real idea of the great shadow that hung over their lives at the moment.

"How are you going to manage, Biddy?" Miss Annersley asked the history mistress after Prayers, while those who were taking picnic lunches with them were collecting their packages.

"I'm going straight to Basle," Miss o'Ryan said. "The train doesn't get there till fourish—I mean sixteen," she added hastily, "so I'm going to Frieda's for *Mittagessen*. What's the news from Freudesheim, by the way? She's sure to ask me."

"Poor Jo!" the Head said with a twinkle.

"I suppose you mean that Margot's down now? Well, it's just as well if they all have it together. At least it means that by—let's see—Monday three weeks at latest, won't it be?—those three can return to school. How are they, by the way?"

"Doing nicely, so Jack said when I saw him before *Frühstück*. Mike's very cross and Margot's sorry for herself at the moment. The other four are over the worst and ought to be out soon. And so far the twins are all right."

"Let's hope they keep all right! Miss Annersley, do you want me to bring our new colleague back in time to come up with all your crowd? Or shall we wait for a later train?"

"A later train, I think. She'll be tired after that long journey. Much better postpone introducing her to the school until tomorrow morning." The Head gave Miss o'Ryan a significant glance and they both laughed.

"Won't it be a shock for the girls?" the latter said.

"For the elder ones. Not many of the younger ones were at school in her day and those that were have probably forgotten her."

"Well, we'll be seeing in due course. Those girls seem to have lined up at last! Shall I go out and join the party?"

"We'll both go. Where's my bag? Got your purse? Then come along!" The Head led the way out of the entrance hall to the drive, where the girls were standing in lines.

"Yes; you look quite all right," the Head said as she passed down the lines of blue-clad girls, all looking very trim. "Prefects, Mlle is waiting for you, so you had better go. Take your time; it's early yet. Your bus is at the gate, Lower IVA, and Miss Lawrence who is in charge of you is there, too. Off you go!"

The prefects turned and left the lines to join Mlle de Lachennais, who was not only an excellent walker but an experienced alpiniste. Lower IVA—eleven of them, since Len and Con Maynard were indulging in German measles, hurried off to clamber into their bus. Then the Head sent Upper Fifth to the head of the column and presently a long winding crocodile was marching along to the little station, which was rather more than a mile away.

It was just as well that the tourist season was coming to an end for the seventy or so girls filled the coaches nearly to capacity. There was just room for the staff who were going down with them, and anyone waiting at the intermediate stations must go on waiting until the next train came down.

"In future, I think I'd better warn the authorities when we're taking all the girls down like this," the Head said *sotto voce* to Miss Denny who was sitting beside her. "We don't want to make pests of ourselves."

"We certainly don't!" Miss Denny agreed. "No one will love us in that case."

Barbara, squeezed into a seat meant for two between Christine Vincent and Catriona Watson, was as excited as anyone. This was what she had dreamed of, but she had never imagined it would come so soon. So far, school had more than come up to her expectations and she thought gleefully of the letter she would write home on the morrow.

"Mummy will be thrilled," she thought. "But I wish Beth could have been here instead of being stuck at Freudesheim."

"Don't you hear?" Christine demanded at this point.

Barbara started. "Oh, did you ask me something? I'm sorry. I was thinking."

"Well, you give thinking a rest for a bit and listen to me!" Christine retorted. "I was asking you if you thought we were likely to see anything of Beth this term?"

"I don't know. I suppose she'll come and see me when the German measles is over, but I haven't any idea how long it takes."

"I said 'us'; not 'you'," Christine told her severely. "She may be your sister, but she was one of the best Head Girls the school ever had. When I was a small kid, I thought she was the cat's whiskers. So did most of us."

Barbara looked startled. "How weird!" she said. "She's —well, she's a dear, of course, but——"

"I suppose it's because she's your sister," Christine began. She got no further, for at that point Mary-Lou, sitting behind with Verity-Anne and Vi crushed in beside her, was moved to wonder aloud what would happen if anything broke?

"Do you think we'd go on sliding down the rail; or would the whole contraption topple over and go *rolling* down?" she wanted to know.

"Mary-Lou, you shut up!" Vi cried with a shudder. "Of all the ghastly ideas!"

Miss o'Ryan had been sitting near enough to overhear this colloquy and she suddenly chuckled. "Don't you try to emulate Joey—I mean Mrs Maynard," she added hurriedly. "And as for anything breaking, there's no need to fear *that*."

"Did Auntie Jo ever think of it?" Mary-Lou demanded with interest.

"I'm telling you! 'Twas in Tirol it was, and she used to try to make our blood run cold by suggesting what might happen. Nothing ever does. The alpine folks are much too careful for that. All these rack and pinion railways are inspected at regular intervals and nothing is ever allowed to slip. Too much would hang on it. So you needn't be shuddering and squealing like that, Vi."

"Are you coming with us, Miss o'Ryan?" Catriona asked, while Mary-Lou subsided into comparative harmlessness for the time being.

"I am not. It's Basle I'm going to. I'm meeting our new maths mistress and bringing her back with me."

"Oh, what's her name, please?" It was not in Mary-Lou to remain subdued for long and this was a question which had been exercising the girls ever since the previous term when Miss Slater, who had been a good many years at the school, had announced that she was leaving and would not be with them in the Oberland.

"You'll know when you come back to school," Miss o'Ryan returned, her blue eyes dancing for no reason that any of them could see.

"Give us a hint," Vi pleaded. "Oh, do, Miss o'Ryan!"

"Not one hint will I give you!" The history mistress was adamant. "You think of the fun you'll be having and all the beautiful things you'll be seeing and wait. Patience is a virtue."

And that was all they could get out of her. For the rest of the brief journey they forgot Mary-Lou's gruesome ideas which was what Miss o'Ryan had intended. Instead, they talked hard about all they expected to see and had still not exhausted the subject when the train finally glided into the Interlaken-Ost station where they all tumbled out and then, having been warned previously what to do, formed into their proper groups and were marched off by the mistresses in charge to start on their expeditions.

CHAPTER EIGHT

Unterseen

HAVING SEEN the rest off, Miss Annersley turned to her own crowd.

"Mercy! What a mob you look!" she exclaimed. "I don't think a throng like this can promenade through Interlaken together. Miss Dene, we'd better revise our plans a little. Suppose we divide them up into two lots. I'll take one and you can have the other. How would that be?"

Miss Dene laughed. "I agree with you. It's much the best thing to do. But how shall we divide them?"

"Pick up sides as we do for games," Mary-Lou suggested with her calm air of equality.

"N-no-o; I don't think that would do," the Head said. "To begin with, I suppose your gang will want to be together as usual. That means yourself, Vi, Verity-Anne, Hilary, Lesley, Christine, Catriona and Ruth, doesn't it?" she smiled.

For once the wind was completely taken out of Mary-Lou's sails. She had had no idea that the Head knew so much about them. Neither had the rest and they all stood staring at her in amazement and looking as they were feeling—supremely silly.

Vi collected her wits first. "Please may Barbara come with us as well?" she asked; and Barbara went pink with pleasure. She had had a very good idea how most of her cousins thought of her. It had been one reason why she had wanted to come to school and, especially, to be a boarder, with no more privileges than anyone else.

The Head agreed easily. "Of course she may. Let me see; that will make nine of you. If I give you six more, Miss Dene, that will divide them up evenly. Who will you have?"

Miss Dene looked the remainder over. "Suppose we add Maeve Bettany and Beth Lane."

"Very well. And as we certainly mustn't separate Ghislaine and Clare on this first expedition, we'll add them. Two more. Gwen, you might join up——"

"And I'll take Francie Wilford for the sixth," Miss Dene put in; whereat Francie's face fell and so did that of her boon companion, Heather Clayton. They had planned to go off together. But though the Head was quite willing to let Mary-Lou and Co. and such steady people as Ghislaine and Clare be together, she was not sorry that two monkeys like Francie and Heather should be parted. She agreed cheerfully and then asked what Miss Dene proposed to do.

"I think we'll cross over to Unterseen," her secretary said. "We can explore round about. Then we'll take a bus and have *Mittagessen* somewhere along the shore of Lake Thun and walk back and have *Kaffee und Kuchen* in Interlaken. There are plenty of *pâtisseries* along the Hoheweg and the girls will like to see the shops as well. The next time we come down, my party can do Interlaken and yours can visit Unterseen. Will that do?"

"Excellently, well. Then will you get off? I don't think I'm fussy, but I don't exactly want to go through the streets looking like a Sunday School treat."

"I do so agree!" Miss Dene murmured. She raised her voice. "Line up in pairs, girls. Mary-Lou and Lesley, lead the way. Off you go!" She flashed a laughing glance at the Head and followed her crowd with Francie at her side.

Miss Annersley called her back for a moment. "Don't forget that you must be at the Interlaken-Ostbahn in time for the six o'clock train. We can't leave it any later for even so it will be dusk by the time we reach the Platz."

Rosalie Dene glanced at her watch. Then she looked at the Head with eyes dancing with mirth though she said nothing. Miss Annersley returned the look, gave a gasp and went pink. To think that she, of all people, who had laid so much stress on the fact that they must become accustomed to using Eastern European time should have fallen into the trap like this!

Not that she made any remark. She merely nodded and turned to call her party to order while Miss Dene hurried after hers and caught up with them at once.

"How do we go, Miss Dene?" Mary-Lou asked eagerly. "Can we walk it?"

"I don't see why not," Miss Dene said. "We go down the Hoheweg and across the bridges over the Aar. Then we find ourselves in Unterseen."

"Lovely! " Mary-Lou heaved a deep sigh of satisfaction. "Miss Dene, just one thing, please. *Need* we croc?"

Rosalie considered the bunch of girls surrounding her at the turning into the Hoheweg. "If you promise me not to lag behind or get too far ahead, I don't see why you shouldn't walk in twos or threes—but *not* more. Only remember: you may *not* cross the road until I'm there. I don't want to have to go back and tell Miss Annersley this evening that I'm sorry, but I've left one or two of you on the road as strawberry jam! "

Peals of laughter greeted this picture before her party took advantage of her permission to break up into groups.

"You come with us, Barbara," Vi commanded. She stopped short and turned to her leader. "How shall we fix things, Mary-Lou? I'm certain Miss Dene won't let *ten* of us go in a bunch. She said not more than two or three."

"That's O.K." Mary-Lou took command of the situation at once. "Chris, you and Catriona can be together. Hilary, you and Ruth and Lesley can make a three. Vi, you and Barbara had better join up and that leaves Verity-Anne and me. What about the rest of you?"

"Don't worry about us," Maeve Bettany retorted. "Clare, you and Ghislaine and I can go together."

"And that leaves Gwen and me—and Francie," Beth Lane said. "Who's *she* going with?"

"You two if you like," said Mary-Lou the ready. "Or she can tag on with Verity and me. Just as you say."

"I'll come with you, Beth, if I may," Francie said quickly. "If I'm with Mary-Lou she'll boss me to death! " she added ungratefully.

Miss Dene had stood back while these amenities were

proceeding. Now she decided that she had better take a hand. She took a step forward.

"Now that's enough," she said firmly. "Francie, that is *not* the way to reply to an offer that was meant kindly, I don't doubt. As for you, Mary-Lou, be careful or you'll be turning into one of those domineering women that no one likes. Francie, if Beth and Gwen will have you, you may go with them."

Mary-Lou had subsided and joined Verity-Anne, her face as red as a peony. Francie's was no better. Between being told to take care to avoid being too bossy and ticked off for bad manners, she rather thought she would prefer the former. Miss Dene chuckled inwardly and, having seen her lambs join up, told them they might start off and joined Christine and Catriona who had invited her eagerly.

"Hurry up!" she said. "We can't stop here all day, blocking up the pavement. We'll be having the police dropping on us for causing a traffic obstruction!"

She did permit them to pause a minute or two to look at the Kursaal, with its beautiful grounds with the far-famed floral clock, concert hall and all the other varieties of pleasure. Then she urged them on.

Barbara had turned round to see the view of the Jungfrau, but the beautiful mountain was veiled in mists today, so she had to turn back and walk along beside Vi who chattered amiably. She was finding that her old feeling of vague dislike had vanished and she had wondered, if some day she and Barbara might be as close friends as Julie and Nancy were. She and Mary-Lou were chums, but she knew well enough that Verity-Anne was closer to her "sister" than Vi herself could hope to be.

"I wonder what there is to see at Unterseen?" she said presently. "Let's hang back a bit and ask Miss Dene."

Miss Dene, when questioned, replied, "A very old church —though it has been modernized, I hear. And there are a number of beautiful old wooden houses. I think you'll like those. Some of them date from the seventeenth century which is a big age for a wooden house. When you see them, you can feel that you are looking at Switzerland as she was during the Confederation of that time."

"Please, what was the Confederation?" Barbara asked.

Miss Dene considered. "It's rather a long story. I think we'll wait till we have *Mittagessen* before I tell you. I'll say this much now. It began with the three clans of Uri, Schwyz and Unterwald, who sent their—their magistrates—though the post wasn't exactly what it is in England—to the Grütli to make a pact of friendship and mutual assistance between them against the Habsburgs who were the rulers of a large part of Switzerland at that time. That was in 1291 when a document was drawn up in Latin and the three clans set their seals to it."

"But why their seals?" Vi asked involuntarily.

Miss Dene laughed. "I imagine because most of them couldn't write."

"But—but they were *magistrates*!" protested Vi, daughter of a barrister. "Oh, and what's the Grütli, please?"

"The Grütli is a meadow. And as for not being able to write, very few people apart from the clergy and religious Orders could either read *or* write in those days."

"I suppose that was in the Middle Ages," Christine remarked.

"The thirteenth century? Quite right, Christine; it was."

"Can you see the document or has it been lost?" Vi asked.

"Oh, it's still in existence—in the archives of the Canton of Schwyz. Whether you can see it or not is another matter. I haven't the least idea."

"But that was only three of them," remarked Mary-Lou who was walking near enough to hear all this. "What about the others? There are dozens of Swiss Cantons, aren't there?"

"Twenty-five, to be accurate—counting the two divisions of Basle, Appenzell and Unterwalden. Each of those has two divisions. But I can't go into Swiss history now. You wait till we have *Mittagessen* and I'll tell you what I know—which isn't much," she added. "You'll have to go to Miss o'Ryan for details. In the meantime, turn round, Mary-

Lou, and walk properly. You'll be bumping into someone or falling off the pavement if you try to walk backwards like that."

Mary-Lou turned round and they went on down the Hoheweg, turning into the Markt-Gasse beside the post office. This led them to the bridge which crosses to the larger island of Spielmatten. Thence, they went over another bridge and found themselves in Unterseen.

"Well, here we are!" Miss Dene said as the last girl joined her on the north bank of the Aar. "Once, this was a village by itself, but now it's been taken into Interlaken. Is there anything special you would like to see first?"

It was impossible to miss Mary-Lou's eager face, so she looked directly at that young woman who promptly burst out, "Oh, *could* we go and see the church? You see, we have a picture in the drawing-room at home of Unterseen and you can see the church tower in it. I'm dying to know if it really is like that and if the farm is still there!"

Luckily for her, for she was anything but lucid, Miss Dene knew the sketch, having been brought up with a similar one in *her* home, and she agreed at once.

"Very well; we'll go there first. But, Mary-Lou, remember that I told you that the church has been brought up-to-date and just what that means, I'm not very sure. But you will see plenty of old houses; that, I do know. Come along, all of you!"

She led the way to the church, only too well brought up-to-date for Mary-Lou, who disgustedly remarked that *that* wasn't like the picture Gran had sketched!

Miss Dene laughed. "My dear girl, times move on and even a little village like Unterscen has to move with the times. Come and see the fountain outside and stop grizzling! At least the mountains are very little changed, if at all." She turned casually to look at the great wall of the Oberland Alps to the south of them and gave an exclamation. "Quick, girls! Look!"

They swung round and exclamations broke from them all. The mists had lifted and the Jungfrau shone forth in all her maiden glory against a matchless blue sky. It was the first time that any of them but Barbara had seen her for, since they had arrived, the mists had blanketed her securely. Now, at their first sight of so much loveliness, they were silenced after those first cries.

At last Vi spoke. "Oh, Miss Dene! How *wonderful*!" she breathed. "Barbara! Did you ever see anything more perfect?"

Barbara flushed. "I can understand why they call her The Maiden," she replied.

"Oh, so can I! She looks like—like a bride, almost!"

Miss Dene, listening to their delighted comments, felt well satisfied with their first sight of the Jungfrau.

"You will see her many times, I hope. At the moment, we are going to visit the fountain which, I am told, is the rallying-place for all the old men and their pipes on a bright day like this. Come along and let's see how far that's true," Miss Dene said.

She took them off to the square where they surveyed the fountain with its attendant gathering of old men sitting on the rim, smoking their meerschaums and gossiping in the slow, gentle dialect of the Oberland.

"I love this!" Hilary said as they watched the water playing. "Look at the weird pipes those old men all have. Aren't they funny?"

"And now, what about *Mittagessen*?" Miss Dene asked. "You must be ravenous by this time. It's nearly—thirteen o'clock." She had nearly fallen into the trap like the Head.

"Let's sit round the rim of the fountain and feed," Vi suggested. "There'd be plenty of room. See! The old boys are beginning to leave."

"No, thank you, Vi! I draw the line at that! But I'll tell you what we *will* do. We'll take a bus a little way out and find somewhere by Lake Thun for a picnic. Now let me see. Where do we catch a bus, I wonder?"

A lady who was passing caught the words and paused to smile and say, "*Bitte, meine Fraülein,* one catches an omnibus to the Lake just across the square. You will see the place marked with a sign. Do you wish some special place?"

Rosalie Dene went scarlet at the friendly speech. Then

she pulled herself together and replied, "*Danke sehr, meine Dame*. No; we only wish to find some quiet spot near Lake Thun to eat our sandwiches and fruit."

"Ah! What you English call 'picnic', *nicht wahr*?" The lady thought a moment. Then she said, "Ah! I have him! You wait for an omnibus marked 'Thunersee'. That will take you to the lakeside and for a fare of fifty centimes each, you can come to a spot that will suit you, I think. Yes; and but ten minutes away is a *Gasthaus* where you may get coffee or milk or light beers and wines, all very good."

Rosalie Dene thanked her for her kindness and she gave them another friendly smile and went off again with a pleasant, "*Guten Tag!*" They all knew *that* one and they chorused, "*Guten Tag!*" as she left them. Then they crowded round their guardian to demand what she had said, since none of them had been able to follow the rapid German very much.

"Do you mean to tell me you didn't understand after all your practice in German last term?" Miss Dene cried. "Girls! I'm ashamed of you!"

"But you both went so fast," Mary-Lou pointed out. "I can follow if people speak slowly, but not if they talk at railroad speed."

"I hope you'll be able to do much better by the end of the term, then!" Miss Dene retorted. Then she condescended to tell them just what had been said before she escorted them to the stopping-place pointed out by their unknown friend. The bus came along a minute or two later and they all crowded in. At last they reached their stopping-place and presently they were all sitting on the grass above the clear, mirror-like water.

"Look at all the reflections!" Hilary said, as she opened her knapsack and pulled out her packet of sandwiches. "Aren't they lovely!"

"And isn't the lake *blue*?" Barbara cried eagerly. "It's the bluest thing I ever saw!"

Miss Dene smiled. "You haven't seen the Tiernsee! I remember it as even bluer than this."

"I don't see how it *could* be," Mary-Lou remarked. "Barbara's quite right!"

Barbara went pink again. She was beginning to get her footing among the Gang, at any rate, and that was something she had not expected to happen for some weeks. Vi just then suggested that they should sit back to back for greater ease and by the time they had settled and most of the others had followed their example, Miss Dene had nearly finished her sandwiches.

Mary-Lou cocked an eye at her and marked this before she said, "And now, Miss Dene, won't you tell us the rest about Switzerland? You said you would while we were having *Mittagessen*, you know."

"What do you want to know?" that lady asked cautiously. "I'm buying no pigs in pokes from you, Mary-Lou!"

"Oh, just about the history. You told us about the three clans palling up and that they sealed the agreement because they couldn't write——"

"Quote me correctly if you quote me at all! I said *probably* most of them couldn't write. It is quite possible that one or two of them could."

"Well, won't you go on from there? Oh, please do!" Mary-Lou pleaded.

"The first thing to tell you, I think, is that the Swiss take their name from Schwyss, the largest of the four Forest Cantons, as they are called," Miss Dene began.

"Why?" Vi asked, jerking upright. "Oh, sorry, Babs! —Why are they called *Forest* Cantons, Miss Dene? Are they all woods?"

"Not in these days, Vi, though at the time of the taking of the Oath, I've no doubt they were. That was in 1291 and there would be very few large towns in them."

"Whereabouts are they?" Hilary asked. "Do you think we can go and see them some time? They sound rather thrilling."

"I'm certain you will, though I doubt if it can be this term. They are the Cantons round Lake Lucerne and I expect the school will have an expedition there though it will most likely have to wait till the summer term."

"Scrummy!" Vi wriggled so violently with delight that Barbara nearly rolled over and was only saved by Hilary catching an arm and steadying her.

"Sit still, Viola!" Miss Dene ordered. And Vi sat still, startled by the use of her full name which was usually abbreviated.

"When did the other Cantons join in?" Mary-Lou asked as she took out an apple.

"Only by degrees. The City of Lucerne was next. Then Zurich, Glarus and Zug asked to join. And by that time, the Habsburgs—I told you they claimed all that part of Switzerland, you remember—realized that if they wanted to retain their hold on the country, they had better do something about it and do it quickly! Leopold II was the Emperor then and he sent an army against the Confederation in 1315, but it was soundly beaten at Morgarten. You see, the Swiss were fighting for their freedom and though theirs was by far the smaller army, they had the greater object in view. After that, every boy was trained in the use of such arms as they used and when, in 1386 Leopold's descendant tried again, his army was so soundly thrashed, that he gave it up as a bad job and so did *his* descendants. After that, the Swiss were able to go ahead with their own ideas."

"And when did the rest come in, please?" Barbara asked eagerly.

"Like the others—by degrees. About a century later though, the Confederation was squabbling among its members over who should have which of the vassal states they had conquered. It nearly came to Civil War among them, but at that time there was living at Fluë a hermit called Nicholas. The Confederation held a Council at a place called Stans and invited him to come and advise them. The result was that the various Cantons agreed to strengthen their early pact by a convention of brotherly love and mutual assistance against enemies. Two more of the great cities who had applied to enter were admitted and so the Confederation now numbered ten."

At this point, Miss Dene stopped and bit into her apple.

"Oh, do go on, Miss Dene!" Christine said earnestly.

"Give me a chance!" she retorted. "You folk have all been munching apples while I've been talking. Now it's my turn."

"Oh, I'm sorry," Christine murmured, turning red.

Miss Dene gave her a grin, finished her apple amid silence from the girls, threw the core into the lake and wiped her fingers on her handkerchief. Then she turned to them and said, "I'm ready now. Want me to go on?"

"Yes, please!"—"Oh, rather!"—"Yes; do! Tell us what happened next!"

"What happened next? Well, Basle and Schaffhausen—where the Falls of Rhine are; and you'll certainly visit *that* some day—and Appenzell were the next to apply and were admitted. And, by the way, please note that all the members of the Confederation weren't—and aren't—all Cantons. Quite a number have always been the great cities. And that hasn't always made for peace."

"Why not?" Barbara asked, making big eyes at her.

"Because the cities had most of the wealth of the country, thanks to the trade. There were times and seasons when they thought that because of that the more rural Cantons should stand back and let them do the ruling. They had external peace for a long time. Countries and great lords thought twice about challenging a nation that had such a reputation as a fighting nation. In fact, the Swiss often served as mercenaries—paid soldiers, Ruth!—to other countries. You all know about the Swiss Guard who were killed to the last man, fighting to try and save Louis XVI and poor, pretty, silly Marie Antoinette from the howling mobs of the Revolutionaries."

"Do we?" Vi asked doubtfully. "I've read *The Scarlet Pimpernel*, of course——"

"Viola Lucy! What was your prose literature book last term?"

"*A Tale of Two Cities*. And I loved it!" Vi said promptly.

"Well?"

Vi stared at her. "Miss Dene, do you really mean that the Swiss Guard came from *here*?"

"Well, where did you think they came from? Of course

I do. And you can all imagine that the Robber Barons and later the other countries thought twice about setting on a country which could produce fighting men like that."

"But, Miss Dene——" Mary-Lou began.

"Yes, Mary-Lou?"

"You said that they had *external* peace. Do you mean that though they made the other countries afraid to tackle them, they kept scrapping among themselves? Because, in that case, how did the Confederation manage to hang together?"

"Oh, it didn't! They had any number of minor civil wars among themselves. Sometimes it was the cities against the rural States. After the Reformation, they had religious wars. And that was the last time the Emperor thought it a good idea to interfere and try to win back the lands his ancestors had lost. However, it came to nothing. Berne called on her men and they rescued Geneva which was being harassed by the Duke of Savoy—and then sailed in and 'liberated' and annexed Vaud which did belong to Savoy and wasn't too pleased about the whole thing, since the Bernese instantly levied heavy taxes to pay for the fighting."

"Did they fight Berne after that, then?" Verity-Anne demanded in her tiny silvery voice.

"No-o; I don't think so. The Vaudois were Protestants in any case and Savoy had a bad record of persecution against them. But they had no fancy for paying the best part of their wealth away to the Bernese. Later, they agreed to differ and at the time when the Confederation consisted of thirteen States, seven were Catholic and six were Protestant. They drew up a fresh Constitution which was revised and completed in 1878. That ended the trouble. Since then, Switzerland has been at peace internally as well as externally. And that is about all I can tell you. Now what about packing up and walking back part of the way, at least to Unterseen?"

"Can we keep to the lakeside?" Hilary asked joyfully. "Oh, good!"

They turned to and tucked their packing-papers into their knapsacks. But Barbara was thinking as she did so.

Finally, just before they set out, she asked, "Please, Miss Dene, how is it that Switzerland is always neutral in wartime?"

"Yes; that's something *I've* wondered about," Mary-Lou put in.

"It's because the Great Powers have always realized—since the Congress of Vienna which ended the Napoleonic Wars—that they simply must have a neutral state in the place where all the vital crossroads of Europe meet. The Congress of Vienna definitely recognized that and the League of Nations confirmed it after the first World War and so has the United Nations. Not even Hitler seems to have been disposed to violate Swiss neutrality. Or at any rate his advisers managed to keep him off it."

"The Swiss must have been jolly thankful about that," Vi said. "I mean, Switzerland is next door to Germany. She could easily have walked in."

"Yes; but that seems to have been one of the few points on which the Germans did *not* lose their heads," Miss Dene said as she got them on to their feet and set them to marching by twos and threes in the direction of Unterseen. "Now keep on walking steadily. When we hear or see any sign of a bus we'll run for it."

It was half an hour before the bus came along and picked them all up, by which time they had walked a good distance. Miss Dene took tickets for them to the Hoheweg, so they did not get out in Unterseen, nor at all until they were half-way up the great main street of Interlaken, when she called them all out and walked them off to a *pâtisserie*, where she treated them all to delicious coffee with what Mary-Lou described as "a *featherbed* of whipped cream" floating on the top and delicious cakes and twists of fancy-bread. After that, they had to hurry or they would have missed the train back to the Platz. As it was they were the last to arrive and caught it by the skin of their teeth

"Still, we did catch it!" Mary-Lou said, leaning back luxuriously in her seat. "It's been a gorgeous expedition, hasn't it? I'll be able to write a really decent letter home tomorrow!"

CHAPTER NINE

A Trial for the School

On Monday, school began in earnest. Barbara had been placed in Upper IVB, much to her delight. She knew that it was mainly thanks to Beth's careful training during the past eighteen months that she had not been relegated to Lower IVA. On the Sunday, when they spent the time between *Frühstück* and Church in writing their home letters, she contrived to snatch time for a short note to her eldest sister, telling her the news and thanking her whole-heartedly for all she had done.

"If you hadn't been so decent about it, I'd have been stuck down with kids like Helen Reeves and Len Maynard," she wrote. "You have been a sport, Beth!"

"I call it quite good, all things considered," Vi said when she heard. "After all, Babs, it isn't *your* fault that you don't know enough to be with us. Once you get into the ways of the school, though, I shouldn't wonder if you didn't just go *steaming* ahead. By this time next year, I expect you'll be with us."

"Yes," agreed Mary-Lou who was present at the interview. She spoke with emphasis. "There's no earthly reason why you shouldn't so long as you don't go and make the silly ass of yourself that *I* did."

Barbara stared at her. "What *do* you mean? How could I make a silly ass of myself by just working? For I jolly well mean to. I'm older than Vi and I ought to be *with* her, at any rate, if I'm not above her. So what?"

"I'll explain. Clem Barrass and I have been chums for ages—long before we ever came to the Chalet School when we were just kids," Mary-Lou replied in her most elderly way. "As a matter of fact, I got here first. Clem didn't come till half-term. I wanted awfully to be in the same form, which was mad seeing she's three years older than I am; but I hadn't any more sense in those days——"

"Got any more now?" someone interjected at this point.

Mary-Lou regarded the interrupter meditatively. "Oh, I think so," she said sweetly. "I may have been a batty kid, but I did at least have enough sense to know it when it was pointed out to me. *Some* people aren't like that, of course. They never can learn!" After which crushing remarks, she turned her back on the offender and went on to Barbara. "We were in the same dormy—by ourselves, too. So I got her to coach me, especially in arithmetic, after we'd gone to bed and I made myself ill. And what a ticking-off Matey did give us both!" she added reminiscently. "It was quite mad, of course. No matter how I worked, it just couldn't be done."

"All the same," Vi put in, "you did set the standard for our lot. You were a new girl, and there you were, simply *rushing* up the form-lists at the rate of no one's business! We jolly well weren't going to have that and we all hoed in like mad and went ahead as hard as we could."

Mary-Lou nodded. "We did. Well, Barbara, when I got better, the Head sent for me and explained why I was being mad and made me promise I wouldn't do such a thing again. Not that she need have done it," she added. "They'd got at Clem while I was in San and she wouldn't coach me any more—not in bed, anyhow."

"But what's all that got to do with me?" Barbara asked, bewildered.

"Just this: don't you be an ass and try to work out of hours. It won't get you anywhere in the end. *I know!*" Miss Trelawney wound up, looking not unlike a wise young owl.

"You'd better not try any games of that kind on!" Vi put in her oar. "You know what Auntie Anne would do if you were ill from swotting too hard."

Barbara knew without anyone telling her and, thanks to the pair of them, was prevented effectually from trying to work overtime.

"All the same," she told herself as she marched with her form through the corridor to their form-room, "I'll jolly well work in form and during prep! No one could blame me for doing that. I mean to be with Vi as soon as I can."

The first lesson was arithmetic with the new maths mistress who had not put in an appearance so far. They knew she had arrived, for it had filtered down the school that she was an old friend of Mrs. Graves, once better known to them as Hilary Burn. Miss Burn had been for some years at the school in the capacity of Games mistress, but had left the previous year to marry Dr. Graves, since when she had spent most of her time in South Africa until the opening of the new Sanatorium at the Görnetz Platz had brought them to the Alps. Rumour said that the new mistress had spent the week-end at the pretty chalet where the Graves lived and had returned to the school late on Sunday night. Neither had she turned up for Prayers that morning, for Miss Wilson, Head of the finishing branch at Welsen, had come up on the very early train to discuss the maths curriculum with her and they had had *Frühstück* together in the Head's sitting-room and stayed there, talking things over until well after prayers.

"We don't even know her name," Ruth Barnes said as they settled into their seats in the big room. "I wonder what she's like?"

"Well, she couldn't be worse than Miss Slater," Clare Kennedy said decidedly. "How I loathed that woman! And how she loathed me back! I'm not sorry she's left."

"Neither am I," Maeve Bettany agreed pensively. "You know, I think the thing was that she hated anyone who wasn't simply *wizard* at maths. She liked Phil Craven all right! Phil could never do anything wrong for her."

"Oh, Phil was a freak!" Ruth said with sudden viciousness. "I never liked her and she's another person I'm not sorry to be missing here!"

"She's gone to join her people in Cape Colony, hasn't she?" queried a serious young person whose name Barbara had discovered to be Dora Ripley.

Maeve nodded. "Sailed last week with her dad who came to fetch her. No; she'll be no loss. She was always being offended about something and sulking all over the place about it. And you couldn't *help* offending her, either," she added. "She got her monkey up at the least thing."

"So did Miss Slater!" Heather Clayton put in feelingly

"You're telling me! She never gave *me* a moment's peace. I used to get so deaved——"

They were on to the new word in a flash.

"So *what*?" Ruth demanded.

"'Deaved', ducky! Nice, isn't it? And not slang, thank goodness! It's Scots and it means—well—muddled and all upside down. I got it from a Scots girl we met when we were staying at Stratford during the hols."

Before anyone could make any reply to this, the sound of footsteps coming down the corridor was heard and they all sat straight in their seats. The door opened and the Head came in, followed by a somewhat plump, very pretty person, sufficiently unlike Miss Slater of the English régime in looks, at any rate, to merit their instant liking for her. They rose politely to their feet and Dora, who sat near the door, closed it while the Head and her companion walked up the room to the mistress's table, where the Head stopped and said, "You may sit, girls!"

The form resumed its seats and sat looking demurely at her.

Miss Annersley smiled at them and then turned to the stranger. "This is Upper IVB, Miss Wilmot. Clare Kennedy is form prefect. Stand a moment, Clare, my dear!"

Clare rose to her feet, blushing wildly, and Miss Wilmot gave her a beaming smile. The Head continued, "Thank you, dear. Sit down now. Girls, this is Miss Wilmot, your form mistress and our new maths mistress. She is an Old Chaletian, though none of you will remember her as she was with us in Tirol. However, she knows the school inside out from experience. For instance, she knows that this is French day and her lesson will be given in French, of course."

She paused, and several people went red at the reminder. They had forgotten and all their chatter had been in English. The Head knew, of course. As Maeve said ruefully later on, she always did. She said no more about it, however, but smiled at Miss Wilmot, spoke a few words in an undertone to which the new mistress replied with a smile and quick, *"Oui, vraiment! C'est bien entendu!"* and then departed, leaving them to get acquainted in their own way.

Miss Wilmot lost no time. "Miss Annersley tells me that as I was with Miss Wilson, no one has taken register," she said, speaking English. "We'll do that first and then I'll have a rough idea of your names. Answer, please!" She went down the list of fifteen, looking steadily at each girl as she responded. Then she shut the register and handed it to Clare with a request that she would take it to the office for Miss Dene.

"Leave it on her desk if she isn't there, Clare," she added.

Clare left the room and presently came back and Miss Wilmot, who had opened a book they all recognized as their textbook, looked up again and called to Ruth Barnes to come and show her how far they had gone in it

Crimson with embarrassment, Ruth left her seat and came to show the new mistress their last term's work. "We got to page 120, Miss Wilmot," she said. "We did all those exercises, but we didn't do the general ones."

Miss Wilmot nodded. "I see. Thank you, Ruth." She glanced down the page. Then she turned to the next and nodded again. "I think the best plan will be for you to do the first four examples of exercise VIII K and let me see how much you remember," she said briskly. "Open your textbooks at page 121 and set to work."

There was a rustle of pages, prolonged in the case of Heather and her boon companion in sin, Francie Wilford, but at last all the form had settled to work.

The example was on compound fractions and Beth had just begun them with Barbara, so that young lady was able to manage the first two with comparative ease. But the third one was stiffer, for it included two decimal fractions Barbara sucked the end of her pencil and tried to remember what her sister had told her.

The other new girl in their form, one Sue Meadows, glanced swiftly at the work and then began to scribble at railroad speed. She was done long before anyone else, took her rough-book up to Miss Wilmot who was busy making out her marks register, and had them all ticked. She was sent back to her seat with instructions to work the last four in the exercise and also to work more neatly.

"Your figures are terrible for a girl of fourteen," Miss Wilmot said, speaking in the French she had employed ever since she had begun the actual lesson. "Take time to shape them properly, Sue. Untidy work won't do."

Sue replied, *"Oui, Mamzelle!"* and went back to her seat and was at it again as hard as she could go while Caroline Sanders, the next to finish, came out with her book for correction.

In the meantime, Barbara was making an appalling mess of the third sum. She was unaccustomed to working with other girls or, indeed, working at any pace but her own. She was rapidly approaching a state when she felt like bursting into tears over it all when a hand was laid on her shoulder and Miss Wilmot's voice said, "Show me your work, Barbara. You seem to be getting into a muddle."

Barbara lifted her flushed face. "I have only just begun fractions like these," she said, speaking in the pretty French she had learnt from her mother whose early years had been spent in France. "I cannot understand this one, though I have tried with it."

"So I see," Miss Wilmot said, eyeing the messy page. She looked at what was legible and then smiled. "But, my dear girl, you should have turned the decimals into vulgar fractions first. You know how to do that?"

Barbara looked at her work. "I forgot that," she owned, twiddling her pencil between her fingers.

"Start again on a clean page, then. And don't rub so hard that you take the surface off the paper. Let me see. I think we'd better tear this out. The paper's worn so thin, you'd go through it. Now go ahead!"

She left Barbara and went to Ruth who had likewise forgotten what to do with decimal fractions in a mixed fraction sum and had made nearly as bad a mess. When Mary Woodley who came next proved to have done the same thing, Miss Wilmot clapped her hands and the girls stopped work only too thankfully.

"Faîtes attention, s'il vous plaît!" And the mistress went

to the blackboard and proceeded then and there to give a brief but intensive lesson on mixed fractions which even Mary Woodley, dullest of girls, could understand.

"Maintenant, vous comprennez la règle, n'est ce pas?" she asked as she laid down her stick of chalk.

"Oh, *oui, Mademoiselle*!" Maeve replied with enthusiasm. And proved it by going to work on the sum and getting it right *first time*!

"And that," as Maeve herself said later, "is unique for me! If she's going to make a chap understand as quickly as that, she jolly well has my vote!"

By the time the bell had rung for the end of the lesson, everyone had done those four sums and got them right. Miss Wilmot told them to work the next four for homework, gathered up her books and left them with a smiling, *"Bon jour, mes enfants!"* and they were left alone.

"I think I'm going to like her," Clare said in careful French.

"I know I am!" Dora Ripley agreed fervently. "She does not—how do you say 'flurry' in French?"

But this was beyond most of them. Barbara waited for someone else to speak. No one did, so she said shyly, "'*Désordre*' is the word."

"Yes!" Maeve cried before Dora had time to thank her. "That's one thing I want to know——"

"En français, s'il vous plaît!" Clare interjected despairingly. *"Toujours en français se jour-ci,* Maeve!"

"Oh bother—I mean——" Maeve hurriedly searched her memory for a French exclamation of disgust, but failed to find one; and then steps were heard outside and the form came quickly to order as Dora held the door open and Miss o'Ryan entered for their history lesson.

Miss o'Ryan, also an Old Chaletian, spoke French and German as fluently as she did her own language and they were soon so involved in trying to follow her remarks, that arithmetic and the new mistress were forgotten. They discovered that they were to do outlines of European history this year. Their new textbooks had not yet arrived, so Miss o'Ryan began with a sketch of the state of Europe at the time of the fall of the Roman Empire. She was careful to speak very slowly and use the simplest language, so even Mary Woodley managed to get some idea of what she was saying. She set them half a dozen questions on what she had told them for homework and was about to leave them when the bell rang for Break, when Heather held her up with an anxious question.

"S'il vous plaît, M'selle, pouvons-nous écrire nos—er—réponses en anglais ou en français, s'il vous plaît?"

"One *'s'il vous plaît'* at the end of the sentence is enough, Heather," Miss o'Ryan told her with a smile. "You must write your answers in French, of course."

"But—but I *can't*!" wailed Heather in English as she surveyed the questions.

"Mais oui; vous pouvez le faire," Miss o'Ryan replied inexorably. "You will use the first part of the sentence I have given you and that means you have half a dozen words at most to add yourself. I am sorry, Heather, but lessons given in French must be answered in French. Have you understood what I was saying?"

Like the Queen of Sheba, Heather had no more spirit left in her. She replied dismally, *"Oui, Mamzelle!"* and Miss o'Ryan left the room.

Naturally, they were all agog to discuss this latest fiat, but Clare took charge at once, ordering them to line up by the door and then marching them off to the *Speisesaal* for their milk and biscuits.

They dared not let loose until they had finished. There were too many Seniors about. But once they were free to go into the garden, they did the best they could with their limited vocabularies to give rein to their feelings.

"*C'est trop* ghastly!" Heather mourned. "*Nous ne pouvons pas parler* at *all!*"

"Cave! Prefects!" someone warned her as Julie and Clem came strolling along in their direction. The prefects were talking quickly and more than one pair of eyes regarded them enviously as the two big girls went past, speaking in French that was fluent and good on Julie's part—like Barbara, she had heard a good deal at home, thanks to their two mothers and their Aunt Elizabeth having spent so much of their girlhood in France—and Clem, who had begun her career at the Chalet School by knowing less, even than Upper IVB, was very quick and had picked it up easily enough, once she chose to give her mind to it.

"Je suppose que nous le pouvons quand nous sommes aussi âgées comme elles," Christine Dawson sighed. "Oh, *comme je*—what's the French for 'long', someone?" No one knew except Barbara and she was shy of putting herself forward, so Christine continued, "No one know? Oh, well —*je* long *pour le mercredi quand nous pouvons parler en anglais tout le temps.*"

That was the attitude of most of them. Luckily for them, however, their next lesson *was* French grammar and when Mlle came in, she was besieged on all sides by requests not to bother about verbs or things like that—this was Heather —but to help them to learn to *talk*.

Little Mlle, who had been with the school from the second year of its inception, regarded them with eyes that sparkled with amusement. "But, *mes petites,*" she protested, "verbs and grammar generally are most necessary if you are to talk and write well."

Then she relented and her three-quarters of an hour was spent in helping them to compose sentences and say them correctly. She even agreed to help them to enlarge their vocabularies by proposing to give them a list of ten new words each day, assuring them that they would soon know a great deal of French if they used any spare moments they had in memorizing even one word.

"By the end of the term, you will all find it much easier to talk if you do this," she promised them. "You will know so many more words, you understand."

They could appreciate this and accepted her list with gratitude.

"*You* won't need it, though," Maeve said to Barbara as they changed into plimsolls for gym which was the next lesson. "How do you talk so easily?"

Barbara explained and Maeve shook her head till the bronze-red curls flew madly. "Lucky you!" she sighed in English—and was instantly and properly caught by Miss Dene who came into the splashery at that moment to escort them to the gymnasium.

Maeve did *not* appreciate being told the correct French for her remark and made to repeat it again and again until her accent satisfied Miss Dene. However, when she had finally got it, she comforted herself with the reflection that at least it was another addition which she would know for the rest of her life. The maddening part was that the rest had also got it without having to accept Miss Dene's rebuke for breaking rules and being awarded an order mark!

Gym in French was not so bad, for at least they were able to work off some of their feelings in marching, jumping and apparatus-work. When their twenty minutes ended, they felt soothed and went back to their form-room for general knowledge with the Head feeling better.

Miss Annersley finished her lesson a little before the end of morning school. Then she smiled at them and spoke in English. "Now, girls! I know you feel that life is going to be very hard for you this term, at any rate. But you all know that one reason why your parents have sent you here is so that you may learn to speak both French and German accurately and fluently. Mlle has told me what she proposes to do and I think it a very good plan. To help you over your first troubles, we have decided that you need have no *dictée* preparation this term; and I will excuse half your repetition. Miss Denny will give you German lists as well and I think that by the end of the term you will find that you are beginning to talk much more easily. And, you know, when you hear nothing but French round you for two days every week and nothing but German on two others, you'll soon pick up words and phrases and begin to use them naturally."

She paused there and smiled at them. Maeve Bettany spoke up at once.

"Do you really mean that we'll be able to talk it as easily as *you* do—or any of the other mistresses, Miss Annersley?"

The Head nodded. "At any rate, if you aren't *quite* so fluent as we are, you must remember that we've been doing it since before any of you were born. But I do mean that if you will really *try* you will find it growing easier every day and then the time will come when you won't even have to think about it, but will just do it. I promise you that!"

"I wish I could believe it!" muttered Heather to Jocelyn Fawcett who shared the dual desk with her.

"You will find I'm right, Heather," the Head said, laughing; and Heather reddened furiously.

Miss Annersley decided that she had said enough. She told them to clear their desks and stand ready to march out to the splashery—and this time she spoke in French. Then she dismissed them, cheered up despite themselves.

Normally, they would have had an hour's needlework after the rest, but the Head knew that once winter set in, there would be many days when it would be impossible for them to go out. She had arranged with the rest of the staff that needlework could be left till that time came. In the meantime, the girls were to be out of doors as much as possible just now. So she rejoiced the hearts of everyone by announcing during *Mittagessen* that that afternoon would begin with open-air exercise.

"The only thing I must insist on," she ended, "is that you must all try to remember to speak French the whole time. Do your best. If you want to say something and don't know how to put it, ask whoever is in charge of you. Now, stand for Grace and then take your deckchairs to Hall for the rest-time. Take your library-books with you and remember that you are forbidden to talk at all until it ends. Ready? Grace!"

CHAPTER TEN

News for the School

"I DON'T LIKE either of those new girls—not Sue Meadows *nor* Barbara Chester; and I just can't think what Vi Lucy sees in Barbara that she's taken to hanging around with her everywhere." Mary Woodley paused and looked at Betty Landon who was in the common room with her at the moment.

"What are you getting at?" Betty demanded. "They're cousins, so you'd expect Vi to give an eye to Barbara for the first week or two, anyhow. Besides, what on earth has it got to do with you who Vi trots round with? She's never been a special pal of yours."

Mary reddened angrily. "I never said she was. I only said I couldn't understand why she stuck like a limpet to her."

"Well, and I don't see that it's any business of yours." Betty eyed Mary keenly. "Of course, I know you'd like Vi to be pals with you, but she doesn't seem to be special pals with anyone. As for Sue and Barbara, I don't know much about Sue, but *I* like Barbara."

"Well, I don't! She puts on any amount of frills about being able to jabber French——"

"Rot! She does no such thing! She told us herself that her mother used to talk to her at home and that's how she knows so much. No frills about that! The fact of the matter is that you're jealous of her with Vi!"

No one, not even her dearest friend, had ever hinted that Betty Landon was tactful, and she certainly had contrived to touch on a very sore point with Mary. Ever since that young person had come to the school, she had cherished a secret passion for Vi Lucy, who knew nothing about it and cared less. Vi had made a big effort to satisfy her mother's request that she would look after her cousin for the first week or two of term. As a result, she was finding that Barbara at home, the petted darling of her mother; and Barbara at school, learning for the first time to stand on her own feet, were two very different people and the second one was a girl with whom she was rapidly developing a close friendship. They were together as much as two people in different forms can be at boarding-school, and Mary was, as Betty had carelessly suggested, jealous.

Mary herself had never had any real friend either. She was a rather heavy, dull girl with a trick of sulking when she was annoyed by anything. She was the oldest in the form, being already fifteen, but her work was so poor all round that it was only by grace of the Head that she was not in Lower IV. Anyone less likely to appeal to quick-silvery Vi, it would have been hard to imagine.

On Betty's last remark, Mary tossed her head, turned her back and walked off in high dudgeon. Feather-headed Betty shrugged her shoulders and departed to seek a partner for the walk that morning. She never gave the matter another thought, which was like her. There was no malice in her—she was merely careless of what she said and did.

Oddly enough, Julie Lucy was discussing her young cousin with her own friend, Clem Barrass. This was a new friendship this term, too. Hitherto, Julie had found all she needed in Barbara's elder sister, Nancy. But Nancy had gone to Welsen and, thanks to peritonitis, Julie had another year at the Chalet School before her. Being a sensible girl, she had decided to try to make closer friends with one or two other people. Clem Barrass, whose own particular friend Gwynneth Jones had remained at the English branch, was in a similar state and the girls had gravitated together naturally, though theirs was certainly a friendship of opposites.

"I'm thankful to see that young Vi has taken Barbara on properly," she said as she and Clem finished packing up the garments to be worn that evening, when the prefects would play hostesses to the rest of the school and were giving them some scenes from Dickens by way of entertainment. "I wondered what would happen for, to tell you the truth, none of us were particularly fond of Barbara at home. She's always been *the* most spoilt little monkey in creation. I suppose that Auntie felt that she was never well and strong like the rest so she had to make it up to her by giving way to her in everything and making the rest do the same. But I can tell you, Babs is growing into a lot nicer girl than I should ever have thought possible."

"She and Vi seem to be regularly in cahoots," replied Clem, purveyor of slang to the rest of her peers.

Julie laughed. "They do—though I'd advise you not to let a staff hear you using *that* expression, my dear! And if you'd heard Vi on the subject when Mummy tackled her about giving Babs a hand in the beginning, you'd know how funny it really is!"

"My dear girl, the early teens are a fussy age at any time," Clem said, as she laid the last dress into the case they would take down to the office which was to act as greenroom. "Vi's a nice kid at bottom, even if she *is* a pest at times like all of them. She'll grow out of it in time."

"Listen to Grandma talking!" Julie mocked her. "Finished? Then come on! I'll give you a hand down to the office with it."

In the meantime, the pair who were causing such very different feelings, were out in the garden, strolling about and chattering hard. Beth had sent her young sister a note that morning, announcing that quarantine was ended and saying that "Aunt Jo" wanted Barbara to come to tea on the morrow and bring a friend with her.

"How super for you!" Vi said.

"Isn't it? I'm longing to see Beth again—*and* Auntie Jo, of course. And Vi; would you be the friend?"

Vi's eyes danced. "Well, rather! What do you think? *I* want to see Bethy, too. *And* the Trips, and Auntie Jo and Uncle Jack, of course. And I'd love to see the inside of Freudesheim. Auntie Jo has lovely things and I've been dying to see what they've done with the house."

Barbara laughed. "I didn't think of that."

"Oh, but I *must* think of things like that," Vi said seriously. "I want to be a—an arranger of houses when I'm grown up. I forget what you call it exactly, but that's what I want to do. So I want to see as many different houses as I can from now on."

"Are the triplets nice?" asked Barbara, who had hitherto had little chance of meeting those young ladies.

Vi chuckled. "Dears, all of them! Con's a bit of a dreamer, but she can tell marvellous yarns. And Len's a pet. As for Margot, she *can* be sweet when she likes, but she does do mad things. She's a pal of Emerence Hope's, by the way."

Barbara laughed. "Is she really as mad as Emerence? What a time their form will have with two of them!"

"Oh, she's in the B division. She's awfully clever, you know, but she only works in bits and pieces, so she won't be with Emerence. Len and Con are, though. I noticed their names when the Head read out the lists at the beginning of term." A sudden, not too pleasant thought struck her. "I say, Babs! Weren't you to live with Auntie Jo and come daily for this term like the Trips and Sue Meadows? What are you going to do about it now?"

"I'm staying on as a boarder," Barbara said placidly. "The Head sent for me while you were practising after *Frühstück* and told me that she'd written to Mummy about it and Mummy said I might choose which I'll do."

"Oh, smash—er—I mean *wizard!*" Vi said, hurriedly correcting herself. "Wizard!" was allowed in the school, but "smashing" most certainly was *not*.

"I'm glad the babies didn't get it," Barbara said, reverting to the German measles at Freudesheim. "And Beth says Stephen didn't either, though he's had to be in quarantine for the full time. Wouldn't it have been ghastly if he'd given it all round in a quite new school?"

A fresh voice brought their gossip to a sudden close as Caroline Sanders came racing across the field to inform them that if they wanted to change their library books that day they had better hurry, for Madge Herbert said she was closing library in five minutes.

"It's O.K.," Vi replied. "We were at library the minute it opened and swopped over. By the way, if you haven't read *The Boy in Red* you'd better try to bag it when Barbara takes it back. It's super!"

"Oh, is it *you* who's got it?" Caroline queried. "Mary Woodley was asking for it and she was mad when Madge told her that someone else had it."

"Oh, Mary Woodley's always being mad about something," Vi said impatiently. "She goes round like a thundercloud whenever anything happens that she doesn't like. There's the bell for the walk! Come on, folks!" And she led the way in a wild race to the Upper IV splashery, where Caroline tucked her own library book into her shoe-locker in direct defiance of rules before she pulled on her beret and coat in readiness for the walk.

Barbara, who had been pulled up for the same thing the previous Saturday, saw her. "Oughtn't you to take your book to the common-room?" she asked Caroline.

Caroline laughed. "I *ought*, of course; but there isn't

really time. I'll just have to risk it for once. I've shoved it right to the back so Matey won't see it."

They thought no more about it, and left the place to join their two forms outside. Neither of them noticed that Mary Woodley was standing nearby and had heard all that had been said. A queer look crossed her face. Before she left the splashery, she stooped over Caroline's locker for a moment. Then she turned and ran with a rather scared look on her face.

Out on the drive, Mary calmed down and walked up to Vi who was alone for the moment as Clare Kennedy had asked Barbara a question and that young lady had moved a pace or two over to answer it. "Will you be my partner this morning?" she asked.

Vi shook her head. "Sorry, but I've bagged Barbara for a partner. Haven't you got one?" She looked round. "There's Dorothy Ruthven alone. She generally has Dora, but Matey yanked Dora off to san when she heard she had earache. Why don't you ask her?"

Mary muttered something and an unpleasant look came into her eyes as she moved off, leaving Vi, who went to join Barbara and Clare. Miss Wilmot, who was in charge of their walk, saw her and came across to ask if she was without a partner.

"I asked Vi Lucy," Mary said sulkily, "but she's booked with Barbara Chester."

Miss Wilmot looked round. "There's Dorothy alone. Dorothy!"

Dorothy came up at once. "Yes, Miss Wilmot?"

"Haven't you a partner for the walk?"

"No, Miss Wilmot. I was walking with Dora Ripley, but——"

"But Matron has taken Dora off to san to see what she can do for the earache. I see. Well, Mary has no one, either, so you two had better partner each other. Run along and line up with the rest. I'm just ready for you."

Without waiting to see if they obeyed her or not, Miss Wilmot turned her attention to Maeve Bettany and Josette Russell who were late and came tearing along the path together at that moment.

"We're sorry, Miss Wilmot," Maeve gasped, "but Miss Annersley sent for us."

"Oh, then, in that case, of course you're excused," Miss Wilmot said with her jolly laugh. "Take your places and hurry up. We're going along the Platz to where that path leads down to the motor road and if we've time you can do some scrambling, so the sooner we're off the better. Ready, girls? Lead on, Hilary and Lesley."

Hilary and Lesley set off and the rest marched smartly after them. In England, they had held their Guide meetings at this time, but so far Guides had remained in abeyance. The Head had decided that until they were in full running order, outside things like Guides must wait, though she fully intended that they should begin presently.

Vi, with memories of the fun you had in Guides, began talking to Barbara about it. "I do hope we aren't going to stop having our Companies. I love Guides!"

"I've always wanted to be one," Barbara said wistfully, "but I never had the chance to join at home. I've read heaps of stories about them, of course, and Beth and Nancy told me lots, too. Mummy said I could join if we had them here, so I *hope* we do!"

Dorothy, walking immediately behind them with the still sulky Mary, and a keen Guide herself, joined in. "Oh, we couldn't possibly drop them! I'm sure the Head will let us start again soon. Only, I wonder who we'll have for Captain? Miss Edwards is in England, now, and Miss Burnett took the Cadets."

"I wonder," Vi said, "if Miss Burn—I mean Mrs. Graves—would come along and take us again. She was a super captain and she can't have much to do in a clean place like this. It isn't as if she had babies to look after, either."

"Yes," Dorothy said eagerly. "That's an idea, Vi! Couldn't we get someone to ask her the next time we see her?"

Mary-Lou, stalking along in front with Verity-Anne, turned her head to remark, "Who's seen her at all? We know she's up here, but she hasn't been near us so far."

"Perhaps she got a sickening of us when she was at school," said Mary disagreeably.

"Rot!" Vi said forcefully. "Burnie wasn't like that. She was always awfully jolly and decent. I expect she's been busy getting her house right and she'll be along soon."

"Girls—girls! Look where you're going!" came Miss Wilmot's voice. "You're straggling abominably! Keep up with the rest, please."

Thus reminded, they hurriedly made up the distance which had widened perceptibly between Mary-Lou and her partner and Catriona and Christine, and the subject dropped for the moment. The rest had to run, too, and by the time Miss Wilmot had her lines in order, they had reached the place where they were to turn off.

"You may break here, girls," Miss Wilmot called. "All I ask is that you won't frighten the natives by yelling. Keep together and remember, you may not go too far ahead. No one is to walk by herself, either, so see that no one is left out."

They broke rank joyfully. The Gang joined up in full force. Dorothy, with hardly a look at her partner, made for Gwen Parry and Carol Younger and Mary was left alone. Mary-Lou saw it, of course, and instantly called her to come and join up with them.

"I can't help it," she said in a hasty undertone in reply to the protesting looks of the others. "You heard what Willy said!" She raised her voice. "Come on, Mary! Room for another!"

Before they could move on, however, there came an interruption. They were hailed by a very sweet, clear voice and they all swung round at once to see a figure racing down the road from the Sanatorium towards them.

"Auntie Jo!" exclaimed Mary-Lou, Vi, Josette, Maeve and Barbara, while the rest shouted, "Mrs. Maynard! Oh, good!"

Jo had reached them by this time. "Hello, everyone! Welcome to the Oberland, though I admit it's on the late side. Don't blame me—blame the family who gave mine German measles! Oh, I'm so thankful it's over and I can pop in and out of school when I like now!" She turned to Miss Wilmot. "Nancy Wilmot! You don't look a day older than when I last saw you in Tirol! Tell me! Do you think I've aged at all?"

"Not in the least," Miss Wilmot said at once. "You're just what you always were—a bit plumper, perhaps. In fact," she added with a grin, "now I look at you, I see you're positively *chubby*!"

"I'm *not*! What a—a horrid thing to say to an old friend! You'll be telling me next that I'm *fat*!" Jo protested.

"Oh, I wouldn't go as far as that," Miss Wilmot said demurely.

Jo glared at her. "I should hope not! But never mind that now, at the moment, I've something much more exciting for you all. I'll give you three guesses among you!"

Miss Wilmot gave it up and laughed. "It wouldn't be you if you didn't come plunging along with the very latest!" she said. "All right, Jo; I can guess, so I'll leave it to the girls. Only tell me one thing. Is it all right?"

Mrs. Maynard nodded. "Absolutely! Of course, you spent a week-end with her, didn't you? O.K.; we'll leave it to the girls. Now, people, three guesses!"

"We're going to have another new mistress?" Mary-Lou queried.

"What a guess! No; certainly not—or if you are, it's the first I've heard of it."

"A new girl—or no—*several* new girls are coming unexpectedly," Maeve suggested.

Jo giggled like one of themselves. "Not *this* term, anyhow! One more; your last shot, so be careful!"

"Oh, I know! Bethy's engaged to someone!" was Vi's brilliant idea. "Who is it, Auntie Jo?"

"Rubbish!" Jo said scornfully. "How could she possibly? Where could she meet anyone? We've both been well and truly tied by the leg with German measles ever since she came!" She stopped and looked at them with a twinkling smile. "What a lot of duds you are, to be sure! Can't you guess? What—none of you? Well, well!"

"Don't tease, but *tell* us!" implored Josette Russell who was one of her nieces.

"O.K., I'll tell you, since you all seem to have left your

brains at school. You all remember Miss Burn who used to be P.T. mistress, don't you?"

A chorus informed her that they did. Mary-Lou added that they had been wondering why she hadn't been along to see them, since they knew she was living near the Sanatorium at the far end of the Platz.

"Oh, you *do* know that, do you? Well, that's something," quoth naughty Jo who was enjoying their mystified faces hugely.

"Oh, go on, Jo!" Miss Wilmot cried. "You know you're going to tell them. Get on with it and stop teasing!"

"Is it something to do with why she hasn't been to see us?" Hilary Bennett asked.

"It is! She's had other fish to fry, I can tell you."

"Well, I wish you'd get on with it and *tell* us!" Josette wailed. "You *are* awful."

"Go on, Auntie Jo!" Maeve joined her cousin's urging. "What *has* Miss Burn—I mean Mrs. Graves—been doing?"

Jo chuckled. Then she relented. "All right! Keep calm and I'll tell you. She presented the school with another prospective pupil first thing this morning."

Miss Wilmot began to laugh. "A girl after all! What a drop for Hilary! She told me they were hoping for a son to start with."

Jo joined in her laughter. "Oh, she's very thrilled with her daughter as you'll find when you see her—which won't be for a day or two, I imagine."

"Do you mean to say that they let *you* in?" Miss Wilmot asked incredulously.

"Talk sense! Of course they didn't! But I saw Phil Graves and he told me they were both delighted. Hilary was sleeping when I called."

"What are they calling the baby?" Mary-Lou demanded.

"Marjorie Edith after her two grandmothers. She'll be Marjorie for every day. I've seen *her*, by the way—just a peep, for she was asleep, too. She's a lovely baby, round and rosy with enormously long lashes. Her nose is a smudge at present," she added as an afterthought. "However, none of my own produced anything better, so we'll hope for the best where it's concerned. Well, now let me look at you all! It's ages since I saw anyone who wasn't covered with pink rash!"

"You've seen Beth," Barbara ventured.

"Who's that—Barbara? My word, young woman, school suits you all right! I'll drop your mother a line tonight and tell her she won't know you when she sees you. What a colour!"—Which she might well say, since Barbara was scarlet with embarrassment at this public notice.—"Are you coming to tea with us tomorrow? Who are you bringing with you?"

"Vi, please," Barbara said shyly. She knew Jo Maynard less well than any of her sisters.

"Excellent! Vi, I'm delighted. And Maeve and Josette, you know you're coming, too, don't you?"

"Rather!" Josette replied for both. "The Head told us just before walk. That's why we were late," she added cheerfully.

Maeve beamed at her aunt. "School's awfully nice, but it'll be fun coming to see you and your new house, Auntie Jo. Is Mummy coming soon, by the way? She said she expected to. Have you heard yet?"

"Yes; I had a letter yesterday. Peggy and your dad are bringing her and *then*"—Jo paused and gave her niece an aggravating look.

"Then—what?" Maeve demanded excitedly. "Go on, Auntie Jo!"

"Well then, Peggy is going back to Welsen for another year."

"Oh, goody! Bride will be thrilled! She said she'd always hoped to have another year with Peg there!"

"So everyone's pleased all round," Jo said. "And now I'm departing and leaving you to finish your walk. You may broadcast my news when you get back—unless I've done it myself in the meanwhile," she added tantalizingly. "I know you'd all go off pop with spontaneous combustion if I said you mustn't!" And with a final peal of laughter and a wave of her hand, she scrambled back to the road and set off down it, leaving Miss Wilmot to cope with a crowd of excited girls.

She did this by reminding them that shrieking was forbidden and bidding them go on if they wanted to do any scrambling. She also requested them to keep to the footpath. There had been a heavy dew that morning and the grass would be very slippery.

They set off, chattering eagerly about the latest news. No one was really sorry, however, when her whistle went and they were told to turn back. Everyone was dying to be first with the information.

And after all, as they found, Jo Maynard herself had done most of the broadcasting, for as they turned in at the gate Betsy Lucy with her chums, Katharine Gordon and Carola Johnston, came flying down the drive to announce with one voice, "Guess the news. Miss Burn has a daughter! We met Mrs. Maynard when we were coming back and she told us."

CHAPTER ELEVEN

Barbara in Trouble

"CAROLINE SANDERS, please go to Matron as soon as you have changed."

Madge Herbert met the two Upper Fourth forms as they finally left Betsy and her friends and sped in to change and prepare for *Mittagessen*. At her words, Caroline's mind at once flew guiltily to her library-book hidden at the back of her shoe-locker and she reddened as she said meekly, "Yes, Madge."

"Well, hurry up and don't keep her waiting, or she'll have even more to say to you than she seems to have already," Madge warned her with a good-natured smile. Then she nodded and turned away and Caroline was surrounded by teasing friends who all wanted to know what awful sin she had committed *now*!

"I can guess," Caroline said in melancholy tones, "though I must say I don't know how Matey got on to it. I put the thing right at the very back of my locker—Barbara saw me do it, didn't you, Barbara?" She appealed to Barbara who still went pink when anyone brought her to public notice and blushed furiously as she replied, "Oh, yes; I saw you do it."

"*And* warned me about it! Wish I'd taken your advice! Bang goes one if not two order marks! Oh dear!"

"But what is it?" Heather asked.

"My library-book. I was late for library and there wasn't time to take it to the common-room when I had got it, so I thought I'd chance it for once. All the same," she added as she changed into slippers at railroad speed, "Matey must have been literally *rootling* in the lockers, if she found it, for I stuck it right at the very back." She stood up and shook herself. "Am I tidy, anyone?"

"As much as you ever are!" half a dozen voices told her with gleeful insult; but she was too apprehensive of her coming interview with Matron to "rise" as she might have done. She peeped at herself in one of the mirrors, pulled her tie straight and left the place. The rest finished changing and went along to their common-room to wait for the gong to summon them to *Mittagessen.*

Three minutes later, the door burst open and Caroline shot in. Her face was scarlet, her eyes flashing. She made straight for Barbara who was standing by one of the windows looking out at the garden and turned to eye her in startled fashion.

"What did you do with my book?" Caroline demanded, going straight to the point.

"Your book?" Barbara went scarlet at the unexpected question. "Nothing, of course. You pushed it right to the back of your locker—I saw you. And that's all I know."

"Oh, yes!" Caroline spoke in biting tones. "And that was why Matey found it lying *on the floor—in front of my locker,* I suppose? And why you've gone as red as a beetroot when I ask you a simple question? You were the only one who saw me do it. *Did* you pull it out again and drop it on the floor to get me into trouble?"

"No; I never did!" Barbara cried. "I warned you what

would happen if you left it and Matey found out. I did do that! But I never touched the thing!"

"Then who did? Just you tell me *that*!" Caroline retorted furiously.

"I don't know. But I do know that I never saw your book after you'd hidden it and that's the plain-down truth!"

Mary Woodley, who had listened to all this with a queer look on her face, now pushed her way through the little crowd thronging round Barbara and Caroline.

"Oh, come, Barbara!" she said in jeering tones. "You don't think we're such mutts as all that, do you? If you were the only one to know what Caroline had done, you *must* know something about it. Or do you think it got legs and walked out on its own?"

Barbara paled and then went red again as she looked round the ring of faces. It was unfortunate for her that none of the Gang were there. Neither was Clare who would have put a stop to this kind of baiting at once, and given her a chance to speak up for herself. The others simply saw that Caroline had a certain amount of right on her side and instantly jumped to the conclusion that Barbara had really played such a mean trick and was lying about it now because she was afraid to face the music. If Barbara Chester thought she could do that sort of thing and get away with it, they meant to show her that she couldn't. So when she sent that quick, rather frightened look round them, there was not a friendly face near.

Mary was quick to seize her advantage. She rammed the charge home. "Come on! Tell the truth and shame You-Know-Who! Didn't you suffer a pain in your conscience over the wicked Caroline and pull the book out and leave it for someone to find so that she would get a good lesson? Own up!"

Her hectoring manner roused Barbara's temper. "Of course I didn't! *I* wouldn't do such a mean thing! I haven't got the nasty kind of mind that would think it up!" she flared as furiously as Caroline herself.

"Meaning that *we* have? Thanks, a lot!" Mary looked significantly at the others. "You hear what Barbara Chester thinks of us? And she's a new girl! She not only gets

Caroline into a row with Matey; she gives us sauce like this!"

The others were beginning to grow angry in their turn and there might have been a fully-fledged row, but just at that moment the gong sounded and put a stop to any further recriminations.

Barbara's chin went up at once and her eyes darkened with anger, but she was unable to say what she thought. Vi saw her and wondered what was wrong but she, too, had to hold her tongue for the time being; and even when Grace had been said and they were sitting in their places, she realized sadly that the meal-table was hardly the place to ask questions of an intimate nature.

Barbara saw her looks and a sudden warmth eased her desolation. Whatever these girls might say about her, she felt sure that Vi would stand by her. It made that meal easier when she caught the glances of one or two people sitting at the table parallel to theirs, as she was bound to do if she looked up.

Chief among them was Mary Woodley who sat next to Betsy Lucy; and on Betsy's other side was Caroline. Mary's looks were full of triumph, but Caroline, who was cooling down now, gave the new girl several puzzled glances.

Barbara cared not a jot for Mary's triumph, but she *had* been inclined to like Caroline who was a pleasant girl if she had not many brains, and the latter's worried expression was not lost on her.

As for Vi, that young lady was more than ever determined to get to the bottom of things. Quite apart from her promise to her mother, she found herself liking Barbara more and more the longer she really knew her.

"She's frightfully new to school," Vi thought as she scooped up the last crumbs of her *Apfeltorte*. "Most likely it's something I can help with. Anyhow, I'm doing my darndest!"

As a result of this resolution, she shook her head when Clem asked if she would have a second helping, greatly to the surprise of that damsel, since Vi Lucy had remarked in her hearing only the previous week that *Apfeltorte* was one of the nicest puddings she had ever tasted and she didn't care how often they had it!

Luckily for her, Mary-Lou was of the same way of thinking and sent up her plate for a second supply, so Clem stopped worrying about Vi and attended to her job. But all the time the rest were enjoying their *Apfeltorte*, Vi was wishing them to Jericho. Never, so it seemed to her, had they been so slow in eating.

Barbara was not anxious to remain at the table, either. Like Caroline, she had begun to cool off a little and she longed to get away somewhere alone where she could think things out. The longer they were, the more she forgot her own grievances and wondered how on earth Caroline's book could have got out of the locker and on to the floor.

"I *saw* her shove it right to the back," she thought. "If she pushed her slippers in as hard as she could, I don't see how she *could* have worked the book out."

Then the bell on the Head's table sounded, and everyone folded her napkin and put it into its ring before standing up. Grace followed and the usual quick clearing of the table, but when that was over, the girls were free to do as they chose for the next half-hour or so.

Barbara made for the door, but Vi was after her and caught up with her before she could vanish.

"Come on! Let's go down the garden," she said, tucking her hand through her cousin's arm. "I want to talk to you."

For a moment, Barbara's face wore a baffled look. Then she suddenly relaxed. "Oh, and I want to talk to *you*, Vi," she said. "I'm—I'm in such a *muddle*!"

At that moment, Mary, who had been watching them, came up. "Like to have a stroll in the garden, Vi?" she asked. "I want to see you about something—rather urgently. Do come!"

"I can't this moment," Vi replied promptly. "I've just asked Barbara to come out with me. It'll wait, won't it? What can you have to say to me that's *urgent*?"

"No, it can't wait!" Mary retorted sharply. She wanted to get in first with her own story.

Barbara freed her arm from her cousin's grasp. "I can

wait, Vi," she said. "If Mary wants you as badly as all that, you go with her. I'll be in the rock garden."

Vi looked at her doubtfully. "You swear you'll wait there for me?" she asked.

Barbara nodded. "I promise you. I honestly do want your advice."

"Righto!" Vi said reluctantly. "I'll be with you in ten minutes. I don't suppose it's anything frightfully much."

Barbara nodded and went off and Vi turned to the triumphant Mary. "I can give you five minutes," she said, glancing at her watch. "Better come to the common-room—it's nearest."

She led the way to the common-room where they could be fairly sure of being alone for a minute or two. Vi waited until her companion was well into the room. Then she shut the door with what was very nearly a bang and faced round on her.

"Now!" she said. "What is it? And hurry up! I can't wait all day."

But now that she had accomplished her end, Mary was bothered as to how to begin.

"Do buck up!" Vi exclaimed impatiently. "What do you want with me?"

Mary took her courage into her hands and plunged headlong into her story. "It's really Caroline's affair," she began. "Only you know what she is, and I do think it's unfair that she should get into a row for something that wasn't her fault."

Vi looked mystified. "What on earth has Caroline's row to do with me?" she asked.

Mary coloured. "Well, she's your cousin——"

Vi interrupted her. "What are you talking about? Really, Mary, there can't be any need to be as asinine as all that! Caroline is *not* my cousin——"

"No; but Barbara Chester is!" Mary interrupted in her turn.

Vi clutched her head with both hands. "What *are* you getting at? First you say Caroline has got into a row. Then you go off on to Barbara. What *is* all this in aid of?"

"It's all Barbara's fault it happened," Mary began.

Vi was up in arms at once. "Don't be such a goat! How could it be Barbara's fault that Caroline's in a row?"

"Well, it is," Mary said doggedly, though she was unable to meet Vi's eyes and turned her own away. "She—she yanked Caro's library book out of her locker and left it on the floor for Matey to find and Caro's in a fearful row for it."

But if she thought that Vi Lucy would swallow a tale like that, she was speedily undeceived. That young lady ruffled up like an indignant bantam and said, "Rot!"

"'Tisn't rot!" Mary protested. "You go and ask Caro if you don't believe me!"

"I jolly well *will*!" And before Mary could stop her, she had swung round, pulled the door open and was flying down the corridor so intent on putting a stop to this lie about her cousin that she forgot all about rules.

Luckily, there was no one about to call her to order, so she got away with it and landed full tilt into the group of which Caroline formed a part, demanding breathlessly, "What's all this rot about Barbara? What have you been saying about her, Caroline?"

Faced by an infuriated Vi, whose eyes were flashing blue fire and whose face was crimson, it was little wonder that Caroline flinched and drew back from her.

"Go on!" Vi ordered. "Tell me what you've been saying and doing to her! Come on, Caroline! Out with it!"

"Well," stammered Caroline, "it—it was just that she *did* know what I'd done with the thing and—and she seemed to th-think I—I oughtn't."

Vi stared at her for a moment. Then she got her breath. "And do you mean to say that you've accused my cousin of playing a beastly trick like that just because she warned you that Matey would raise the roof if she knew you'd shoved your book into your locker instead of taking it to common-room? You must be crackers!"

"Sh-she was the only one who knew wh-what I'd done!"

"Well, that's where your toes turn in, for I knew about it myself! I heard what you both said. I suppose next thing you'll say that *I* had a hand in it!"

"Oh, rot!" Heather Clayton interposed. "Of course, no one would think you would do such a thing, Vi."

"Then why should you think it of Barbara?"

Someone murmured something about her being new and not used to school. Vi was down on her in a flash. "What's that got to do with it? You start to get decent ideas from your home people, I should hope. Besides, we weren't the *only* ones in the splashery. All the rest were there too."

"No," Caroline said eagerly. "We were the last out. Everyone else had gone."

Vi thought back, frowning until her black brows nearly met over her pretty nose. "No, we weren't!" she said triumphantly. "There was someone after us. Now who was it?" She thought hard. "I can't remember; but I know there was someone else there besides us. Anyhow, whoever did that with your book, it wasn't Barbara. Besides, we left together, she and I, so she *couldn't* have done it!"

"It—it does seem as if we must have made a mistake somewhere," Caroline faltered. "*Thank* you!" Vi's dignity was immense. "I'm glad you can see sense when it's pushed down your throat! Perhaps you'll tell Barbara that you're sorry you've spoken to her as you did? And now, if that's all, I'm going to her."

She strutted off, her head in the air, leaving them gazing after her with consternation on their faces. Vi was a very popular young person with her own kind and she was also one of the Gang. Some of them thought uncomfortably of what Mary-Lou, Hilary and Lesley would have to say to them if they ever got wind of this and wished they hadn't been so ready to accuse a new girl just because she *was* new.

Meanwhile, Vi had gone to the rock garden where she found her cousin waiting for her, a very determined look on her face.

"Oh, Vi!" she exclaimed as that young woman appeared. "I'm so glad to see you! I thought you were never coming and I really am in a—a jam!"

"I've just been hearing all about it," Vi told her. "Here, I say! You *are* a frog! Have you been standing still? Oh, you goop! Come on! I'll race you round this path. Are you ready? Then—*off*!"

She set off at full pelt and Barbara had nothing to do but race after her. When they finally pulled up near the doorway once more, she was flushed and panting and quite warm. Vi felt her hands and then nodded.

"That's better! Now, Babs, I've just been having things out with Caroline and the rest. They're a set of idiots, of course, but I *think* I've made them see reason. Anyhow, Caroline is going to tell you she's made a mistake and she's sorry. So *that's* all right!"

Barbara looked at her. "Was that the urgent thing Mary wanted to see you about?" she demanded.

Vi nodded. "It was. And I told her exactly where she got off! Don't think any more about it."

Barbara gave her a queer look. Then the bell rang and they had to go to get ready for the afternoon expedition. But as they went in, Barbara was considering. While she had waited for Vi, she had done some hard thinking and she had remembered that Mary Woodley had been in the splashery with them. What was more, she was sure that the elder girl had not left the place before they did. That being the case, unless Caroline had really contrived to send her book on to the floor herself, it meant that only Mary could have played the trick.

"But why pick on me?" Barbara thought as she joined the stream of girls making for the splashery. "I haven't done anything to her—I hardly know her. Why should she blame *me*? I can see why Caroline might have thought I'd done it—though I think it's horrid of her to think it—but why should Mary have backed her up like that? And—and why did she want to drag Vi into it as she must have done?" She began to change her shoes as she pondered this. As she tied her shoelaces, an idea came to her. "Oh, what an idiot I am! Of course! They all like Vi—and I don't wonder! She's a perfect dear! I expect the truth is Mary doesn't like her being so chummy with me. I know Vi doesn't like Mary and has no use for her. Trying to break our friendship wouldn't get *her* anywhere. If I *had* been mean enough to do such a thing, Vi would be furious with me all right. But what earthly good could it do *Mary*?"

She had to give it up then, for Vi was claiming her as a partner. What was more there was a positive clang of triumph in her cousin's voice as she said, "Come on, Babs! I'm ready and you're my partner for this! Get cracking, can't you?"

Mary, watching from the other side of the splashery, sniffed loudly and significantly.

However, that was all. She fully realized that her unpleasant plot to end the close friendship between Vi and Barbara had failed and she had done herself no good by it, either. Vi had made that very plain by her little speech. She would have been wiser to let things alone, for it had only stiffened Mary's dislike of her cousin and made her the more resolved to do something to show "that Barbara Chester" that she wasn't wanted.

On this day, she paired off with Emerence Hope who was eagerly looking forward to the return of the Maynards on Monday. Emerence and Margot, the youngest of the Triplets, were bosom friends and Emerence had been lonely without her usual comrade-in-arms. In her joyful anticipation of what Monday would bring, she had overlooked the fact that she needed a partner for the afternoon's trip until everyone else had been booked up except Mary. She made a grimace behind that young person's back when she found what her fate was to be. However, she had learned—somewhat painfully—that at school, at any rate, she had to do as she was told and take the rough with the smooth on occasion, so she joined the elder girl without demur.

They set off, escorted by five mistresses, since both Upper IVs and Lower IVA were off on this expedition which was to be by mountain train to the valley above the Görnetz Platz whence they would walk down again. The train journey would last only twenty minutes and the walk should take not longer than two hours. They had been told they might take sweets and fruit with them for the return journey as they were not going anywhere for *Kaffee and Kuchen*. If they did it this way, they could be home before darkness fell. It was made easier by the fact that the road passed through two tiny hamlets where there were stations so that if anyone was too tired to go on, she could be put on the first downward train.

The Middles had all been looking forward to the trip ever since it had been promised to them on the Monday of that week and now they set off, talking excitedly of what they hoped to see. What none of them knew was that, before they saw the Chalet School again, they were to have one of the most alarming experiences of their lives.

CHAPTER TWELVE

Adventure for the Middles

THE ROSLEINALP was much higher than the Görnetz Platz and when the girls tumbled out of the little mountain train, they felt the difference of the keener, thinner air at once. The sun was shining, but they were glad of their gentian-blue winter coats and the thin woollen handkerchiefs in white striped with crimson which they wore tucked snugly round their throats.

"Brrh! " Barbara shivered. "Isn't it cold up here! "

"Yes; but it makes you feel awfully fit," her cousin replied. "I feel as if I could do a ten-mile walk easily! " She looked round. "This is the Rösleinalp, isn't it? Well, doesn't that mean 'Rosebud'? Where are the roses? I don't see them.

"Plenty of alpenroses about," Miss Derwent told her. "All the same, I rather think that it gets its name from the Alpenglück which dyes this shelf nearly crimson on occasion—or so I'm told," she added. "I've not seen it for myself."

Barbara had been sniffing like a dog who encounters a strange new smell. "What a queer smell there is—sort of sharp and sourish! What is it, Miss Derwent?"

"Don't say 'sort of'! " scolded the English mistress who was down on that particular expression on all occasions.

"As for the smell, it comes from the glacier beyond—over there. Look, girls!" She flung out her hand towards the north-west and they all swung round to gaze. "That's the Eismeer over there. We are much nearer it up here than we are down at the Platz, of course."

"How lovely and—and *glittery* it is!" Verity-Anne exclaimed.

"Isn't it?" Barbara stared at it rapturously. "Oh, Miss Derwent, couldn't we just walk as far as it? I've never seen a glacier before in my life—or not so near."

Miss Derwent laughed. "You most certainly could *not*!"

"But why not?" Mary-Lou demanded. "It looks only about half an hour away."

Miss Derwent laughed again as she exchanged glances with Miss o'Ryan who stood nearby. That lady joined in the talk at once.

"Indeed, then, and Miss Derwent is quite right. In this clear air, distances are deceptive. 'Tis a good two hours' walk away it is and some nasty bits of scrambling before you get there. Oh, no, you two! 'Tis waiting you'll be until you know a little more about climbing than you do at present. By the time we got there, if we went, we want to be half-way down again." She stopped and looked at Miss Derwent who, as Senior mistress, was in charge of the expedition.

Miss Derwent nodded. "Girls! I want your attention, please! You may have half an hour to explore. Then we must set off on our downward journey. We are going to divide up into three parties as I don't want to overwhelm the natives. There are thirty-nine of you, so that gives us just thirteen for each group." She turned to Mary-Lou. "Mary-Lou, if I let you and your Gang go together, will you promise me to behave yourselves?"

"We'll be wingless angels!" Mary-Lou rejoined promptly.

The mistresses all broke into peals of laughter at this large promise. When she had recovered her gravity, the Senior mistress said, "My dear girl, I never ask impossibilities of anyone!" She paused and Mary-Lou went pink. "All I want," she resumed, "is your word of honour that you will keep together, do as you are told at once and without argument, and remember not to yell at the tops of your voices. Can you promise me that much, do you think?"

Mary-Lou held her tongue and it was left to Vi, Hilary and Lesley to reply eagerly, "Oh, yes, Miss Derwent!"

"Very well, then. You may go in a bunch. Miss o'Ryan, I'll hand them over to you—Oh, one moment! There are only ten of them——"

"Eleven, now that we've got Barbara Chester." Mary-Lou was never put down for long.

"Oh, you've adopted Barbara, have you? Very well, then; eleven. I said *thirteen* in each group, so you need two more." She glanced round and called the first couple she saw who could be relied on to behave reasonably well. "Clare and Ghislaine, you'd better join with them. Come along! Now, Miss o'Ryan, I think perhaps you'd better get off at once. Remember that if any of them seem to be tiring,"—she glanced at Barbara and Verity-Anne, neither of them over-strong—"leave them at the station at either Oberhofen or Unterhofen to catch the next train down. You've plenty of money for fares?"

"I have so," Miss o'Ryan replied. "We'll set off, then. 'Tis a fine enough day now, but at this time of year you can never be telling what may happen!"

Wherein, she spoke more truly than she knew.

Miss Derwent nodded. "Off you go! *Auf Wiedersehn!* We'll meet at the school!" She smiled at them and then turned to settle the other two parties and Miss o'Ryan called her charges to come with her and led them across the short, rough turf towards the tiny village.

Barbara walked along with the rest in a state of complete happiness because of what Mary-Lou had said about her. The Gang were apt to be a very select crew and by this time she knew that if they had not liked her for herself, not even the fact that she and Vi were cousins could have gained her admission to it.

Mary Woodley, who had also heard, looked after the cluster of girls and her face darkened. She knew that her first attempt at breaking up the friendship between Vi and

Barbara had been a complete failure and she was none too happy about her own position if anyone ever found out that she had been the last to leave the splashery that morning. It was a good thing that Vi had forgotten and she hardly thought that Barbara knew. Otherwise, she reasoned, judging the new girl by her own standards and thereby cheating herself badly, that young woman would have been certain to say something about it.

"Mary Woodley! Will you kindly wake up and pay attention to me!" Miss Derwent's voice in its sharpest tones broke across her thoughts. "I've spoken to you three times already! Will you go over to Miss Moore's group?"

Mary jumped and reddened.

Carol Younger, who had been assigned to the same party, yanked her across to join them. "Wake up, you ass!" she said in an undertone. "You don't want a row for not paying attention on an expedition, do you?"

Assuredly Mary did not. She lined up with the rest in charge of Miss Moore, the geography mistress, and Frau Mieders who took domestic science, and Miss Derwent sent them off before she rounded up the remnant and marched them away to the far side of the little shelf with Miss Armitage as her partner.

Meanwhile, Miss o'Ryan was keeping her girls moving at a brisk pace. Like them, she felt the keen nip in the air up here and, mistress as she was, she shook in her shoes as she thought of what Matron might say to her if any of them started colds or chills thanks to her own negligence. She led them round a curve of the shelf and then halted them for a moment, saying, "Look!" with outflung hand. They looked and a gasp of delight went up at the sight of the Jungfrau.

"How lovely she is!" sighed Barbara who was beginning to develop marked artistic tendencies.

Mary-Lou startled them all by quoting in a deeply reverent voice, "'I will lift up mine eyes unto the hills from whence cometh my help'. I always feel like that when I see mountains," she added. "Somehow, they make you see how awfully *big* God is. And yet He can be so near to you when you get stuck as well."

No one commented on this remark. A good many of them felt the same; but it took Mary-Lou to put it into words. Miss o'Ryan reflected on this as she called them to move on again and wondered if, in the future, the Chalet School would have yet another writer to its credit.

"We can't stand about," she said briskly. "It's much too cold after you've been accustomed to the Platz. Now let's have a peep at the village and then we must take the downward path. I don't want to be caught by the dark."

The village hardly deserved that name. There were half a dozen chalets and a *Gasthaus* which was rather larger. There were no shops, but you could buy post-cards and stamps and oddments of woodcarving, hand-made lace and silk ribbons in a room at the *Gasthaus*. The young mistress let the girls spend ten minutes in buying some small souvenir of their first visit here. Then she hurried them on.

"The others will be coming for their turn and we mustn't hold them up," she said as she hounded Hilary Bennett out on to the grass. "Over there, now, and turn down by that path. And I think, once we reach it, we'll go in twos. Mary-Lou and Josette, you can lead. Come along, now, and don't straggle."

At the head of the path, they got into line, Vi calling Barbara to join her. Maeve was without a partner for once, so she tagged on to them. Miss o'Ryan saw to it that Clare and Ghislaine, last of the pack, were well up with the rest and then went to the head of the little column.

The path led down over the short, sweet turf with its low bushes of alpenroses, now bare of their blossoms. On either side, the tall, black-trunked pines stood sentinel and before long, the grass had vanished and they were passing among the trees.

"I almost expect to meet the Wolf," Vi murmured to Barbara and Maeve as they marched steadily downwards.

"Yes; *I* feel rather like Little Red Riding Hood," Maeve agreed with a giggle.

"Only we haven't any butter or eggs or a cake," Barbara chimed in.

"No; but I've got a slab of chocolate!" Vi exclaimed, tugging at her coat-pocket to get it out. "Here you are!

Let's see—thirteen of us; no, fourteen, with Miss o'Ryan, and it's in twelve lots. D'you think I can manage to break it up fairly evenly?"

"I've got some myself." Barbara fished it out. "If we broke them both up, we could manage all right. That would be a piece each and some over for later."

"Mine's mint lumps." Maeve produced the bag with a flourish. "Shall we start with the choc first and have them later when we feel colder?"

"I feel cold already," Barbara said with a shiver. "The sun's gone in—or is it going under the trees?"

"Prob'ly a bit of both," Maeve replied. She glanced up through the branches. "The blue's gone, anyhow. How grey the sky is! Finish breaking up that choc, Vi, and dish it out and then we'll link."

But Miss o'Ryan had already noticed the change in the weather. She called to Clare and Ghislaine not to fall behind and told Mary-Lou and Josette to keep the pace going. She was weatherwise and she did not like what she saw.

"She's getting windy," Maeve commented shrewdly. She looked up and round again. Low-hanging clouds now seemed to press down on the tops of the great pines and there was a queer hush in the air which was beginning to affect the girls. They talked in lowered voices and their laughter died away.

"I don't like it," Barbara said nervously. "Something's going to happen."

Vi finished breaking up the chocolate and then gave her cousin's arm a squeeze. "Don't worry, Babs. If we're going to have rain or anything, we'll just hurry on to Oberhofen and get the train from there. It can't be so *very* far away now. We've been going down for quite a while now. Then we'll soon be back at school. I hope *Kaffee und Kuchen* will be ready," she added with a giggle. "I'm simply ravenous! I could eat an elephant this very minute!"

Maeve, on Barbara's other side, also took her arm, regardless of rules. "So am I—ravenous, I mean. What about sharing out that choc, Vi? It 'ud be better than nothing, anyhow."

"O.K.!" Vi removed her hand from her cousin's arm.

"I'll just go the rounds. I suppose Miss o'Ryan won't make a fuss if I do?" she added.

"Of course she won't. Thanks; I'll have a piece, since you're so pressing. And so will Barbara. Thanks a lot! Now you go and be polite with the rest."

Vi laughed and ran off to the head of the column to hand the chocolate round. One or two of the girls pointed out that they had their own, but Miss o'Ryan told them to take a piece and eat it.

"Vi has broken hers up and you haven't," she pointed out. "A piece of chocolate will help you. You can share yours later on. Thank you, Vi!"

She accepted the piece Vi offered her, glanced round and then went flying back to whip in Clare and Ghislaine who had dropped behind again. They could just hear the voices of the next party behind them. Miss o'Ryan, still acting as whipper-in, glanced up anxiously at the sky and her face puckered in thought. The next moment, bidding Clare and Ghislaine to keep up with the rest, she was racing back to the top of the line.

"Mary-Lou! You're the best runner we have here. Go back to Miss Derwent and tell her from me that it feels to me like snow. Ask her to hurry the girls as much as possible and also to send someone back to warn Frau Mieders and Miss Moore—though Frau Mieders has probably done it, anyhow. She's lived in Tirol," she added. "And Mary-Lou! If it does begin to snow, don't try to come back to us. Stay with Miss Derwent. Understand?"

"Yes, Miss o'Ryan." Mary-Lou wasted no more time. She set off at her best pace which was not very quick at the moment, since the gradient was steep and she had to run uphill. Miss o'Ryan turned to watch her a moment and then began to hustle the rest of her flock who had heard her words with amazement.

"Keep a good pace, girls, but don't try to run. The path is very uneven here and a sprained ankle won't do us any good. With luck we'll be at Oberhofen before it starts. Josette, join up with me until Mary-Lou comes back."

They went on at a quickened pace and the mistress kept a look-out for anything that would show her their goal. If only they could reach the little platform which was all the station either Oberhofen or Unterhofen had, it would not be so bad. And they ought to do it easily, she thought. But she proved to be too optimistic. Things were made worse by a light mist which began to rise, blotting out what light there was faster than anyone had anticipated.

Then Mary-Lou came flying back to say that she had told Miss Derwent, and Frau Mieders and Miss Moore had already joined up with the former.

"And they all think we must be nearly at Oberhofen," Mary-Lou wound up breathlessly. Then she stumbled over a rock and fell—which nearly proved disastrous for the little party, for by the time Miss o'Ryan had steadied her and made sure that she was not hurt, the sound of the voices of the others had died away and the mist was thickening.

"On you go! " Miss o'Ryan said briskly. "Not much further now, girls."

Barbara was plodding along as sturdily as any of them, but she was beginning to tire. She said nothing, but Vi guessed it and she tucked her cousin's arm through hers, with the remark that Babs had better hang on to her a bit or she'd be conking out and that would be a nice mess!

Maeve took the hint and Barbara found that she could manage, even though she was longing to give up and sit down. But she knew very well that to do that would be to risk the safety of all concerned, so she plodded on pluckily.

Miss o'Ryan saw them and called to the others to link up. "Keep close together, girls! " she said. "We can't have any stragglers. Ghislaine, take my arm. Is someone seeing to Verity-Anne? Clare, you join up with Leslie. Watch your feet, girls, and tell me the instant you see any lights or hear any fresh sounds."

"Think it'll be a bad snow-storm?" Mary-Lou asked casually of Josette.

Josette looked serious. "If it's anything like it was in Canada, it jolly well will. Don't let's talk about it, Mary-Lou! " For her thoughts had gone back to some of the storms she had seen during her two years in Canada.

"Try to keep going steadily, girls," Miss o'Ryan said

firmly as Ghislaine murmured something to her about aching with tiredness. "It can't be far now and then you shall rest as much as you want. Mary-Lou! Is Verity-Anne managing all right?"

"Quite well, thank you," came Verity-Anne's own voice.

"Barbara? You able to keep up?"

With an effort, Barbara pulled herself together and replied as jauntily as she could. "I'm quite O.K., thank you, Miss o'Ryan."

Biddy o'Ryan passed over the forbidden slang and said no more. Maeve squeezed Barbara's arm with hers. "You're jolly plucky, anyhow!" she murmured.

Barbara flushed and for the next few minutes, forgot her aches and pains. Then Josette gave a sudden exclamation. "It's snowing, Miss o'Ryan!"

"I know that as well as you!" the mistress snapped. "Keep going!"

The flakes were just beginning to fall, a few at a time, very slowly and lazily; but for anyone who knew the Alps, it was a danger-signal not to be missed. Biddy o'Ryan, with her early schooldays all spent in Tirol, knew what to expect. First these odd flakes. Then the same, but a little heavier. Finally, a dizzying, whirling dervish dance which made it next-door to impossible to see where you were going. The only thing she could do was what she was doing—keep the girls going as quickly as she could. And then the path, which so far seemed to cut straight down, suddenly forked!

They stopped perforce. Josette brushed the clinging snow from her long lashes and asked, "Which fork do we take, Miss o'Ryan?"

Between the increasing snowfall and her wild anxiety for the girls, Miss o'Ryan had almost ceased to think of anything but getting them down. She wiped the snow from her own face and stared anxiously round. And then help came. A long yodel pierced the muffling fog. Biddy o'Ryan pulled herself together and put all her voice into a clear yodel which was answered promptly—and nearer!

"Oh, thank God!" she half-whispered to herself. Then,

aloud, "Stand where you are girls. Stamp your feet and swing your arms to keep warm. We're all right now!"

The new hope roused them and they obeyed her as well as they could. Then, looming through the mist like giants, came two figures which grew smaller as they approached the little group and finally resolved themselves into two brawny mountaineers.

"Ah! Then you are here!" exclaimed the elder of the pair, a very big man with a short curly beard. "*Das Fraülein* with the other young ladies begged that we should hunt for you and bring you to the Bahnhof."

"The young lady with the other young ladies?" Biddy repeated dazedly. "Why—how did they get in front of us?"

"You must have missed the opening, *gnädiges Fraülein.* It is an easy mistake to make in weather like this. But we will not stay here. You shall all come to my home where my woman prepares hot milk and coffee and bread and honey."

"Missed the opening?" Biddy o'Ryan seemed to herself to be able to do nothing but repeat his remarks.

"*Ja, gnädiges Fraülein.* Where the big rock stands below a cleft." He suddenly swooped down on Barbara and tossed her over his shoulder. "So! *Das ist besser!*"

His companion had done the same by Verity-Anne and was eyeing Ghislaine speculatively. She shrank back against the mistress. She had no wish to be carried. But Verity-Anne laid her head down on the broad shoulder and calmly went to sleep. Barbara contrived to keep awake by dint of rubbing her eyes; but she was thankful to know that she need walk no further at present. Then she lifted her head and looked round.

"Lots of the others are just as tired as me," she murmured.

Her bearer took no notice. He was speaking to Miss o'Ryan again. "Follow me, please. Soon we will at my house be. The other lady, ah! how afraid she was for you and *die Mädchen*! But all is well now. Turn this way, *Fraülein.*"

He turned to the right, still carrying Barbara who had shot her bolt. The right fork led almost at once out on to a shelf and a few steps farther along stood a chalet into which he led them. A small, dumpy woman greeted them in Low German so broad that even Miss o'Ryan hardly understood her; but there was no mistaking the kindness in both voice and face. Barbara slid from her perch to the floor where Vi and Maeve grabbed her and pulled her over to the big stove to thaw out. And then cups and bowls of hot milk, of milky and very bitter coffee which was mainly chicory came round, accompanied by hunks of bread with dabs of honey on top and they feasted. Even Verity-Anne roused up enough to take her share. But once it was down, she drowsed off again on Miss o'Ryan's lap. The others listened hard to the German talk between their mistress and the big mountaineer as he explained that he and his son Franz would stop the down-train so that they could go down in it to Platz.

"That will be in half an hour from now," he said, with a look at the cuckoo clock ticking solemnly away on the wall. "Until then, please rest yourselves."

No one needed to be told that. Between their weariness, the warmth of the little house and the meal they had just had they were all inclined to be drowsy. Miss o'Ryan herself would hardly have been able to keep awake if it had not been for her anxiety. She was worried about Verity-Anne's sleepiness; but when she spoke to Herr Reisinger about it, he laughed with a deep rumble and told her that it was only natural sleepiness and the girl was all right.

"Twenty minutes to rest, *mein Fraülein*," he said, "and then you will don hats and coats and Franz and I will take you to catch the train."

Franz nodded solemn agreement and Miss o'Ryan gave it up. At least she would have Verity-Anne and the rest safely in Matron's keeping in an hour's time.

"Though how we are to get back to school from the station is more than I can say," she thought. "Oh, well, I'll tackle *that* problem when it comes."

She must have drowsed herself after that, for the next thing she knew, she was being gently shaken by Mary-Lou with the information that the train was due in less than ten minutes' time and they must be going out. This time, there was no need to fear the storm. The two men had brought big lanterns hung on the end of long poles and when they heard the distant sound of the train, they waved them vigorously and it drew up for just long enough to take the party on board. Ten minutes later, they had reached the Görnetz Platz safely. Nor was there any need to worry about how they would get back to the school, for Dr. Maynard and one of his colleagues were waiting for them with cars and they were all bundled in and whisked off home.

Barbara was beginning to drowse once more when they drew up before the big door of the main block. The weary crowd was decanted, though Dr. Jack had to carry Verity-Anne, for she had dropped off to sleep again. In fact, she made minor history in the school that day, for she went on sleeping through being carried up to the dormitory, undressed, popped into a hot bath, dried, and tucked up in bed, and never woke until noon next day.

The rest managed under their own steam. Matron and the prefects came round with light supper for them before lights were switched off and they went to sleep.

But the big shock came next day. There was no snow to be seen at the Platz, but the rain was coming down in torrents and the garden was a sea of mud. Furthermore, as they all learned at their belated breakfast, there never had been any snow at the Platz, though it had rained hard enough since half-way through the afternoon of the day before.

"But I don't understand," Barbara protested to Mrs. Maynard that afternoon when they were sitting in her big *Saal*, talking over the previous day's events. "It snowed like mad up at Unterhofen. You just couldn't see where you were going. And yet everyone says there wasn't a vestige of snow here! How could that be?"

"Oh, that's easy," Jo replied cheerfully as she produced a box of chocolates and handed them round. "Even Unterhofen is much higher than we are here. When you've been a little longer in this part of the world, you find that they're often having young blizzards on the upper shelves, while we have nothing worse than rain here. Also, you'll find that when we are enduring fog and rain, the chances are that *they* are rejoicing in glorious sunshine. It's largely a question of height, you see."

"Well, anyhow," observed Beth, who had been eyeing her young sister keenly, "it doesn't seem to have done you any harm. I think we'll say nothing at home about your latest adventure. Mummy would have fits and there isn't the slightest need. And now that's settled, Jo, what about that new game you invented for this afternoon? Fetch it out and let's see what we can make of it!"

And it was so!

CHAPTER THIRTEEN

"Quite an Asset to the Form!"

SCHOOL would have seemed very flat next day after that exciting expedition, but no sooner had the school assembled in Hall after Prayers than the Head informed them that that afternoon she would meet them all there at fifteen o'clock and tell them about the Christmas play.

A buzz of delight broke forth, but she hushed it at once. "One moment, please. My doing so will depend on *you*. If I have bad reports of a form from any mistress, I'm afraid the play must wait a little. So please let me have no complaints of anyone."

As a result, when fifteen o'clock came—three, by English time—a full school was waiting for the Head in Hall.

Miss Annersley appeared dead on the stroke of the hour, a thick bundle of manuscript in her hand. She took her place at the desk on the dais and then smiled round at them.

"Sit down, girls," she said, "and make yourselves comfortable. This may prove rather a lengthy session and I'd rather have all the squirming and wriggling over before I start business." When everyone was still at last and all the young faces were upturned to her, she held up her sheaf of papers.

"Now, girls," she began, "Lady Russell has provided our play for this year as Mrs. Maynard is still too busy. But Madame has written a good many plays for us in the past and I can assure you that this one is as charming as any of them."

She paused a moment and the girls seized their chance and clapped vociferously. Then the Head held up her hand and the applause ceased.

"I have just one or two things to say before I begin to read it to you," she said. "First of all, this year, we shall have a new audience. The Welsen branch will all come to see it, of course; and I shouldn't be surprised if we didn't have a visit from some of our other Old Girls. But in addition to that, there are the people up here. Many of them are too ill; but there are many who are here because they are not really ill yet—only threatened and it is hoped that a long visit up here will prevent it's ever being more than a threat. Life can be very dull in such circumstances, and we hope our play will give them all a new interest. I want you to try to realize how hard life must be for these poor folk at times. Now, we have the chance to—to give them a break, as you girls say. Do your best to make it a *good* one!"

She finished speaking and while she pulled her chair round in front of the reading-desk, some of the mistresses came in and quietly sat down in spare seats on the long green forms that half-filled Hall. Miss Annersley opened her MS., looked round to see that everyone was ready and then spoke again.

"It is called," she said, "*Strangers at the Inn*. The setting is an old inn and the scenes are set in different centuries. In every case, strangers come to the inn to seek shelter on Christmas Eve. We work backwards—I mean," she added as she saw that some of the younger girls looked puzzled, "that we begin with the present century. Then we have a scene during the Napoleonic Wars; one during the Thirty Years War; one during the Hundred Years War; and one dealing with the time of the Children's Crusade. Finally, we have the first Christmas Eve when Strangers did indeed come to the inn and a Little Child was born in the stable because there was no room for Them in the inn itself."

"I think it sounds marvellous," Julie said, speaking for all the Seniors.

"One last word. As you know, Miss Lawrence has been taking the singing so far. But our old singing-master, Mr. Denny, is recovered from his long illness and is coming to join us at the end of this week. So he will see to the carols."

Julie led the burst of cheering that greeted this. All the older girls had known and liked their somewhat eccentric singing-master, brother of Miss Denny, and "Plato" to them without exception. They had missed him during the year and more that had elapsed since his long illness began and were delighted to hear that he was returning.

"I thought you would be pleased," the Head nodded. "Well, now I'm going to read the play to you—or as much of it as we can manage before *Kaffee und Kuchen.* We'll finish it after Prayers this evening and the younger Middles will sit up an extra half-hour or so for that reason."

The two Lower IV forms broke into clapping, but the triplets, close together as usual, looked at each other. Then Len stood up. "Please, Miss Annersley——"

The Head glanced down at her. "Yes, Len?"

"What about us—Con and Margot and me? Oh, and Sue Meadows, too? We all go home before *Abendessen* and Sue goes at the end of school."

"I haven't forgotten you. You're all spending the night with us. And once the heavy snows of winter come, we are seriously considering making you all boarders. You could hardly come to school during a blizzard, you know."

"Oh, thank you!" Len spoke very properly as she sat down again, but she squeezed her hands together delightedly.

No one knew how Sue Meadows felt about it. She was new that term, having come to the Platz as company for her cousin. The doctors had said that the delicate little girl must not spend another winter in the damp climate of England, so Sue had been borrowed to be a companion for Leila and had been sent to the school by her aunt so that her education should not suffer.

She left school the moment lessons were over, for she was old enough to be trusted to do her preparation alone. The girls in her own form had tried to be friendly but she would have none of it, so latterly they had left her to herself. She sat between Barbara and Clare and they both shot a quick glance at her, but her face told them nothing. Meantime, the Head had opened at the first scene and was beginning to read so they left it.

Miss Annersley's beautiful voice made music of Lady Russell's lovely words and the girls were spellbound as she read the first two scenes. Then the bell rang for *Kaffee und Kuchen* and she closed her MS. and stood up.

"*Kaffee und Kuchen* is to be early, girls, and when it is over, you are to go straight upstairs to change for the evening. Sue, you and the Maynards are in Primrose dormitory. Someone will show you where to go. Come down as soon as you are ready and go straight to prep. *Abendessen* will be at half-past eighteen and we will have Prayers immediately after, which will give us a good two hours before anyone's bedtime. Stand—turn—march!"

Miss Dene swung round on the music-stool and struck up a jolly march and they left Hall. But once they were in the *Speisesaal*, they all talked at once. Miss Annersley had used English throughout, so they took it for granted that even though it was a German day and goodness knew most of them needed all the practice they could get in German, English it would be for the rest of the day. That being so, no one was at a loss for language. Eventually, Julie marched to the staff-table and pealed the Head's bell loudly.

As the sharp "pr-r-ring!" rang out, they fell silent and all turned guiltily to look towards the table. Only Julie was there, however. But she was enough!

"Yes," she said sweetly. "And do you *really* want someone to come down on us and remind us that this is German day? Because, if so, just go on making all that noise. You won't be disappointed, I assure you! Speak *quietly*, please, and don't all talk at once!" She waited a moment for this to sink in and then went back to her seat and the school resumed its gossip in rather more subdued tones.

As soon as the meal was over, they raced upstairs to change into their evening frocks of gentian-blue velveteen. Joey Maynard had been over during the afternoon with her daughters' possessions and someone had walked the mile or so to the chalet where Sue's aunt was staying and brought Sue's. Vi took the four upstairs to the Primrose dormitory which had been empty so far and left them there.

When they had changed, they hurried downstairs where Con left Sue at the door of Upper IVB and went on to her own form-room.

Most of the girls were there already when Sue entered. She went to her desk and sat down to open it.

"Arith and French exercise and that awful history question of Miss o'Ryan's and rep," Heather informed her. "Take out everything you need and put it on the floor. Once prep begins, you can't open your desk again."

"Thank you," Sue said politely as she fished for the books. Heather opened her arithmetic and heaved a sigh. "How I do *not* like arith! Problems, especially!"

"Shut up!" said Maeve Bettany who liked it no better than she did and who was already clutching at her thick curls in desperation.

Most of the girls were equally hard at it and when Julie Lucy entered to take charge she found a roomful of silent workers. She heaved a sigh of relief, sat down and opened her *Æneid*.

"Let's hope no one wants much help," she thought as she began to hunt for a predicate. "I can do with all my time! Ah! *Got* him!" And she settled down to her construe with an easy mind.

Sue went at her sums with a speed and assurance that filled Heather and some of the others with envy. They had half an hour for the subject and then must change when Julie gave the word. If you finished your work before the set time ended, you might go on to the next thing which frequently gave you a few minutes in hand at the end. Then you might either finish what you had left undone or, if everything was prepared, you might read your library book.

When Julie said, "Change work, please!" Heather

heaved a sigh and set aside her unfinished arithmetic for French which she found fairly easy. Finally came repetition. Heather was a quick learner when it came to that and by the time half the quarter-hour was up, she knew the twelve lines of "The Ballad of the Revenge" which they were learning and was able to turn back to her sums once more.

Before she tackled them, she glanced aside at Sue. That young lady was sitting with her eyes glued to her anthology, a frown of intense concentration on her face and her lips moving as she repeated the words over and over in an effort to fix them in her memory. She was clearly making heavy weather of it.

"Well, I'll be a monkey's uncle!" Heather thought as she considered the problem she had had to leave. "I thought Sue was a born genius at everything!" Then she gave it up and concentrated on her arithmetic which occupied her until the bell rang for the end of prep.

Sue gave the poetry a look of despair as she packed her books away. "Oh, dear!" she said aloud. "I shall *never* know it by tomorrow!"

"I don't understand," Heather said bluntly. "It's an awfully easy thing to learn."

Sue turned to her. "To you, perhaps, but I'm no good at learning by heart. I'd rather do twenty sums than have to learn one verse of poetry!"

Heather gasped. "Well, I'll be gumswizzled! I loathe and abominate maths in any shape or form, but I love learning by heart! It's the easiest thing on earth!"

"Yes—to you! That's what I said. It's hardest of all to me."

Barbara joined in the talk—Julie had left the room—"Don't you really like rep, Sue? How weird of you! But then," she added plaintively, "look what a pot you are at maths! I suppose nobody can be good at everything!"

"Of course they can't!" Clare chimed in. "But I say, Sue, if you don't like learning by heart, what *will* you do if they give you a longish part in the play?"

"Tell them I can't do it," Sue retorted grimly. "I don't

see why they should, either. I'm new and they can't possibly know whether I'm any good at acting or not—I may say I'm *not*!" she added.

"Well, they can't know about me, either," Barbara sighed. "but I'd love some sort of speaking part even if it's only, 'The carriage waits, my lord!'"

Clare gave her a quick look. "You're much more likely to be given some sort of angel to do. No one is going to miss that curly mop of yours. It's just *made* for a halo!"

Barbara giggled. "Oh, Clare! What awful rot you talk!"

"No rot at all. We haven't the kids now—the Juniors, I mean—and anyhow, there are to be archangels. I should say it would be exactly your cup of tea!"

"In the meantime," remarked Julie's voice behind—she had come back to find her fountain pen—"the bell has rung for *Abendessen* and the rest are lined up. Postpone this highly interesting conversation of yours, please, and tag on and be quick about it!"

With the Head Girl speaking and looking like that, they had no option. They were silent and went to join the line which Julie promptly marched off to the *Speisesaal*.

As soon as *Abendessen* was over, they divided for Prayers, after which they met again in Hall where the Head read them the remainder of the play. As soon as she finished, all the Middles had to go to bed and when next morning came, Sue herself vanished as soon as she could to do her best with "The Revenge" so they had little chance of talking to her. Wednesday meant Games for both divisions of Upper IV and you never got any chance of talking then, besides which, they had to make up for yesterday's freedom and talk German until sixteen o'clock which, as Barbara mournfully remarked to Vi, tied them down horribly. Games over, they had extra prep and Sue never stayed for this and vanished after they went in.

"All the same," Clare said to a select group consisting of Barbara, Heather, Vi and Josette as they sat down for *Kaffee und Kuchen*, "if she really comes as a boarder once the snow starts, I shouldn't be surprised if we didn't find Sue Meadows quite an asset to our form."

"Who's swallowed the dicker?" Maeve Bettany jeered, overhearing this. And in the wordy squabble that followed, Sue was forgotten for the time being.

CHAPTER FOURTEEN

Berne

THE NEXT important happening in this first term in the Oberland was the half-term holiday which came at the end of October. Lessons ended at midday on the Friday. The afternoon was spent at games, a team from the Welsen branch having challenged the school team at netball. It ended in a draw of eight all and then the elder girls were entertained to tea, followed by a short dance.

On the Saturday, making the most of the bright October sunshine, everyone went for a scramble and returned to the school happily tired after a glorious day in the open.

Sunday was enlivened with sudden showers of rain. Everyone watched the weather with a long face, for the Head had announced that expeditions had been arranged for the Monday—if it were fine! She had refused to say any more, thus leaving them in a state of pleasing uncertainty as to what might happen.

"I'd like to know just where we are going," Julie Lucy said as she sat with the other grandees of the school in the prefects' room, eating apples. "Personally, I'd like to do the Jungfrau trip."

"Shouldn't think we'll get anywhere if this goes on," Annis Lovell said decidedly. "As a matter of fact, I'd rather do one of the big cities, myself—Lucerne, or Geneva, or Zurich. Any of them would do me."

"It's much more likely to be somewhere nearer home," Clem Barrass put in. "What about Berne? We haven't seen that yet and it's the capital, after all."

Julie nodded. "Jolly good choice if it's to be a city. I'd

like that myself—What in the name of goodness is that? It sounds like a baby elephant falling downstairs!"

She tossed the core of her apple into the waste-paper basket and sped off to find out what was happening as she spoke and the rest followed her. It turned out to be no baby elephant, but Mary-Lou. That young woman had caught her heel on the top stair and crashed to the bottom, ending up with one foot twisted badly under her. She had also banged her head well and truly against the newell-post and was half-stunned into the bargain.

"No trip for you tomorrow!" Matron informed her when she had finally discovered the extent of the damage.

Mary-Lou looked at her with heavy eyes. "I suppose not," she agreed. "Ow! That hurts, Matron!"

"Sorry; but you've given your ankle a nasty sprain and it must be properly strapped up or you'll be lame for weeks," Matron told her inexorably. "Don't try to talk. You'll only make your head worse."

Mary-Lou, who was beginning an outsize in headaches, groaned as Matron deftly strapped up the ankle, and subsided for the moment. Later on, however, when she was lying in bed in a darkened room, she put out a hand and caught Matron's apron.

"I say, Matey, I'll be able to be up by Tuesday, won't I?" she asked.

"That all depends on how you are." Matron came to a standstill. "Now be a good child and try to sleep. If your head is better by bedtime, Clem and Verity-Anne may come to see you for a minute or two."

"Well, there's no need to let Mother know until we go home for the hols, is there?"

"None at all, if you'll do as you're told now." But Matron's eyes were much kinder than her tone. Everyone knew that Mary-Lou really did try to take care of her mother ever since the news of her father's death had come from the Amazon country, nearly five years ago.

"Thanks a lot," Mary-Lou murmured. "Tell Clem and Verity-Anne to say nothing in their home letters then, please."

Matron promised and then, once more adjuring her

patient to go to sleep, left her. But later on, the Head was bearded in her study by an anxious-eyed Clem, who begged that she and Verity-Anne might be allowed to stay from the expedition and be with Mary-Lou next day.

"I know it's her own silly fault," Clem said, "but Verity-Anne will be miserable if she has to go. And—well—the Trelawneys have been awfully good to Tony and me and I'd like to pay back a little if I can."

Miss Annersley knew all about it and she gave consent at once. So, as Matron already had seven cases of streaming cold in San as well as one from Lower IVB with a bad bilious attack, nine people would be out of it. In addition, all the elder girls with relations at Welsen had been invited there for the day and Joey Maynard was giving a party for the triplets, which meant that another dozen would not be going.

"So if we send what's left of both Lower Fourths off to Grindelwald, we can divide the rest up into two parties which will be much easier for all concerned," the Head told the staff when they were having coffee later on.

The school woke next morning in fear and trembling as to what the weather might be doing. However, they had their fears for nothing. The rain was over, a fresh breeze was blowing and a pale November sun was shining down bravely. The girls dressed at top speed and never were beds stripped and cubicles tidied in shorter time.

They were going down to the valley by the nine-ten train. At Interlaken they learned they would take the ten o'clock express to Berne and there they would spend the day. The Seniors would be in one party with Mlle at the head and the Middles in the other with Miss Denny in charge.

They set off for the station at ten to nine, sped on their way by the party from Freudesheim who had turned up in force to line the road and cheer as they passed

"I must say," Julie remarked to her partner, Madge Herbert, "that Mrs. Graves might have chosen another day for her daughter's christening. We'd all have loved to be there."

"That was just why," put in Miss Wilmot who was near enough to them to hear her. "Hilary—I mean Mrs. Graves

—said she didn't want a *mob* present! Oh, well, you'll be seeing plenty of them both before long, I expect.

At Welsen, quite a number of girls left the party to be greeted by a bunch of people who were headed by Peggy Bettany, eldest sister of Maeve, former Head Girl of the school and a most popular person. Peggy waved cheerfully to everyone and Miss Wilmot, once the train was gliding downwards again, turned to Veronica Worsley who happened to be sitting next to her to demand, "Who is that girl? I seem to know her face."

"That's Peggy Bettany," Veronica replied.

"Peggy Bettany?" gasped Miss Wilmot. "One of the Bettany twins, you mean?"

"Yes; I believe she *has* a twin brother," Veronica said, staring a little.

Miss Wilmot said no more; but she moved over to the seat Mlle was sharing with Miss Denny and squeezed in beside them. "Tell me! Have I any white hairs?"

They stared at her amazedly. "But no, my dear Nancy," Mlle said at last. "Why do you ask such a thing?"

"Because I've just seen a vision!" Nancy Wilmot said dramatically. "I behold a pretty—a *very* pretty grown-up girl who seems vaguely familiar to me. I ask what her name is and am informed that she is Peggy Bettany—*Peggy Bettany*! I last saw that young woman as a leggy infant and here she is, a young lady. I *must* be ageing when people I knew as small babes are *grown-up*! Not," she added reflectively, "that Peggy seems to have grown very far."

"Peggy always was on a miniature scale," Miss Denny said. "All the others are long enough, even Maeve. As for Bride, the girl's a young giantess."

"Eheu fugaces!" Miss Wilmot sighed deeply. "Well, since I'm here, are there any words of wisdom you'd like to whisper into my ear before I return to my own seat?"

"None," Mlle said with finality. "You will be with Miss Denny and she will tell you all you need to know. In the meantime, *ma chère* Nancy, *you* are not small. We were already two in the seat and they are not made for three."

Miss Wilmot chuckled, got up and went back to her own seat. As she passed between the girls, she glanced at them.

Mary Woodley was by herself in a back seat, her face very black. The maths mistress paused beside her.

"Well, what's wrong? You don't look much like a jolly expedition. Aren't you well?"

"I'm quite well, thank you," Mary muttered sulkily.

"Then why not look cheerful about it? And why sit by yourself? There's a vacant seat by Josette Russell. Run along and share it with her and don't sit here, glooming alone," said Miss Wilmot breezily.

Mary got up and went to the seat indicated. She went reluctantly. In addition to hating Barbara, who was with Vi as usual, she had also been industriously pitying herself. There she was, alone and without a chum while even that wretched Barbara Chester had a pal! She forgot that to *have* a friend you must *be* a friend, and she had been ready to blame everyone else but herself.

Josette looked up as she arrived and interrupted the chatter she had been having with Hilary Bennett and Clare Kennedy who sat in front to move up and make room.

Neither Hilary nor Clare liked Mary, so they dropped the talk with Josette and that young woman calmly turned her attention to the newcomer.

"Aren't you thrilled to the back teeth?" she queried. "*I* am. I've been dying to see Berne ever since I read Auntie Jo's last book—'Werner of the Alps'. Read it?"

"No; I've not been able to get it from Library yet," Mary said.

"I've got my copy at school with me. I'll lend it to you if you like. Remind me to give it to you tomorrow. I don't suppose there'll be time for it when we get back." Josette wound up with a chuckle which deepened the dimples in her cheeks and made her blue eyes nearly close.

By this time, they were speeding through the environs of Interlaken. They reached the little Interlaken-Ost station next minute and had to tumble out and line up for the march down the Hoheweg to the Interlakenbahn where they just managed to catch the Berne train. A porter was on the look-out for them and waved to them frantically as soon as he saw the bright blue coats and berets, so they were able to scramble in safely.

Josette, missing Maeve, her usual "pair", since Maeve had gone to Welsen where her mother had taken a small chalet for the next two or three months, decided that it would be a good idea if she and Mary cheered each other's loneliness and stuck firmly to her. For once, the Gang drifted off in couples instead of keeping together, so that Barbara and Vi; Christine and Catriona; Hilary and Lesley were all in different parts of the carriage; and Ruth Barnes had chummed up with Heather Clayton.

"That crowd miss their Mary-Lou," Miss o'Ryan murmured to Miss Wilmot as they gazed out of the window at the end-of-autumn landscape past which they were speeding. "She keeps them tied up when she's there. You know, some day, Mary-Lou is going to be Head Girl and *won't* she make them all toe the mark!"

Miss Wilmot laughed. "In some ways, she's Joey Bettany over again—much more so than any of Jo's own girls, so far as I've had anything to do with them."

"I wouldn't say that," Miss o'Ryan replied cautiously. "Con has her dreamy side and all her love of and feeling for history. Len has her protectiveness. When did Jo ever fail to rush to the help of anyone who seemed to need it? Len is just the same there. As for Margot, she has all her mother's love of mischief. They've split up her qualities among them; that's all."

"Well, you know them better than I do. You may be right," her friend allowed.

"I know I am," Biddy o'Ryan said with calm assurance. "Hello! This looks like the beginning of Berne. Better get them in order."

"We meet here at half-past eighteen," was Mlle's last remark to Miss Denny as they parted to go and take charge of their groups.

"Very well," Miss Denny agreed. "Hope you all enjoy yourselves."

"But yes; I think we shall do that," Mlle replied, laughing.

"Where do we go first?" Hilary Bennett asked eagerly when they had been shepherded out of the station into the Bahnhofplatz after the Seniors had departed.

"To see the famous clock," Miss Denny said. "Into line, all of you! We can't waste time if you are to be there when it strikes eleven. Miss o'Ryan and Miss Wilmot, will you lead the way? Turn left and then straight on along the Spitalgasse and the Marktgasse. Miss Burnett, we'll act as whippers-in. I don't want any laggards just here."

They marched off smartly, headed by the two young mistresses, and made their way through the busy crowds in the two shopping streets. Miss o'Ryan pointed out the old Church of the Holy Ghost in the Spitalgasse, but there was no time to do more than look at its exterior. Their most urgent quest was the clock-tower, rather jaw-breakingly known to the Bernese as the Zytgloggeturm.

They reached the far end of the Marktgasse two minutes before the hour and joined the little groups of visitors and school-children who were all gazing up at the square-towered gateway with its ancient astronomical clock.

"It looks *aged*!" Barbara said in awestruck tones as she stared at it.

"Sixteenth century," Miss o'Ryan told her and those near enough to hear her.

"What is the *exact* date?" Vi asked.

"Some time in the fifteen-twenties. I'll have to look up the exact year later. Now stop talking and watch."

At that moment, the clock began to strike and, to the joy of the Middles, a troop of bears marched solemnly round in a circle as soon as a painted wooden cock had crowed three times. A man sitting at the side with a staff in one hand and an hour-glass in the other, counted the strokes by opening his mouth at each one and striking with his staff. Up in the belfry, the fully-armoured figure of the Duke of Zähringen of that time struck the eleven strokes on the bell with a hammer. Then the cock crowed once more, the bears stood still and the sight was over for another hour.

"Ooh!" Hilary breathed rapturously when the tiny pageant was over. "How simply super! Why don't we have clocks like that in England?"

"We do—there are one or two, though nothing so elaborate as this," Miss Denny told her. "Don't forget that here we are in the land of clocks and watches." Miss o'Ryan, who was still standing near them, put in her word.

"And while you are remembering, Hilary, you might be remembering that slang isn't allowed, even on a holiday. You keep your eye on your tongue, my child."

There were smothered splutters from Miss Wilmot and Miss Burnett who were also nearby and she swung round on them to demand in rapid French and an undertone, "And what's the matter with you two, may I ask?"

"You!" Nancy Wilmot told her with fresh chuckles. "Keep your eye on your tongue, indeed! For a really lovely example of an Irish bull commend me to that!"

Biddy o'Ryan looked offended. Then she began to laugh, too. "She knew what I was after all right, though. Look at the red face of her, will you!"

The mistress looked at Hilary's scarlet cheeks and laughed again. Then, in mercy, Miss Burnett raised her voice. "Where are we going next, Miss Denny?"

"The bear-pit, I think. Get them into line and start them off down the Kramgasse. We'll walk for the present. Plenty of time to take trams later on when everyone is beginning to feel tired. Through the gate and straight ahead till you reach the far end of the Gerechtigkeitsgasse. Then turn left down the Nydegg and cross the Aar by the Nydegg bridge and the bear-pit is just on the right. You can't miss it."

"Please, Miss Denny, *may* we buy buns and things to give the bears?" Vi implored.

"Yes; but wait until we are there. They have stalls round about where you can buy everything—carrots, peanuts and buns. Lead on, please, and don't loiter!"

It was just as well Miss Denny had added this to her directions, for when they came to the river, the girls showed a decided tendency to stop to gaze down at the turbulent blue-green water, tearing along eighty-two feet below.

"How cold and dark it looks!" Lesley Malcolm shuddered. "And how—how *relentless*! I'd hate to fall in! I'm certain I'd never get out alive!"

"Get on and stop giving us all the grues!" Christine commanded. "Sally-Go-Round-the-Moon is waving hard at us. We'd better scram!"

"How did Miss Denny ever get such a mad name?" Barbara asked as they hurried across the bridge in answer to her urgent beckoning.

"Don't ask me!" Vi gave a giggle. "I only know she's *always* been called that. Auntie Jo would know. We'll ask her some time—if we remember."

At the bear-pit, they found that there were stalls all round where they soon bought all they wanted in the way of titbits for the bears. Then, duly armed, they crowded eagerly round the railings to look down into the pit where three shaggy adults and two or three cubs were going through their tricks to encourage the gazers to add to their daily diet with the delicacies dear to their hearts.

Presently Miss Wilmot, who had been having a word with the keeper, provided them with the sight of the occasion. She had presented the man with a tin of condensed milk which he pierced in four or five places before tossing it to the father of the family. The gentleman grabbed the tin and proceeded to perform such antics that even Mary Woodley was soon doubled up with laughter. He licked the top, but found that didn't help much. Then he shook it, and finally he held it upside down between his fore-paws, and the sticky creamy contents oozed slowly out over his muzzle and paws and down his tummy on to the ground in thick blobs where the youngsters rushed to lick them clean. But the most of that condensed milk went to its proper owner and he got himself spotless before he had finished with it.

The girls simply screamed with laughter at the sight and so did the other visitors.

"How did you come to think of it, Nancy?" Miss o'Ryan asked when at last Miss Denny ruled that they must move on.

"I saw it happen once in the Zoo in Regent's Park," Nancy Wilmot explained with a chuckle. "It was treacle in that case—golden syrup, rather; but I guessed it would work just as well with condensed milk and I couldn't remember the German for treacle."

"Well, it was a real success," Biddy said cordially. "Which way now?"

"Over the bridge again and turn along the Junkerngasse," Miss Denny said. "I want the girls to see the old houses there."

So they walked down the street with its beautiful old houses where at one time the aristocracy of Berne used to dwell, and then cut down a side street and came into the Spitalgasse again where they were treated to a sight of the Bagpiper Fountain after which they turned back once more through the Marktgasse and then into the Kornhaus Platz where they saw what must be a fountain of fountains, the Ogre, with its horrible figure of a great ogre in the middle of devouring one baby while others are close at hand around him! And round this really ghastly figure dance a ring of the jolliest bears imaginable.

"What a—what a simply *horrible* thing!" Lesley commented.

"Awful!" Vi agreed. "Why ever did they make a fountain as ghastly as that? It's enough to give any kid nightmares. I know I'd have been scared stiff of it when *I* was a small kid!"

"That was the idea," Miss Denny told them cheerfully.

They stared at her. "Frighten children, you mean?" Barbara asked. "But *why*?"

"At one time, a very deep ditch ran past here which was dangerous to children so they erected this frightening figure to keep them away."

"But where's the ditch gone to?" Josette demanded, gazing around.

"Filled in and built over years ago. You're probably standing on what used to be the edge of it. Only the Ogre remains now to show where it was. Well, what about *Mittagessen*. We are having it at the Kornhauskellar which is a noted restaurant and there it is on the other side of the street."

"Why is it noted?" Vi asked.

Miss Denny chuckled as she solemnly replied, "It has a barrel that holds 10,000 gallons of wine or beer."

A concerted gasp greeted this piece of information.

"Not really?" Barbara asked doubtfully. "But—*could*

there be? And who could afford to fill it—unless they used water, of course," she added.

Miss Denny laughed. "You forget, my child, that the barrel was made years ago when both wine and beer were very much cheaper. However, you'll see it presently I hope. Come along! " She swept them all off across the street and presently they were all sitting down to a meal which, they were told, was typically Bernese.

They began with a thick vegetable soup, and followed it up with *Bernerplatte* which turned out to be cabbage boiled together with thin strips of smoked ham, smoked sausages, potatoes and carrot. It was good, but so very filling that it was just as well that the sweet was of the lightest—meringues, blanketed in whipped cream and adorned with *glacé* cherries.

"I hope we don't have to start off on a lot of walking at once," Mary said to Josette as she finally laid down her spoon.

"I feel that way, too," Josette giggled, before she buried her nose in her glass of still lemonade.

"*I* don't feel as if I could move *at all*! " Barbara sighed from the other side of Josette. "I don't think I've ever eaten so much at one meal in my life! "

"It must be the example of the Ogre," Vi chuckled. "*I've* done myself rather proud too, if you come to that."

However, they discovered that much exercise was not required of them for a short while. They were taken to see the fabulous beer-barrel. Then, when they left the Kornhauskellar, they climbed on to one of the trams which run through all the main streets of the city. By the time they reached the Bundesplatz where they descended in order to visit the Bundeshaus—the Swiss Federal Parliament House—most of them had recovered from the first effects of their lordly meal and they thoroughly enjoyed all that the guide told them as he led them round. He pointed out the lovely ceiling paintings in the long Promenade room; the Hall of the National Council where the seats for the members were arranged in a great semicircle, while behind the President's chair was a wonderful painting of the Rütli, the meadow in which the Confederation had been born.

"Where next?" Hilary asked eagerly when they had seen all he could show them for one time and were out in the Platz again.

"Another tram and the Natural History Museum," Miss Denny replied.

Vi pulled a long face behind the mistress. "I loathe museums!" she murmured to Barbara.

She had to stop there, for Miss Denny was speaking again. "We won't stay very long there," she told them. "There are one or two things I know you'll enjoy seeing, but once we have inspected them, we'll finish with sight-seeing—after all, we want to leave a few sights for another time!—and go shopping before we have *Kaffee und Kuchen*. Partners, please! We have to cross the road to catch our tram."

They *did* enjoy the Museum, despite Vi's remarks. Among other things, they saw some wonderful scenes of wild life in Africa and—most delightful of all to them—Barri, the famous St. Bernard who saved so many lives and is now stuffed and at the Natural History Museum as a monument to the sagacity and heroism of his fine breed.

But after that, they visited the shops under the arcades—or "*Lauben*", as the Bernese call them—which give coolness in summer and shelter in winter. No one had much money to spend, but everyone contrived to buy one or two souvenirs of their visit. Then they went to a *pâtisserie* where they had the sort of luscious tea with cakes of cream and nuts and honey and chocolate that everyone enjoys once in a way.

And that was really the end of the trip for, when they had finished their meal, they had to hurry to the station to catch the train for Interlaken.

"Enjoyed yourselves?" Julie Lucy asked of her young cousin and sister when she saw them.

And the weary mistresses had their reward, for everyone within hearing replied: "*Rather!*"

CHAPTER FIFTEEN

The Snow Comes

"BABS! BABS!"

"Uh-huh?"

"Are you awake?"

A pause. Then, in sleepily sarcastic tones, "Oh dear, no! I'm talking in my sleep. Didn't you know that?"

"Well, I like that!" Vi began indignantly. Then she stopped and chuckled softly. "No; but seriously, are you really wide awake?"

"Of course I am! You haven't given me much chance of being anything else," Barbara grumbled as she turned over in bed and then sat up and shivered violently. "Ur-m, isn't it *cold*? What do you want, Vi?"

"H'sh! Don't make a noise, whatever you do. It's early yet. Mustn't rouse the rest, 'specially Clem or she'll have something to say. She's a pet, all right; but she's a lot stricter than Katt Gordon was. I can't think why Matey had to move Katt over to Pansy and send Clem here. 'Tisn't as if we weren't a well-behaved dormy—taking us all round!"

By this time, Barbara had snuggled down once more under the *plumeau* and blankets, so her reply was rather muffled. "Did you dig me out just to yarn about Katt Gordon and Clem Barrass?"

"Rather not! What I really meant to do was to ask you to hop out of bed and see what the weather's doing—if you were awake, that is. I heard Miss Moore say last night that she wouldn't be surprised if we had snow before today."

"Well, I like your style! Hop out yourself if you're as anxious as all that to know," her cousin advised indignantly.

"It's so awfully cold," Vi replied plaintively.

"I know that, thank you. I've been sitting up for a minute or so."

"Yes; I heard you. That's why I thought *you* might as well be the one to find out if the snow has really come." Vi responded calmly. "I think it must have done, 'cos it's so pitchy dark and it's nearly seven. What about it, Babs?"

Barbara began a protest. Then she suddenly stopped as the funny side of it struck her. She buried her head under the bedclothes and shook with laughter. She had no wish to disturb the others before the bell went. She had been long enough at school now to know what they would have to say in that event!

Vi heard her choking and wondered what could be wrong. She raised her voice anxiously.

"Babs—I say, Babs! You're all right, aren't you? I didn't mean to offend you or anything, you know."

Barbara wriggled up from under the clothes to reply, "Don't be a goat! Of course I'm not offended. Only your cheek suddenly struck me as funny——"

At that point, the rising-bell cut across her remarks and, from the cubicle in the corner where Matron had established her a fortnight or so before, came Clem's voice: "Up you get, all of you! Show a leg, there—show a leg!"

It was Saturday, so English was in order. Sundry sounds of reluctance and grumbling came from one or two of the cubicles—notably, Emerence Hope's—but thuds showed that the girls were obeying the prefect, and Clem, standing between the curtains of her own cubicle, saw a minute later a bare leg poking out from every other. She had instituted this practice herself on being transferred to the dormitory, being comfortably certain that once a girl was out of bed she remained out of bed. The answer to Vi's question as to why she had come to them was to be found in the fact that Emerence loved her bed and Katharine Gordon had found it difficult to get her out when the rising-bell sounded. Clem had no trouble after the first morning when she had marched in on a happily drowsing Emerence, hauled all the bedclothes off her and tossed them over the chair and left her bitterly complaining. So far as Emerence was concerned, it had settled the matter. She might—and did—complain; but she got up with the rest.

The only cubicle without Clem's established sign was Mary-Lou's. That young lady had been brought back to Leafy from San the previous day, and was to go back into school again, much to the relief of all concerned. The cases of cold had all recovered a few days before and the sociable Mary-Lou had been very bored by herself. Her ankle was securely strapped up and her head was all right again and Dr Maynard had told Matron that there was no need to *add* to work by keeping her where she was.

Now she raised her voice. "I say, Clem, I can't get up. Sorry; but Matey made me promise I'd stay where I was until she came to help me."

"I didn't mean you," Clem replied, appearing with a suddenness that was quite stunning between the curtains and looking down on her with a grin. "If that's what Matey said to you, I fully agree you'd be wiser to stay where you are. How does the foot feel?"

"Quite O.K. so long as I don't try to walk or stand too much on it. It aches then, all right. Anyhow, both Uncle Jack and Matey say I can come back into school, thank goodness! I was fed to the—Heavens! What's cooking now?" For a wild squawk had made both her and Clem jump at that point.

"I can guess." Clem came in, went to the window and pulled the curtains back. "You sit up and look out and then you'll know."

Mary-Lou hauled herself up and turned to stare out of the window. "Oh, my goodness!" she gasped. "The snow!"

"You've said it!" Clem bethought herself of her duties and retired to say briskly, "Now then, you kids, don't stand there, gaping at it! Anyhow, what are you doing in some-one else's cubicle, Emerence? And you, too, Janet? You *know* visiting isn't allowed. Go back to your own. First baths people, scram! The rest of you, strip your beds and if you've time, say your prayers. You can stare at it all you like when you're downstairs. There just isn't time now."

There was not, as they knew all too well. They obeyed her on the word. Matron arrived and went to see to Mary-

Lou at once, but they all knew that her ears were pricked for any sounds of dilly-dallying and even Emerence hurried this morning.

Once they were in their own quarters, they made a concerted rush to the windows where two or three people were already staring out. Never, in all their lives, had they seen snow like this—not even on that eventful walk before half-term. As Miss Moore had prophesied, the storm had begun during the night and now it was coming down wholesale. The flakes whirled round and round in a dizzying dervish dance that, as Barbara said, made you feel positively giddy simply to look at! The sky, heavy and yellowish-grey, seemed to be lying on the tops of the trees and already the netball posts, which they could see faintly through the wild snow-mist, were heaped up at least a foot deep at the base.

"Well!" Clare Kennedy remarked as she peered out into the faint, greyish light, "there's one thing certain. Neither the Trips nor Sue Meadows will be at school today!"

"No," Hilary agreed. "No one would let kids like the Trips stir out into a storm of this kind and Sue lives much too far away. Their chalet is a good mile off!"

Vi nodded. "I couldn't agree more. I don't wonder the Abbess says they must be boarders during the winter. I wonder if it'll go on like this all day?"

No one could tell her that just then, but they proved it for themselves. All day the snow came down, silently, relentlessly, and when, at half-past three all the curtains were drawn, shutting out the wintry scene, it was still falling.

"It—it's almost *terrifying*!" Verity-Anne said in awe-struck tones before she pulled the curtains together. "I didn't know snow *could* be as awful as this!"

Mary-Lou, who was seated at her desk, chuckled. "I'm glad I've seen it for myself. I mean, one's read about it, of course, but you have to see it really before you can even *begin* to know what it's like. Are there enough desks for B division, by the way? It's a nuisance their lights have gone bad on them. We shall be awfully crowded in here for prep."

"They brought in folding-desks for themselves before art," Catriona said. "And here they come."

The next moment, the door opened and Upper IVB marched in, bearing their preparation. Something had gone wrong with the lights in their room and both those of Lower Fourth. It mattered less for the younger girls, for they always did their work together in Hall with a mistress in charge. Upper IVB had been told to come to A division as theirs was a large room and next door to B's.

They took their places quietly and then, as there was still a minute or so to spare, Mary-Lou went on airing her ideas.

"You know, I've always admired Captain Oates for going out into the blizzard, even though he *knew* he must die."

"Then why did he do that?" queried Ghislaine Thomé.

"He wanted to give the rest of the party a chance to get back safely," Mary-Lou explained. "He couldn't walk himself, because his feet were all frostbitten and they had to drag him along on a sledge. You can see for yourself how *that* slowed them up. Yes; I've always admired him, but I admire him ten times more now. Imagine going out into *that*! And I suppose it would be even more awful at the South Pole."

"Very much more awful," said Miss o'Ryan from the doorway where she had arrived in time to hear this. She came in briskly and deposited an armful of exercise books on the mistress's table. "Sit down, girls. About Captain Oates. He not only had the snow to face. There was a howling gale blowing at the same time—one hundred and twenty miles an hour, I believe. The man who deliberately faced that and the blizzard in order to give his friends a better chance of life was a real hero. To do such a thing takes stark courage. For believe me, girls, he did know exactly what he was doing and he did it in cold blood without any of the excitement of battle to work him up to it. Well might Captain Scott write of him, 'He was a very gallant gentleman'!"

Clare was murmuring something to herself.

"What's that, Clare?" Mary-Lou demanded.

Clare blushed. "It was just—I was thinking of what St. John says Our Lord said."

Biddy o'Ryan nodded at her. "'Greater love no man hath than this, that he lay down his life for his friends.' Yes, Clare; that is the finest epitaph Oates could have."

There was a moment's silence. Then the young mistress called them to order. "Come along, girls! prep now, please."

When the bell rang for the end of school, Miss o'Ryan gathered up Lower IVB's history which she had been correcting and said a last word before she left them.

"I'd like you to be thinking of this, girls. How was it that Captain Oates was able to brace himself to such an action? See if you can work it out for yourselves, now." Then she left them.

"Well, why?" Vi demanded when they were safely in their dormitory, changing for the evening. "I should say it was because he was a brave man, anyhow."

But Mary-Lou, brought up for the first ten years of her life among older people, was able to see farther into it than her friend. "I think," she said soberly, "that what Miss o'Ryan wants us to see is that it was because he felt it was his duty. If he had stayed with the rest, having to be dragged all the way, it would have made them a lot slower and none of them could possibly hang out long enough to get to the next place where food was cached. That's another thing, you know. The food was running short already and they were growing weaker because of that. But if he wasn't there, it would leave more for the others and they'd be saved the extra work, too. I mean," she added, "what I think Miss o'Ryan means is that duty was a sort of second nature to him. He was *accustomed* to putting it first. So when it came to doing a thing like that, he was able to do it, even though it *was* in cold blood."

It snowed all night and when the girls rose next morning it was still snowing as if it never meant to leave off. The snow was drifting badly now, and when they got downstairs it was to find that the ground-floor windows were drifted half-way up and it would mean burning the lights all day.

"Looks as if we are going to be completely snowed up," Vi said at *Frühstück*. "Wouldn't it be awful if we were— though it would be exciting," she added thoughtfully.

"Yes; and won't it be exciting if we haven't enough food to carry on?" someone said.

No one had thought of that, and one or two of the girls looked alarmed at this unpleasant idea. Clem Barrass quickly put a stopper on it.

"What awful rot! As if the folk in charge won't have thought of it!" she said with her usual blunt common sense. "You seem to forget, Carol, that a lot of them lived in Tirol for years before the war and they know just what to expect."

"Yes; but this is the *Alps*," Carol insisted.

"So is Tirol. Didn't you know that? Tirol is simply a continuation of the Alps. They stretch right across Central Europe. You look at your atlas when you go to your form-room. Anyhow," she went on, anxious to turn their thoughts from possible short commons, "once this stops and it's possible for us to go out, we'll be having winter sports—sledging and ski-ing, for instance. We might have a snow-fight—Seniors, versus Middles."

She succeeded. Her table promptly forgot all about food at this charming notion.

"How soon do you think we'll be able to go out?" Mary-Lou demanded.

"Not knowing, can't say. It all depends on when the snow ceases. Also, on how soon it freezes hard enough to be walked on. You couldn't manage on this," she added with a grin. "You'd sink right through and vanish from sight and then we'd have to get spades and dig you out—*if* we knew where you were."

"It *looks* solid enough," Christine objected. "Doesn't snow sort of pack down?"

"Not yet," Clem replied with authority. "I know what it was like when we spent that winter in Norway ages ago. No, my lambs; we're tied to the house until it's frozen."

"But doesn't it freeze as it falls?" Barbara queried.

Clem shook her head. "If it did that, my lamb, we'd have hail—not snow. Well, at any rate we can get on with rehearsals for the play. And it might be a bright idea to ask if we can have an extra Hobbies meeting on Saturday afternoon. We aren't going to have much of a show at the Sale next term unless we get cracking about it."

"We're going to miss Tom Gay and her marvellous dolls' house," Mary-Lou said sadly.

Clem laughed. "Oh no, we aren't! Welsen are having two stalls of their own at the Sale and Tom is hard at work on a grand dolls' chalet this very minute. Any more coffee, anyone?"

"Yes, please," came from three or four people and, while Clem filled up the cups with the milky coffee, the rest discussed the Sale.

It was an annual event, held in the Easter term. The proceeds went to support free beds for poor children. It was a grand affair, for they generally had a pattern, as, for example, a Chinese bazaar; or a Fairy-tale one. The last they had held in England had illustrated that charming allegory of the Victorian writer, A.L.O.E., "THE CROWN OF SUCCESS". Matron made pounds and pounds of jams, jellies and marmalades during the year and presented them with a goodly proportion of it for one stall. The girls themselves filled the others mainly with their own work. For the last five or six years, Tom Gay had made them a dolls' house for which there had been a competition with the house as the prize. This always brought in a big sum. Her last effort had been a toy village of a size to make it possible for several small children to play with it at once. This was as well, for it had been won by the great doctor, Sir James Talbot, and he had announced his intention of sending it to a hospital for tubercular poor children.

The Ozanne twins were clever at woodwork, but the school had never had anyone so good as Tom at carpentry and they had all bemoaned the fact that when she went to Welsen, they would have to do without her houses, so Clem's news came as a great relief.

"I call that wizard of Tom," Mary-Lou said. "Only, is it to be just a draw, or do we have to think up a competition for it? For I don't know how we can suggest anything new. You had to guess the name of the village last time, but that was only because it *was* a village and not a single house."

"I can't tell you," Clem informed her. "Anyhow, I don't suppose they'll bother *us* about it. It'll be Welsen's affair. Hurry up and finish, you people. The Head's looking our way and everyone else seems to be done."

The snow continued all that day and the next, but on Thursday morning they woke up to find that the long storm had ended. A clear sky of baby blue was overhead and the sun was just beginning to peep between the mountain peaks in the east. The sound of spades told them that someone—several someones, in fact—was hard at work, digging out paths and they hurried over their dressing in order to get downstairs and see if there was any chance of going out.

They had to wait till the end of *Frühstück*; but then the Head announced with a smile that the men had been digging out paths through the garden and as soon as beds were made and Prayers over, they were to put on their nailed boots and winter garments and they would be allowed to have an hour outside, so long as they kept to the paths.

"The snow is still soft and loose," she said, "and we don't want to have to dig any of you out. But, according to the radio, frost is expected tonight and once it comes, you shall make your first attempts at ski-ing. Also, you may try tobogganing on that slope that runs up the mountainside behind the chalet where Sue Meadows' aunt is living. But for today, you must be content to keep to the paths."

She prepared to sit down, but Mlle, who sat next to her, touched her arm and spoke in a low tone but with some urgency. She nodded as she listened. Then she turned again to the eagerly waiting girls.

"Mlle reminds me that the Staff intend to entertain you on Saturday evening," she said, looking at them with dancing eyes. "It is not for me to say how they mean to do it, but I am assured that it is something you will all enjoy very much. Now, will you finish, if you haven't already done so, and I'll say Grace and you can be off."

She did sit down then, having given them plenty to occupy their minds for the rest of the day and roused their curiosity to the highest degree.

CHAPTER SIXTEEN

Winter-Sporting

THAT NIGHT brought the frost which the radio had prophesied and when the girls got up next morning, it was to a world that glittered and sparkled beneath a pale blue sky flecked with white clouds through which the sun shone fitfully.

"Oh, my only Aunt Jemima! Doesn't it make your eyes feel muzzy if you look at it for long!" Vi exclaimed as she gazed out of the common-room window. She drew back and rubbed her hand over her eyes. "D'you think they'll let us wear our hats?"

"I wouldn't know," Hilary responded, taking her place, "but they'll let us go out all right. With frost like that, the snow must be as hard as a rock!"

"Isn't it lovely, though!" Barbara sighed with satisfaction. "It looks as though diamonds were scattered everywhere!"

Mary-Lou, who had just come down, also sighed. "It's grand for the rest of you, but I doubt if Matey will let me put even a toe out-of-doors. It must be as slippery as old boots and she'll be scared stiff in case I fall again."

As the bell for *Frühstück* rang just then, no one was able to give her any views on the subject. However, when the meal was ended, the Head rose to tell them that when they had finished their bedroom work, they were to change into breeches, windbreakers and socks over their stockings, for they were going to make their first attempts at ski-ing.

A murmur of delight went round the tables. Then the Head called Mary-Lou's name and that mournful person looked up with a sudden brightening which increased as

Miss Annersley proved once more that the staff thought about *all* their charges.

"Matron would rather you didn't try to walk at present. This frost has made the snow very slippery and we don't want you to have another fall. You might break something this time," the Head told her with dancing eyes. "However, you need fresh air as much as anyone, so we've borrowed a chair on runners and one of the mistresses will push you along in it and you can see the fun even if you can't take part in it just yet. Mind you wrap up warmly, all of you. Pullovers under your windbreakers, please. There is no wind, but the air is so cold, it stings like a whip and Matron doesn't want anyone in San if it can be helped."

Mary-Lou was one broad beam as she toiled up the stairs with the rest of the Gang in attendance. "Sporting of them, isn't it?" she observed.

"Yes; but then they generally *are*," Vi responded. "I say, if we've got to wear hoods, my eyes will be watering in half no time!"

But she found out that even that had been taken care of. When they came down to the splasheries to get into their boots, Miss Dene was waiting for them at the foot of the stairs, a big case beside her on a little table and she fitted each girl with a pair of coloured glasses which she was instructed to put on before she went out and to *keep* on.

"But *why*?" Emerence asked as she tried hers on.

"To save you from snow-blindness," Miss Dene told her. "The effect of the sun on the frozen snow is dazzling and can be almost blinding at times. These glasses will prevent that. Run along, Emerence, and get ready. Margot—oh, you have your own?"

Margot Maynard, who had come down with her sisters, nodded. "Yes; Mamma brought them when she was over last night. She said we'd need them, she expected."

Rosalie Dene laughed. "She remembers all right!"

"We had to wear them in Canada, too," Len put in.

"So you would. Well, be off, then. I've plenty to do at the moment."

They went scuttering off after Emerence and the distribution of glasses went on.

The girls hurried into their boots and then found why shawls, of all things, had been put on the school inventory. Each had a warm crimson one of good size and they were instructed to fold them cornerwise and then throw them over their shoulders, crossing the ends over their chests and tying them at the back so as to hold down the points across their backs and cover their chests completely.

"I'll be *boiled*!" Lesley proclaimed as she settled hers.

"You'll be thankful of it when you know how cold it is outside," Miss Derwent told her. "That's right, Lesley. Put on your glasses and run along."

The result of donning the glasses was peals of laughter as they looked at each other.

"What a complete guy you look!" Mary-Lou told Vi with a chuckle.

"I know I do if you're anything to go by!" Vi retorted smartly. She ran to the side-door and stared out at the glittering snow. "Anyhow, you *can* look at the snow without being dazzled to death, so looks don't matter. I shall jolly well keep *mine* on when I'm out!"

"Girls—girls! Stop gossiping and pick up your ski-sticks and line up outside!" came from Miss Denny who was ranging up and down the corridor like an anxious sheep-dog. "Go out as soon as you are ready and don't block up the corridor."

"What about our skis, Miss Denny?" Julie Lucy asked.

"They're coming along on the wood-sledge. You'll have quite enough to do to keep your feet at first and you couldn't possibly hope to get anywhere *on* them as yet."

"It *looks* easy enough," murmured Julie, glancing at Miss o'Ryan and Miss Wilmot who were skimming along the lines with an easy, bird-like movement.

Miss Denny replied only with a chuckle and Julie went out to find that the mistress had spoken the truth. The frost had made the snow as slippery as glass and the girls had all their work cut out to keep their feet. Thanks to heavily nailed boots and ski-sticks, they were able to do it, but by the time they had reached the *Elisehütte*, they were all glowing between the bite of the air and their hard work.

"Carol! You've got a *colour*!" Vi exclaimed, suddenly

remembering their chatter in the train when they first came. "And *doesn't* it improve you! I told you so!"

For once, this most unpopular remark brought only a beaming smile as Carol replied, "Oh, do you think so? I've noticed I didn't look so no-colour this last week or two, but I wondered if I was just imagining it."

"It's not imagination; it's really so," Hilary put in.

Carol opened her lips to say something, but her remark became a loud, "*Ow!*" as she skidded and was only saved from falling headlong by the arm of Miss Wilmot, coming up behind them, extended in time to catch her. Two minutes later, Mary-Lou riding in state in the chair on runners pushed by Miss Dene moving easily in her skis, came flying past. Mary-Lou waved exultantly to her chums and then she was gone.

"Don't you *move* on skis!" Barbara said with amazement. "Miss Dene looks almost as if she were flying! Oh, I hope I can learn to manage quickly!"

"So do I," Vi chimed in. "Oh, here's the *Elisehütte* and there's Sue waiting for us. Hello, Sue!"

Sue came down the path carefully and went to Miss Annersley and said something. The Head nodded and turned to Mlle to say a few words. Then she beckoned to Sue to join up with someone and the long crocodile moved on while Miss Annersley went up to the house where a lady was waiting for her and took her in at once.

"Come on, Sue!" Clare, who was just behind Barbara and Vi, called her. "You can tag on to Heather and me."

Sue came—cautiously. "How awfully slippery it is!" she said. "Oh, look at Miss o'Ryan! I'd simply love to be able to go it like that!"

Maeve heard this and turned round. "Peggy says that just at first it's simply ghastly. Your toes *will* keep on crossing."

"*What!*" It came as a concerted shriek from all near enough to hear.

Maeve gave a giggle. "The toes of your skis. Peggy says they just *rush* together, no matter how hard you try to keep them apart, and then over you go!"

"Oh, well," Clare said easily, "I suppose it'll just be a case of sticking to it till you get your balance," she added.

"Halt! " called Miss Derwent who had taken over. "Anyone who knows anything about ski-ing, go over to that side. The rest of you, stay where you are. Now, let me see. H'm! Clem and Zoé, Jean Ackroyd and you three Maynards. Right! Get your skis and you can amuse yourselves about here. The rest of you, keep to the level until you've got your balance—which won't be *this* day," she added *sotto voce* to Nancy Wilmot. "Clem, don't start anything mad on the slope, will you? You can take charge of the other five. If anyone gets to doing anything more than staggering about, I'll send her to you."

She turned to look at the rest. Then she rapidly counted all the staff who were present. This included Miss Dene who had run Mary-Lou into a sheltered spot near a clump of firs and was watching the fun. "Five of us—and the Head, when she comes."

"That may mean any time. We can't wait for her," urged Miss Burnett.

"You can count me in on this," Rosalie Dene put in, leaving Mary-Lou and the chair to look after themselves. "Mary-Lou's all right where she is for the moment, and I'll call Clem and Jean to take her for a run presently. I'll give a hand with this lot in the meantime."

"Oh, good! Then that means groups of about eighteen each——"

"Less than that! Here comes Mlle! " Miss Denny put in as Mlle, who had been to the station to drop the mail-bag for the next train down, came flying up to them. "That makes seven of us—say fifteen each."

"I'll take fifteen of the Junior Middles," Miss o'Ryan said.

"Thanks; that'll be a relief! Peggy," she turned to Miss Burnett, "will you take the rest of them? If you two will go right over there, then they'll be out of the way of the older girls. I'll be responsible for the rest of the Middles with Rosalie to help me if you and Miss Denny will take charge of the Seniors, Mlle."

"But of course! " Mlle nodded cheerfully. "Then we

should begin at once, for it is cold for the girls to stand still." And off she went to collect all the Seniors and take them away to another part of the area, Miss Denny going with her, while Miss Derwent and Miss Dene called the elder Middles to order and first made sure that all skis were strapped on securely.

"Now then," Miss Derwent said, "a ski-stick in each hand. Slide your feet forward and try to keep your points apart. That's all you need to do just now. Off you go!"

Off they went. Vi cautiously slid one foot forward. Then she slid the other keeping her eyes fixed on the treacherous ski-points and willing with all her might to stay apart. She took one more step; they rushed together and over she went!

Luckily, although the snow was crisp enough for walking, it was not frozen deep and when Vi landed full-length, she sank through into a soft blanket from which she was speedily rescued by the laughing Miss Dene, who got her to her feet and set her off again after she had brushed the fine, powdery snow off her.

Meanwhile, Barbara was advancing by tiny, mincing steps and had contrived to make seven of them when her ski caught in a snowed-in bush and over *she* went—with a wild yell which made Clare jump and lose *her* balance. In fact, most of them were unable to manage more than three or four steps before they fell. It was good fun, though, for the under-snow was soft and dry, so no one was hurt, though a good many of them would be very stiff before bedtime and there were bellows to mend in some cases.

It was left to Emerence to supply *the* sensation of the morning. Her balance was naturally good and a girl who had done surf-board riding at Manly Bay in Australia was better able to tackle the skis than most. She got on quite well, and presently was moving fairly easily over the ground. Peggy Burnett had her hands full with Nan Wentworth and two or three more of the little ones who were nervous and left her to herself. Thus it was that Emerence, proud of her prowess, found herself right in the middle of the area between the three groups and Clem, who was flying down the slope, got a perfect view of the event.

"It was one of the funniest things I ever saw!" vowed Clem later on in the prefects' room. "She was doing really quite well when she suddenly—goodness knows why!—made a terrific stride. Then she tried to bring the other leg forward and couldn't, she slipped and before you could say 'knife', there she was, down on the ground, doing the splits as perfectly as any professional acrobat! And her *face*!" Clem screamed with laughter in which all the rest joined her.

As she said, it was not merely the performance itself, though that had been funny and sudden enough to set them all laughing. It was Emerence's expression as she realized what had happened. She had looked startled, baffled, frightened and suddenly meekly proud of herself all in the same moment. And how, as Mlle said to her compeers, she had managed to avoid breaking either of her skis, was a miracle!

The people at the Sanatorium might almost have heard the yells of laughter that greeted Emerence's exploits and she had added one more to the many tales which Chalet School girls remembered as long as they lived. She was not hurt, though she admitted that she felt as if she had been badly stretched. In fact, she insisted on trying again, once she was up. Whatever else she lacked, it was not pluck.

Twenty minutes later, the Head arrived, looking none too pleased, and was at once surrounded by a throng, all trying to relate the young Australian's latest to her. Emerence herself came forward at her beckoning with a grin.

"Are you sure you haven't hurt yourself, Emerence?" the Head asked shakily.

"No, thank you," Emerence replied. "Of course, I feel rather as if I'd been racked a bit,"—with a sudden memory of her last history lesson—"but it's wearing off now."

Miss Annersley nodded and turned away to help some of the other girls and by the time she decided they had had enough, her brow was clear and she had regained full self-control. When she later retailed the story to Joey and Beth, she let herself go and her laughter pealed through the *Saal* at Freudesheim.

The girls were very loath to give up the fun, but the Head was firm. She knew that they would all be stiff by bedtime and she was anxious that none of the less robust girls should be over-strained. The wood-sledge had come up and she ordered little Nan Wentworth and two or three more of the Junior Middles on to it, adding the Ozanne twins who were never very strong, and Dorothy Watson. She eyed Barbara meditatively, but that young person's rosy cheeks and glowing eyes gave no sign of real fatigue.

The girls set off on their homeward journey, with the prefects to act as whippers-in and the mistresses strolled along—so far as you *can* stroll on skis—in a bunch and the Head gave them her news.

She had called at the *Elisehütte* to ask Mrs. Elstob, Sue's aunt, to let the girl be a boarder for the rest of the term. They were at the beginning of winter and might expect other snowstorms just as fierce as the recent one. That would mean that if Sue remained a day-girl, she must lose a good deal of her work.

Mrs. Elstob was not at all ready to agree. She pointed out that Sue was there, in the first place, to give her delicate cousin companionship which could not be if the former were a boarder. Miss Annersley had done her best, however, for Sue's own sake and at last Mrs. Elstob had agreed that she should be a weekly boarder, provided she might come home for an hour each afternoon if it was fine, to amuse Leila.

"Well, at least you've gained so much," Miss Derwent said. "Poor Sue! I was at the Graves' last Sunday, and Hilary told me that Leila Elstob is the most petted little piece of selfishness you could find anywhere. Sue hasn't too easy a time, from all I can hear."

Miss Annersley looked grave. "I'm sorry for Leila herself. It's tubercular disease in the hip and it's gone very far. Jack Maynard told me that they were doing all they could, but anything might happen. The child has very little strength and they're afraid to operate. They hope that if this place suits her, they may be able to do it later on; but at present she's just as well where she is. She frets for her mother when she is away from her, and that's no help."

They had reached the school by this time, so no more could be said. The girls and staff had to hurry to change and the afternoon work of needlework and art was rather languidly performed that day, for everyone was healthily tired.

Late in the afternoon, the snow had begun to fall again and, according to the radio that evening, was likely to continue for the next twenty-four hours at least.

"Anyhow," Vi said, summing it up when they were undressing that night, "we had a super time this morning, and tomorrow we have Hobbies in the afternoon and on Saturday there's the staff party."

To which Barbara, dropping her hairbrush, replied, "Isn't life *wizard*?"

CHAPTER SEVENTEEN

Staff Party

"WHAT *I* want to know," observed Mary-Lou as she got into her velveteen frock, aided by Barbara and Vi who had constituted themselves as ladies-maids to her for the next week or so—"But it's only until your foot's better," Vi had warned her—"what I am *dying* to know, I may say, is just what the staff are going to do with us tonight?"

"Oh, hang on for another hour or so!" Verity-Anne said in her soft little voice. "If you died now, you'd never know."

Verity-Anne was famed for saying the most outrageous things in that silvery voice of hers which made people ignore the outrageousness at the time, though they realized it later when they had had time to think over what she had said.

On this occasion, Mary-Lou only said cheerfully, "Oh, I'm not going to—to——"

" 'Shuffle off this mortal coil'!" Barbara helped her out, having come across the quotation in her literature class the day before and watched her chance to drag it into conversation somehow.

"What?" Mary-Lou demanded, staring at her.

"Shakespeare said it," Barbara explained.

"Oh!" Mary-Lou gave her another look and then decided to let it go.

"It must be something awfully funny," Emerence gave as her opinion. "I had to go past Hall this afternoon and I heard them all shrieking like anything. I say, Barbara, could you fix my collar, d'you think? I've been fiddling with it for ages and I *can't* get the points even!"

She produced something that looked like a well-chewed piece of string.

Barbara shrieked when she saw it. "Emerence Hope! What on earth have you done with it? You can't possibly wear a thing like that! You'll have to find another if you can. I couldn't do anything with *this*!"

"Then come and take your pick," Emerence invited.

"Don't you, Babs!" Vi cried. "Emerence, you *know* we aren't allowed to go into each other's cubeys unless it's absolutely necessary. You bring those collars out here if you want Babs to choose."

"Oh, bother vou!" Emerence grumbled. "Clem's not here now."

"That's not to sav she won't come back, any time. Or Matey might pop along to see if Mary-Lou's all right. Why should Barbara get into a row to please you?"

"Oh, all right. I'll bring them." Emerence went back to her cubicle and emerged again with a boxful of dainty collars and cuffs.

"However many have you got?" demanded Mary-Lou who, like most of the girls, owned only four sets.

"A dozen of each. Here you are, Barbara. Get something that'll go with these cuffs, do! There isn't time to change the cuffs as well."

"There isn't!" Barbara glanced at them and began turning over the collars with careful fingers. "This is exactly the same. You must have got hold of an odd set—unless you have two of that pattern. I'll have to pin it, though. Anyone got any gold safeties?"

Two or three people produced enough small gilt safety-pins for the purpose and Barbara pinned the collar into place with accuracy and neatness. Emerence surveyed herself in the long wall-mirror with complacency when it was done.

"You're bonser at that sort of thing, Barbara. Thanks a million! Oh, and if you ever run short of cuffs and collars, borrow from me. I've plenty."

"Thanks a lot, but you know I can't. We aren't allowed to borrow," Barbara replied as gratefully as she could in the circumstances.

"Then take a set—yes, do! I've lots more than I need and you've saved me from a row with someone," Emerence suggested, for, whatever her faults, she was generous enough with her possessions.

"I've plenty, thanks, but it's awfully decent of you."

"Well, the offer's open if you ever want to take it," Emerence returned, going to her cubicle with the rag.

"Hi, Emerence! What are you doing with that thing?" Mary-Lou demanded.

"Shove it into my hanky drawer."

"Well, just you put it into your soiled-linen bag. If Matey finds it with your hankies, you'll get into a row!"

"I'd forgotten that. O.K.; and thanks a lot!" Emerence pushed it into her bag and, when Matron arrived a minute or two later to make sure that all was well with her patient, the girls were ready and the cubicles were in their usual spick-and-span condition.

"It's still snowing," Janet Forster was announcing from the window at the far end.

"And likely to go on for the next day or two," Matron said, advancing on Mary-Lou. "How is the foot, Mary-Lou? Now remember; you are not to stand about. I don't want you laid up again. You're more bother than you're worth, when you do silly things like this!"

Mary-Lou looked meek. "My foot doesn't hurt at all, Matron," she said.

"Glad to hear it! Let me see your cubicles. Yes; quite all right. Have you all got clean handkerchiefs? You may need them before the evening's out." Matron's lips suddenly twitched. "That's all right. Yes; you'll do. Run along downstairs."

But what she had said had aroused their curiosity.

"What are we going to do, Matron?" Vi asked eagerly.

"As if I would tell you! You must wait until the time comes. Didn't you all hear me tell you to go downstairs? The gong will sound for *Abendessen* in a minute or two, now. By the way, don't eat *too* much. I'll tell you that, anyhow."

Then she left them and the girls went down, wild with curiosity. They guessed that the Staff had provided refreshments, though, and that was a relief, for *Abendessen* that night consisted of soup followed by a milk pudding which was not very satisfying, especially as helpings were small.

"Is this all we're getting? Let's hope we have something else later on or I'll be awake all night, I'll be so famished," Hilary muttered to her next-door neighbour.

"When Matey came into our dormy to see to Mary-Lou, she warned us not to eat too much," Vi said detachedly.

"What a hope! No one's giving us any chance!" Hilary scraped the last remains of semolina from her plate and laid her spoon down.

Once *Abendessen* was over, the Head stood up. "Prayers now, girls. Catholics, go to the gym as usual. The others, remain here. Mlle, will you send your flock back here when you have finished Prayers and they can all wait together."

Mlle nodded and laughed. She took her girls off and then Miss Annersley reminded her own lambs that they were about to address God and must think while they did so and not be satisfied with words only.

It was a timely reminder, for some of the younger ones, at any rate, were growing very excited and in a far from prayerful mood. The Catholic girls came to join them presently and they talked quietly until Miss Dene appeared with a list and called, "Vi Lucy, Nan Wentworth, Madge Herbert, Nella Ozanne, Mary-Lou Trelawney. Go to Hall, please, all of you."

Full of excitement, they went along the corridors to Hall where they were met at the door by Miss Denny, who sent them into the room one at a time. While they waited their turn, she pinned a number on the back of each. They were passed on to a kind of ante-chamber, made with screens, where one of the younger mistresses tied a half mask of black material round their heads and then put a hood over their hair, carefully tucking away all stray ends and curls. Then they were sent into Hall itself where they greeted each unknown figure with smothered giggles, for their last instructions had been not to speak and not even to laugh if they could help it.

It was an unexpected beginning to the evening and the hopes of the girls rose high. It was really surprising what a difference it made when all you could see of someone else's face were the tip of her nose and her mouth and chin. No help could be got from dresses, either, since all wore the same blue velveteen with embroidered collars and cuffs.

One by one, the girls came in and took their seats in more or less solemn silence. Some of the younger mistresses gave way to half-smothered laughter at the sight of the masked and hooded creatures sitting so primly round the walls. But apart from that and a giggle or two from the more easily excited ones, there was a stillness in the great room that could be felt.

When the last girl had taken her seat, Miss Annersley, who had been sitting in her big chair on the dais, chatting quietly with Mlle and Miss Denny, rose and explained. "Each of you has a number. On those tables over there, you will find trays of pencils and piles of paper. Beginning at this end, get up, march round and take one of each as you pass. You are to write down the names of as many people as you can guess in the next twenty minutes. You may not speak one word and you must try not to laugh. Now do you all understand? Don't speak. Just nod."

They all nodded like so many blackavized mandarins and the staff exploded at the sight. When there was silence again, she added something more to her remarks. "As everyone can guess Mary-Lou Trelawney, she may put her own name on the list to make it quite fair. Now that is all. Off you go!"

With one accord the crowd bounced up, marched round the room and finally broke into knots and the fun started.

Everyone headed her sheet with Mary-Lou's name. Dorothy Watson was easily guessed, too, for her front teeth were banded with gold. Most folk got Annis Lovell, for that young woman had a bad habit of striding which no one had been able to cure so far. Six-foot Polly Winterton was another easy mark. But for the rest, it was a case of making wild shots and hoping some of them would come off. When Miss Annersley struck her bell as a sign that time was up and they were free to speak once more, a perfect chorus of dismay went up.

"I've only twenty-two names!" came from Julie Lucy. "Some of those are quite wild guesses, too!"

"Me, I have only four!" cried Ghislaine Thomé.

Mary-Lou's lips parted in a complacent smile. "I've got thirty," she said.

"Take off your headgear!" the Head called, stifling her laughter with difficulty. "Hand in your lists first, though."

Then the mistresses were among them collecting lists and they were free to pull off hoods and masks and a fresh series of exclamations arose.

"I put Verity-Anne down for Nan Wentworth!" from Vi in deep dismay.

Barbara, finding herself next to Julie, said mournfully, "And I put *you* down for Betsy. I thought I recognized your brooch."

"We both have them, you goat," came from Betsy herself. "And I'm half a head taller than Julie, too." Then she chuckled. "Far as *that* goes, I put *you* down for Blossom Willoughby."

"Isn't it extraordinary what covering up your head and half your face does for you?" observed her own chum, Ailsa Thomson.

"Time for the next round!" the Head announced. "Go and sit down at those long tables. One for each form and they're all marked, so you can't make a mistake. Hurry, girls!"

The girls fled to the long trestle tables which had been screened off until now and when all were seated, they were told to open the envelope lying before each of them. The Seniors found slips of paper, each with something written on it. The Middles had little squares of cardboard, each with a printed letter. This had been Miss Denny's idea and she came on to the dais to explain.

"Seniors, your slips put together will compose a recipe. I don't say it's a cookery recipe each time—it often isn't. Some are for cements, or polishes or home-made medicines and so on. You have to arrange your slips in order, find out the use of each and then put all the slips back into the envelope, writing your name and what you think the recipe is on the front. Middles, you have each twenty-five letters. You are to make words out of them. You will get one point for four-letter words; two points for five-letter words and three for anything longer. Write your words and name on *your* envelope and put the letters back. Don't lose any. We may want them again." She paused with an eye on her watch. Then she said, "Go! You have exactly ten minutes."

Fresh groans arose as the girls emptied the contents of their envelopes.

Annis found, "Sweet oil 1 pt., turpentine 3 oz., hogs' lard ½lb., beeswax 3 oz., simmer slowly. Use when cold," and uttered a startled yelp before she finally called what was a cure for chilblains, furniture polish.

As for Clem, faced with, "2 oz. turmeric, 6 oz. coriander seed, ½ oz. powdered ginger, 2 drs. cinnamon, 6 drs. cayenne pepper, 4 drs. black pepper, 1 dr. each mace, cloves and pimento, 4 drs. nutmeg, 1½ drs. fennel seed. Powder finely, mix well, dry and bottle," she gave it up, merely writing, "This seems to be a very *hot* recipe." Later, she was told that it was an old recipe for curry powder, whereat she remarked demurely, "Well, I *did* say it was hot!"

As for the rest, the younger girls satisfied themselves with four-letter words for the most part, but Mary-Lou the ambitious, contrived one ten-letter word, one of nine and then found herself left with K Z J J A and O. As she couldn't possibly make a word out of that mixture, she had to break up the others and hadn't quite finished when Miss Denny called, "Time! Hand in your envelopes, please!"

While the girls had been busy over this brain-teaser,

some of the staff had been setting up the screens to form an oblong. Forms were set round outside and they heard a clatter as if someone were emptying a few pounds of nails on the floor. The first twelve girls were called, mounted on the forms, each given a bamboo with a long cord attached to which was tied a toy magnet, and they had to fish and see what they could catch.

"Only one shot each," pronounced Miss Wilmot who was running this with the help of Miss Armitage and Miss o'Ryan. "You cast, draw your line along and then haul up."

"What are the fish, Miss Wilmot?" Julie asked from her perch.

"Ah! That's the question!" Miss Wilmot gave her a bland smile and looked provoking.

Julie gave it up, meekly took the bamboo and slung her line over. She heard a clinking noise and Miss Wilmot, come to watch, told her to draw up. She hauled up and saw, clinging to the magnet, a small steel ring with a bone key-tag tied to it. She looked at it eagerly. "17" was marked on it.

"What's this?" she demanded.

"What else but the size of the fish you've caught?" Biddy o'Ryan told her. "Mind you keep it safe, Julie. We had to borrow key-tags from everyone we could and they've got to be returned."

Julie jumped down with a laugh and passed the rod to the next-comer. Then she stood to one side enjoying the fun. Before three minutes had passed, everyone near enough to see it was in fits of laughter. Catriona was on the small side and she gave her line a good swirl in order to land it over the screen. Unfortunately, it caught in Miss Denny's hair and when she extricated it, three hairpins came with it and her hair came tumbling down. Then the Ozanne twins, "fishing" from opposite sides of the "pond", contrived in some magical way to get their lines entangled, Vanna gave a violent tug when Nella was not expecting it and that young person plunged on to the screen below her and brought it down flat, landing in spread-eagle fashion on top of it.

No harm was done, except to the screen. That was a light affair not intended to uphold eight stone or so of girl, and one of the cross-bars was snapped when they got it set up again.

Several people caught nothing at all. Several others had rings that represented the poorest quantities of fish. Then luck changed. Barbara landed a ring labelled with a magnificent "129" and hugged herself with glee, since this was top, so far. But Clare completely outdid her, for when she hauled up her line it was to find that she had "hooked" no fewer than *three* rings and when the weights were added together, it was found that she had caught 502 lbs. This remained top score and when Betsy Lucy, last of them all, jumped down and announced that her catch was a mere 9 lbs., Miss Annersley announced from the dais where she had been nearly weeping with laughter that they would now have light refreshments in the *Speisesaal*. After that, there would be a boat race to wind up. She then smiled at Julie and invited her to take her arm.

Blushing at this unexpected honour, Julie obeyed and they headed a line to the *Speisesaal* where they found the tables laden with sandwiches, pastries, creams, jellies, fruit, nuts and sweets and, to wind up with, ices. Lemonade, ginger beer and fruit drinks were also provided and when everyone had eaten her fill boxes of crackers appeared, and a few minutes later, everyone was adorned with a paper hat of some kind.

"Be careful with them," the Head said warningly. "They are part of the boat race; you can't enter if you haven't a paper hat or cap."

"But how, I ask you, can we have a boat race up here?" Madge Herbert remarked to Annis when they were making their way back to Hall.

"Don't ask me! But aren't the staff *brains* to have thought all this out?" Annis rejoined.

Arrived in Hall, the Head informed Mary-Lou that this was one competition in which she might not take part.

Mary-Lou's face fell, though she only said meekly, "Very well, Miss Annersley." But she let herself go to the others when the Head went off to the other end of Hall.

"Oh, *why* did I have to fall downstairs?" she moaned to her neighbours.

"You didn't—it was your own stupidity," Clem informed her bracingly. "Anyhow, don't grouse. This is the only thing you've been out of."

Mary-Lou fell silent, but she thought the more and, when twenty girls were all seated on small mats, each given a short-handled broom and informed that they were to propel themselves to the other end of Hall by means of the brooms and, to give a final touch of difficulty, without losing their headgear, she nearly wept.

With peals of laughter, the twenty girls chosen to open the event, sat down on their mats, settled their paper adornments as securely as they could, gripped their broom-handles and waited for the word.

Matron gave it. She eyed them all thoughtfully. Then she said, "One—two—three—four—*off*!" and the whole fleet set off.

The mats slid easily enough over the highly polished boards; but when you are bending forward to put everything you can into a good shove and then swinging backwards as your mat slides along, a paper cap is not the easiest of headgear to retain. They might straighten the things, or even hold them on; but once a cap fell off and touched the floor, its owner was disqualified and had to leave the race.

Meanwhile, Miss Derwent had set Mary-Lou at a small table with paper and pencil and told her to write down the name of each girl she fancied for winner in the heats. If she was right, she got five marks; second place brought her three; third meant one. Mary-Lou set herself to watch critically, but before a minute had passed, she was holding her sides and gasping for breath. Julie had given herself such a violent shove-off, that she had shot forward ahead of everyone else. All very well if that had been all; but for some unknown reason, her mat swung round so that she was facing the starting-point and had to swivel herself round somehow which meant that quite half a dozen others got ahead of her.

Katharine Gordon, with a bishop's mitre perched precariously on top of her brown locks, kept giving alternate wild clutches at it and equally wild shoves with her broom. Clem and Annis collided in mid-stream, so to speak, and both rolled over on the floor in such shrieks of laughter that it was fully a minute before they could sit up and get out of the way Hilary Wilson, in an effort to avoid Clem's wildly thrashing feet, steered straight into Mlle, who was standing to one side, shaking with mirth which changed to a yell as her feet were swept from under her and she collapsed on top of Hilary who gave vent to a smothered howl, for Mlle, though tiny, was no light weight when she came on you full force like that.

Mary-Lou was recalled to her share in the business by Rosalie Dene who suddenly exclaimed, "Look at Madge and Nora! I believe they're going to be ties!"

That brought the critic to her senses, and she hurriedly wrote down Madge Herbert's name. But Miss Dene proved right, for it was dead-heat between them. They ended up a mat's-length away from Blossom Willoughby who was a good second. Mary-Lou was awarded 2½ marks and the mats were raced back to the end of Hall and twenty more competitors took their places.

The second heat was won by Verity-Anne of all people, though she was racing against big girls like Polly Winterton, Edris Young, Betsy Lucy and Hilda Jukes. Verity-Anne was a canny young person and she had noted in the previous heat that those who drove hardest were apt to swerve and had to waste time getting straight again. She set her mind on keeping one dead straight line and beat them all as a result. Mary-Lou the loyal had naturally put her name down and was awarded five marks. Then she settled down to view the third heat in which she was wildly wrong for, being intrigued by a very showy beginning from Polly's young sister, Lala, she put her name down, and half-way through, Lala's green crown was wafted from her head to land neatly before Matron, so Lala was out of it and the race went to Carola Johnston.

In the next heat, a record was created, for *every* girl lost her cap, Elinor Pennell letting hers go just as she reached the winning-post. However, it was only just, so Miss Burnett, who was refereeing, adjudged her winner.

The last two heats followed the pattern set by the earlier ones and fell to Sybil Russell and Emerence Hope respectively. And then Emerence was disqualified, for Matron was moved to investigate the reason for her ability to ignore her pink dunce's cap and found that the young sinner had run the end of a hair-grip through the edge just before she started.

"Cheat!" cried Vi who had been early out of it, having dropped *her* cap almost at once.

"No one said we mustn't!" Emerence retorted defiantly.

"No one thought it necessary," Julie Lucy replied from just behind them. "It serves you right. That makes young Barbara winner."

Then came the grand finale. Madge, Nora, Verity-Anne, Carola, Elinor, Sybil and the secretly exultant Barbara were seated in a row and then the Head calmly informed them that this time they had to make the round of Hall before coming up the straight to the winning-post—her own big chair, by the way.

They set off and found that turning corners was a very tricky business indeed. In fact, the three big girls got involved with each other almost at once and by the time they had sorted themselves out, the rest were sailing away round the third corner. Sybil was well in front of Elinor, and Verity-Anne and Barbara were level, just behind. Barbara went ahead at this point, passed Elinor and looked like catching up with Sybil. Then Verity-Anne, setting her teeth and with a look of almost savage determination on her small face, sent her mat past Elinor's, past Barbara's and caught up with Sybil.

The girls were wild with excitement and shouting for all the competitors at the full pitch of excellent lungs and Mary-Lou, not sure whether to yell for Barbara or Verity-Anne—since both were members of the Gang—compromised by yelling first one and then the other while she bounced up and down on her chair in a way that was none too good for it.

And then Elinor spurted again. She passed Barbara,

passed Verity-Anne, who was tiring, passed Sybil and, with a final violent shove, imitated Hilary's exploit, for she drove straight into Miss Denny who was standing near the chair, cheering madly. Miss Denny felt herself going, clutched wildly at Miss Armitage and Miss Derwent who were on either side of her and not prepared, and the three of them fell in a heap—luckily *not* on Elinor who had the sense to roll out of the way just in time.

That ended the evening. The horrified Head glanced at the clock and saw that it was not far from half-past twenty-two. She called for silence while Biddy o'Ryan and Nancy Wilmot hurriedly brought in a table loaded with parcels, and gave out the prizes, informing each winner that nothing must be opened that night. They were all to line up at once and go straight to bed.

Julie jumped on to a nearby chair and called for three cheers for the Head and the staff. The school was more or less worn out by this time, but they pulled themselves together and the resultant cheers nearly took the roof off. Then, led by the prefects, they marched off upstairs and the staff party was over.

CHAPTER EIGHTEEN

"Strangers at the Inn"

"ARE YOU all ready, girls? Remember what I told you. There is to be *no* talking behind the scenes. I'll deal with whoever talks myself when the play's over." Miss Dene stopped there and looked round the assembled girls with an expression that made everyone resolve to hold her tongue, however much she might want to say something. Then she went on. "There's the overture beginning. First episode, go and take your places. And whatever you do, be ready to come in on your cues. Off you go! Good luck!"

Miss Dene went to take her place, with her copy of the play and waited while the orchestra, provided by girls from the Welsen branch and conducted by Mr. Denny, drew to the close of "A Fantasia on Christmas Carols" and then swept straight away into the opening carol, "Brightest and Best of the Sons of the Morning" which was sung by everyone behind the curtains. As the last sweet note died away, curtains were drawn swiftly apart by Miss Wilmot and Miss Armitage to disclose the bar parlour of a modern "local". A bar had been made of folding desks and brown paper at the right of the stage and behind it was standing a charming barmaid, Edris Young, handing out glasses of cold tea—well-sweetened—raspberry vinegar and very yellow lemonade to a gathering of three men and two women. Standing beside the fire, which was ingeniously made of red and yellow crinkled paper with small electric light bulbs beneath to make it glow, was the landlady, talking to a six-footer gentleman with a bag in either hand and his hat on his head.

The gentleman was engaging a room for the night, saying that he was a doctor who had been called to a consultation and now could not reach home because the road was blocked with snow and his car had run into a drift. The landlady told him she had only one room but that was at his disposal. The other customers joined in as he finally sat down with a glass of lemonade before him and the landlady bustled off to see about the room.

Then there came a tramping of feet and voices from outside rang out in the old Welsh carol, "The Shepherds' Carol". The waits had arrived. The barmaid hurried to open the door and they came in with their shoulders covered with snow—salt, as a matter of fact—blowing on their fingers, swinging their arms round themselves and showing as clearly as they could that it was bitterly cold.

By this time, the landlady had rejoined them and she and the barmaid and another girl went about with plates of cake and glasses of liquid. They accepted them and when they had finished their feast—the pieces of cake were very small—they offered to sing another carol. Before they could do so, there came a bang on the door. One of the waits flung it open and standing there were a man, a woman and a small girl. The landlady bade the three come in and shut that door before everyone was frozen.

When they were in, she demanded to know their business. They explained that they were trying to tramp to the nearest town, but could go no further, and begged for food and shelter for the night.

The landlady shook her head. She had no room at all. She was sorry; but there it was.

"Just for tonight," the man begged. "Anything—even an outhouse. It's so late and the storm is so wild."

The tall man came forward. They might have his room and he would sleep down here in the bar-parlour if the landlady would consent. He added, "This is Christmas Eve and we all know what happened on the first Christmas Eve. A Man, a Woman and a Baby had to find shelter in a draughty cave where the beasts were stabled." For the sake of the First Christmas, he offered his own room to the wanderers.

The landlady agreed to that and began to talk of supper for them and bread and milk for the little girl. She sent off her second help to see to it and the man said, "Our little Mary will sing her thanks to you."

He took his fiddle out of its case and nodded to the small girl who came forward and sang the quaint Czech carol, "*Rocking*". Verity-Anne had a lovely voice with a lark-like lilt in it and she sang the charming words with great distinctness and with every note as pure and round as a chorister's. A sigh of pleasure rose as the last beautiful note died away. Jean Ackroyd played well, too.

When the carol ended, the landlady brought a basin which she gave to the child and then told the elder pair that their supper was ready in the kitchen and when they had had it, there would be a room ready for them.

"He's right," she said, nodding to the doctor. "I couldn't turn the worst tramp from the door on Christmas Eve."

The woman thanked her gratefully and then said that she would sing for them if she might before they left the bar-parlour. The landlady agreed and Blossom Willoughby, to the accompaniment of the orchestra, sang a carol which Lady Russell had written and Jacynth Hardy, an

Old Girl who was already bringing laurels to the school both by her 'cello playing and her composition, had set.

Who comes this way by the cold starlight?
A man and a Lady fair and bright.
They make their way to Bethlehem—
Oh, who will there find room for them?
Nowell, Nowell, Nowell.

They stand outside in the wind and gloom.
They are come so late that there is no room:
The only shelter the inn can yield
Is among the beasts brought in from the field.
Nowell, Nowell, Nowell.

So into the cold dark cave they go
Where the soft-eyed cattle are sleeping below
And there, on the hay in an empty stall
Is born Lord Christ Who is King of all.
Nowell, Nowell, Nowell.

Oh, all good people in cot or hall,
Give welcome to strangers, one and all,
Lest turning away the mean and poor,
Ye turn Our Lord away from your door.
Nowell, Nowell, Nowell.

This was Blossom's début as a soloist, and the entire school held its breath in case she should be attacked by stage fright. But she gave no sign of it and her beautiful deep alto notes made a complete contrast to Verity-Anne's soprano.

The curtain fell as she ended and while the staff hurriedly made changes in the scenery, the choir broke forth into the old English carol, *"The Moon Shines Bright"*.

The next scene showed an inn at the beginning of the last century. Women in full Tirolean costume hurried about and the landlord urged them on.

"Let the Little Corporal and his men do their worst," he

said. "We'll keep the Holy Season as well as we may. And thank God I have more than one cellar. So make haste, my lasses! They may have done their worst for us, but we've enough for a Christmas feast tomorrow and God will see to the rest."

A thundering knock at the door made everyone shiver with terror lest the French should have come back and a stout landlady came hurrying in.

"Open the door, husband! Don't keep them waiting!" she cried.

The landlord opened the door and there stood a cluster of fugitives—a man and his family. He had been wounded in battle with the French and had managed to escape to his home, only to find that the enemy were coming. His wife and children had fled with him and they were trying to get to the coast where they hoped to find a ship to take them to England. But his wife and the children were worn out and he was exhausted by his wounds—Ruth Wilson wore a most gory-looking bandage round her head and had one arm in a sling—and they feared for the baby.

"Yes; come in—come in!" the landlord cried hospitably. "I can keep you all safe as I kept my best barrel of beer and our Christmas goose safe."

The door was shut. Julie, carrying tiny Felicity Maynard, and hoping desperately that the baby would not suddenly be frightened and begin to yell, sat down and the five children clustered round her, Con Maynard closest, so that her little sister might see one face she knew well. Luckily, Felicity was charmed with the bright lights. She sat up on Julie's knee and looked round with a gurgle which made her proper mother, sitting in the visitors' seats in front, turn round to a lady just behind her to remark softly, "I rather wondered what would happen, but she's a born actress, bless her!"

"You turn round and don't draw attention to me!" the lady retorted. "What an ass you can be, Jo!"

The squelched Mrs. Maynard meekly turned back just in time to see her youngest daughter stretch out fat hands to grab the rim of Julie's poke bonnet and tug with all her might. Luckily, Con kept her head, she pulled the ribbons loose and the bonnet came off and Felicity spent the rest of the scene placidly investigating it.

The landlord told his guests that they would celebrate Christmas with him. Then the curtains fell while the choir sang, "Sing Good Company, Frank and Free".

There was a good deal to do for the next scene and the choir sang the whole of William Dunbar's lengthy carol, "*Rorate Coeli Desuper*", while all the comfortable furniture was rushed out and a couple of benches and a trestle-table put in their place. Jo had her daughter returned to her by Miss Derwent and Felicity, very pleased with herself, snuggled up to her mother and went to sleep.

When the curtains rose, it was on a very different scene. The "fire" had been screened by curtains and at the back stood a brazier with a small red glow amongst the black that seemed to fill it. Wooden bowls stood on the table round which sat two or three dirty shaggy men who looked complete cut-throats. It had been found necessary to cut out two episodes, as time had to be limited, so this was the Children's Crusade episode.

Valerie Arnott was the landlord and a villainous creature she looked in ragged shirt and breeches, wooden sabots, and a kind of nightcap dragged over one side of her head. Rosalind Wynyard as her wife was also in torn clothes and produced a most unnatural look of downtrodden meekness which had its funny side for those who knew her.

"What a set of rascals! " the most important visitor there whispered to the Head who sat beside her. "I wouldn't trust myself alone with one of them in broad daylight! "

"Scoundrels, the whole lot," Jo agreed from in front. "I'd no idea we had such desperadoes in the school, Hilda! "

Then the scene opened with grumbling from all the men. Times were bad, landlords worse. As for the Children's Crusade, it was sheer insanity. Still, there was good in all things if you looked for it. Doubtless by the time it was over there would be very many fewer mouths to feed!

The wife timidly suggested that the poor mothers would be heartbroken. Her loving husband threatened her with his fist and told her to hold her tongue and go and find something to do. She gave a squawk and fled while he enlarged on how he would behave to the unfortunate Crusaders if they reached *his* inn.

And then the door was flung open and a mob of boys poured in with a few little girls. All were untidy and Margot Maynard's left eye was tied up with a cloth so filthy that her mother wondered aloud where on earth they had found it? But all wore the Crusader's cross. They thronged in and begged food and drink from the landlord. True to his word, he shouted at them. Let them begone for a pack of lazy young vagabonds!

The leader—Mary-Lou—stood her ground. This was Christmas Eve. They were children as Christ had been a Child. In His Name they begged food and the shelter of the barn for the night. Josette Russell came to add her pleadings. Finally, Maeve Bettany joined in.

"In the Name of Christ," she said. "He may even be in our band. Would you turn *Him* away?"

The landlord relented. He shouted to his wife to bring the brats some soup and she came in, looking remarkably cheery at this. The Crusaders promptly closed ranks and sang, "How far is it to Bethlehem?" while she set bowls all round the table and the curtain fell as they finished and crowded round on the benches.

Once more, there was a longish interval, for everything had to be removed. This was the last scene of all—the scene of the First Christmas. The orchestra played Mendelssohn's "Christmas Pieces" and then the choir sang three carols— "Three Kings from Persian Lands afar", "Masters in this Hall" and, finally, "In the fields with their flocks abiding", with the glockenspiel giving very softly a bell accompaniment. It ended and the glockenspiel remained playing alone, louder and louder until the Hall was filled with triumphant pealing as the curtains were swept up to show the lowly stable. A long trough stood dead centre, in it, Sybil Russell, leaning against a truss of hay, with a big Bambino on one arm, at her feet, Dr. Graves' cocker spaniel. Behind her stood St. Joseph—Nora Penley—holding a lantern in one hand and resting the other on the neck of a little donkey belonging to Emil, one of the men who worked at the school. He himself, clad as a shepherd, stood at the foot of the trough with his golden-skinned little cow, Suzette. All round the walls stood row upon row of angels—great archangels, in robes of glowing colours with wings to match soaring above their heads and, kneeling all round the crib, little angels in pink and blue, green, yellow and mauve.

As the audience gazed at the scene, the orchestra swept into the "Gloria" from Bach's "Mass in B Minor" which Mr. Denny and Miss Lawrence had arranged for trebles in four parts and the whole school, with the exception of the Madonna and St. Joseph, burst into the glorious anthem. It ended, and a sudden silence fell. Then the scarlet-robed archangel came forward and led into the stable the shepherds from the hills. They knelt and offered their crooks and the Madonna smiled at them with a sign of acceptance.

They were followed by the Crusaders who had found time to make themselves clean and tidy and who all wore white cloaks hiding their rags with the scarlet cross on one shoulder.

The Blue archangel led in those from the Napoleonic scene and then came the moderns led by one in violet and gold. All knelt before moving quietly to one side or the other to mingle with the angels.

The stage seemed full, but there were still the Three Kings, who came in with an archangel whose golden robes were set off by wings of green and scarlet. They knelt to offer their gifts of gold, frankincense and myrrh before they, too, went to one side. Then the Madonna lifted the Bambino and rocked him gently as the angel choir sang the beautiful old Breton carol, "Sleep, Holy Babe". The curtains fell on the last long note; but only for a few seconds. For the last time they rose and now the Madonna was standing, holding up the Babe for the adoration of the universe; and angels and humans, all kneeling humbly, sang the "*Adeste*" in its musical Latin form.

That really was the end, so far as the play was concerned. But the Head had a surprise in store. She had left her guests and now appeared before the curtains.

"Thank you all," she said. "There can, of course, be no applause for the play; but I know you will all be pleased to see the author. May I present to you—Lady Russell!" She beckoned and Lady Russell, looking thoroughly taken aback, joined her on the stage where she smiled and bowed her thanks for the applause she received.

"Thank you all," she said. "I should like to tell you that we hope to offer you other plays. I know that our Welsen branch is giving you a pantomime next term, and we are also hoping for a pageant in the summer term and we hope you will all come to that, too. Finally, on behalf of the entire school, the Welsen branch as well as this one, I wish you all a joyous Christmas and a Happy New Year."

She withdrew, then the audience slowly dispersed.

"I could wring your neck, Hilda Annersley!" Madge Russell proclaimed when they were alone at last. "Couldn't you possibly have held your silly tongue?"

"Not possibly!" Miss Annersley said firmly. Then she added, "Are you satisfied?"

"Quite satisfied. The school has got off to a decent start. Thank you and all the staff more than I can say!"

In the *Speisesaal* the girls were talking the play over.

"Well," said Mary-Lou, when they began to turn to other things, "our first term is nearly ended. I think we've made a good beginning. As for you, young Babs, your own mother won't know you when she sees you!"

Barbara bolted a mouthful of cream bun before she replied. "I know it! And I'd like to say something myself. I always wanted to come to the Chalet School, but if I'd really known before what a—a *smashing* school it is, I'd have wanted it ten times more!"

From her place at the head of the prefects' table, Julie called out, "I dare say; but you be careful with your language, my child! There's still time for a few more fines in the box!"

"What about *that* part of it?" Vi asked with a giggle.

Barbara stuck to her guns. "I don't mind even slang fines so long as I'm at the Chalet School!"